I0823946

This Wretched Beauty

A Dorian Gray Remix

A Clash of Steel: A Treasure Island Remix
by C. B. LEE

So Many Beginnings: A Little Women Remix
by BETHANY C. MORROW

Travelers Along the Way: A Robin Hood Remix
by AMINAH MAE SAFI

What Souls Are Made Of: A Wuthering Heights Remix
by TASHA SURI

Self-Made Boys: A Great Gatsby Remix
by ANNA-MARIE McLEMORE

My Dear Henry: A Jekyll & Hyde Remix
by KALYNN BAYRON

Teach the Torches to Burn: A Romeo & Juliet Remix
by CALEB ROEHRIG

Into the Bright Open: A Secret Garden Remix
by CHERIE DIMALINE

Most Ardently: A Pride & Prejudice Remix
by GABE COLE NOVOA

This Wretched Beauty: A Dorian Gray Remix
by ELLE GRENIER

This Wretched Beauty

A Dorian Gray Remix

ELLE GRENIER

FEIWEL AND FRIENDS
New York

Content warning: *This book contains mentions of child abuse, violence, and anti-queer rhetoric.*

A Feiwel and Friends Book
An imprint of Macmillan Publishing Group, LLC
120 Broadway, New York, NY 10271 • fiercereads.com

EU representative: Macmillan Publishers Ireland Ltd, 1st Floor, The Liffey Trust Centre, 117–126 Sheriff Street Upper, Dublin 1, D01 YC43

Our books may be purchased in bulk for specialty retail/wholesale, literacy, corporate/premium, educational, and subscription box use. Please contact MacmillanSpecialMarkets@macmillan.com.

Library of Congress Control Number: 2025015222

First edition, 2026
Book design by L. Whitt
Feiwel and Friends logo designed by Filomena Tuosto
Printed in the United States of America

ISBN 978-1-250-32978-3
10 9 8 7 6 5 4 3 2 1

Author's Note

In many ways, this is a book about shadows and what takes place within them. Queer spaces existed out of public sight in the Victorian era, and, while obscurity provided some protections, it also had its shortcomings. By confining certain topics to the shadows, we leave people without the language to describe their experiences—and, as a result, we leave them vulnerable to the types of abuse they can't communicate. This is especially true for young people still learning to navigate the world.

As a result, *This Wretched Beauty* tackles some difficult subjects: mental illness, abusive guardians, the death of parents, body horror, gender dysphoria, substance abuse, and abusive/coercive relationships. While all these topics are present throughout the book, I have tried, when possible, to write trauma not through the many events at its core, but through the ripples left in its wake. As such, much of the abuse discussed exists in the margins, relying on the dynamics between the characters to imply what is happening behind closed doors. I hope this can provide some shelter from the harshness of Dorian's reality. Still, if now is not the time to dive into this world, I respect your call to heed your own instincts. I've certainly made the same decision myself in the past.

Of all the things I want to promise at the start of this book, happiness is the biggest—but that term feels too gray, too likely to mean different things to each of us. Instead, I'll leave you with this: Whatever bruises and scars gather along the way, there is always room for a better tomorrow.

To Camille,
who changed my life by introducing me to a book

London, 1867

1
London Gray

I often catch myself thinking about broken glass.

It's a violent image, far more than it has any right to be. Such tiny shards, smaller than the eye can see, yet able to shred paper, canvas, or even skin in an instant. Once, it belonged to something ornate, something with purpose, but the second it breaks it becomes a curse. Years of misfortune as a punishment for . . . what, exactly? Ruining something that never mattered to begin with?

The shard glistens between my thumb and my forefinger, mocking me with its silence. If Grandfather heard the window break, he hasn't bothered to do anything about it. I wait a little longer, tilting the glass to watch the light dance atop it. A few strands of hair fall over my eye, blocking the top-left corner of my vision.

I suppose it'll be time to cut it soon—or, more likely, it has been for a while now and I simply hadn't noticed. It's hard to keep track of when hair moves from fashionably long to something Grandfather might condemn as sloppy and unkempt.

It isn't until I see the glass stain red that I realize how tightly I'm clutching it.

A stubborn part of my brain insists I should be feeling some kind of sting where the blood flows. It's an oddly peaceful feeling, staring at the red trickling down my index finger like the creek behind our estate. The waters have mostly been still since the groundskeeper set up some rocks halfway down, silencing the rush that used to sing me to sleep. Grandfather insisted it kept him up at night, so now its lullabies are little more than a pleasant memory. I might miss it, had I not learned long ago that nothing in my life is mine to grow fond of.

My bedroom window looks even smaller now that it's broken. Jagged shards jut out from its edges, each one a dragon's tooth trying to keep its hostage locked in. There's enough space for my body to squeeze through, but I know better than to assume I'll make my escape without a few cuts and scrapes.

I step one leg out the dragon's mouth, feeling around with my foot until I find the solidity of the trellis under me. Once I'm confident that my balance is steady, I lift the second leg to bridge the gap. The dragon gets one bite on my neck before I escape its grasp—I take a second to rearrange my hair and cover the cut. My shirt tears a little under its teeth, exposing a glimpse of my lower back to the night sky.

There's something romantic about climbing out my window in the dead of night. The air smells of rebellion and adventure, the kind of night where something magical might happen if this were a stage play or a novel. I can picture some young ingenue sneaking out this way, desperate to break free and find some great fate of her own. Maybe she'd meet a handsome man from a rival family, or one who's betrothed to some princess or duchess. Whatever the case, their love would be star-crossed. There's no point reading any romance where the odds are in their favor. Happiness needs to be earned in the face of impossible odds, or there's no beauty in it. Even joy becomes ugly when it grows mundane.

The scratch of the trellis on my fingertips is soothing. Looking down and seeing how far I am above the ground exhilarates me. My breath catches in my throat as my brain reminds me, unprovoked, that one missed step might lead to my death.

I picture Grandfather walking out in the morning to find his only heir's body broken beside the rosebushes. Would he know I fell escaping him, or would his mind fly to a more dramatic conclusion? I wonder for a moment if it might sadden him to lose the last family he has—and to know that, once again, he's to blame for the loss.

A splinter off the trellis pricks my finger and snaps me back to reason. Grandfather would never walk our gardens. They were Mother's domain once, and Grandmother's before that. The great Lord Kelso has no time for such frivolous things as flowers. The news of my death would be well on its way through society gossip networks before it ever reached his ears.

I'm sure the scandal of it all would get some reaction out of him, at least.

The feeling of solid ground beneath me is as disappointing as it is reassuring. My heart quiets down, yet my breathing refuses to follow suit. *You're still in danger*, it insists, but if it knows what the threat is, it doesn't say. Grandfather's face flashes in my mind, stormy with the look he wears whenever he says my name: as if acknowledging my existence is blasphemy in and of itself.

Overhead, the moon shines bright and full, its pale light washing any life or color from my skin. An observer might mistake me for a ghost haunting the estate, some reminder of shame and tragedy tainting the Kelso name. On nights like this, it's hard not to believe such things.

How can I consider myself to be living, knowing any glimpse of a life I might scavenge comes only at nighttime, when there's nobody around to see me?

The walk into London proper is crisp and dark but much more flattering than the harsh lights the moon and streetlights provide. Smoke and fog offer cover, even as they fill my nose with their bitter, harrowing smell. It's as if the city itself is ill, buckling under the weight of all the factories and chimneys that rise as quickly as the pox. Even the streetlights struggle to break through the miasma around me. Each new one flickers in the distance like a near-dead star guiding a sailor as best it can. It's not much, but I navigate by reflex more than anything now. Papa's gallery calls to me from across the city, promising its warmth and conversation and ambience; a few moments of life in all its brightness and boldness. No matter where I am, I think I'd be able to find my way there.

Shadows lurk behind every corner, ready to strike the second I pass by them. Grandfather has warned me time and time again that London is a dangerous place at night, full of brigands who'd love nothing more than to attack a lord foolish enough to wander around. But shadows aren't a threat—even the more ominous ones. They're part of the backdrop, lending a tone of risk to any secret adventures one might take.

It's on nights like these I wish I were an artist. I'd turn every wisp of smoke into a series of gray ribbons dancing around London, each shadow into a figure, each light into a glowworm. The buildings would form groves of towering tree stumps, silent and unforgiving. But as much as I may have the vision and the taste, I've always lacked the skill. I remember begging Grandfather to hire tutors when I was younger, but he'd insisted it was a waste of time. I had enough on my plate learning "proper subjects" without wasting my time studying anything as frivolous as Beauty.

I doubt studying art would be any different from my Latin lessons, anyway—I see it everywhere, and I understand it just fine, but I lack the language to express it. Despite my best efforts, I can't translate my thoughts into it, at least not in a way other people can understand.

Maybe the fault is with my thoughts, then. It's possible that *I* am the one who doesn't make sense, that no language could translate the things I see. It'd take a fool to feel misunderstood so often without wondering if I might be the problem after all.

Papa's gallery helps with that, at least somewhat. It's full of such fascinating people—*eccentrics*, Grandfather would call them in the same tone he says my name—and I understand them. They sit and talk about new styles and movements and all these ways strangers are experimenting with form and beauty as concepts, and it makes me want to join in. They might appreciate the mystique of a black night or the exhilaration of shadows if I could express it to them.

What is destruction, I long to ask them, *if not a way to create? What is absence if not a presence to be felt?*

Entering the gallery never feels like making an entrance. Chaos already pulses in every direction, ebbing and flowing in perfect harmony with the conversation. Paintings line the wall with shades I've never seen, warm yellows and bright pinks that have no business together but somehow work amidst the madness. The chatter is much louder than is proper, each conversation drowning out the other until the rise and fall of voices feels like a melody I don't know. A smile eases onto my face as I look around, as utterly lost as I always am here. Drowning has never seemed a more pleasant concept than it does now, letting wave after wave of life crash over me. There's nobody I have to be, no impression to consider, when to most of these people I'm little more than a fly buzzing on the wall.

"Dorian!"

Papa's voice manages to be loud and booming without ever being brash. Instead, it has all the sudden charm of someone bursting into song, guided by the gentle lilting of his Parisian accent. He breaks free from the crowd and pulls me into a hug. He smells like fresh paint and red wine, overpowering in its sweetness but welcoming in its warmth. We sit in the hug for a while, taking in each other's presence like it's a luxury vintage stored in the cellar for only the most special occasions.

“It’s been too long since I last saw you, soleil,” Papa says as he pulls away. “Your hair’s getting long.”

I run my hand behind my neck, shrinking under his words. There’s no coldness or judgment in his tone, but I’ve heard the phrase leave Grandfather’s mouth too often not to apologize on reflex. Papa winces at my defensiveness—perhaps it would be kinder of me to keep my distance and spare him the pain of seeing Grandfather raise me in the exact way he and my mother risked so much to protect me from.

“I’ll cut it soon,” I promise.

Papa shrugs. “It’s quite fashionable these days, you know. I’ll never understand why the English feel obliged to be so traditional at all times.”

“Grandfather says—”

“It makes you look like your mother. Even your grandfather should be able to appreciate that.”

I open my mouth to tell him we both know why Grandfather wouldn’t care to hear his point, then close it. I don’t see Papa enough to waste my time arguing with him about a man he has every reason to despise. I spend enough time dwelling on what Grandfather thinks of me as is; this should be one of the few places I can leave him behind and think only about what I want for myself.

“Don’t listen to him,” a second voice calls from behind Papa. “You’ve got so much of your father in you. He’d see it too if he could look past the hair for two seconds.”

And so the dance reaches its last step. Grandfather insists I look like him, but softer; Papa compares me to my mother, and then Fabián decides I’m my father’s son after all. Between the three of them, I wonder if I take on whatever appearance people want to see—like a blank canvas, or a mirror that reflects the expectations of whoever's in front of it.

What would it mean to look like Dorian instead of someone else's reflection? I can't picture it. My features come to mind easily enough—hair caught between copper and gold, eyes slightly too big for my face, a mouth overpowered into a pout by my bottom lip—but they feel disjointed. Like items on a list rather than parts of a whole. There must be something I'm missing, some piece that ties me together. There's little I wouldn't give to know what it might be, but the few places I've been able to look haven't offered any answer.

I watch Papa and Fabián bicker back and forth, fading in and out of focus as they go on. It seems strange for business partners to disagree as much as they do, but there's no denying Papa's much happier now that he doesn't have to run the gallery alone. Besides, selling Fabián's frames has done wonders for the business; each one of them is a work of art on its own merit.

"I hope I'm not interrupting."

I turn to find a young man I've never met, broken free from the crowd chattering behind him. The bags under his eyes have the heaviness of someone who's spent months away from their bed, and his smile wears the tired ease of someone who's content to sit and watch the world turn without them. Splatters of green paint decorate his lightly calloused hands, though that's not unusual for Papa's clientele. Artists have a way of wearing their work. If anything, the fact that he has managed to keep the stains to just his skin is an achievement.

The painter's eyes do not bounce off me like others do. They bump into me, halt, and then pierce as easily as if I were made of water. His gaze burns, but it isn't unpleasant. It reminds me of the sun on a hot day, when I've been out too long but can't pull myself from the gardens: Staying in the warmth too long will hurt later, but I can't bring myself to go back inside quite yet.

Is this how it feels to be seen?

"I think I ought to be the one apologizing," I answer, pointing to the crowd behind us. Their conversation has halted as if this painter's presence were the only thing keeping it afloat. While I may not know who he is, this man has obviously captured the attention of tonight's gathered crowd. "It seems I've pulled you away from your audience."

"Perhaps I should thank you, then. I never intended to have an audience today, but I suppose I should have known better than to show my face after years of absence and expect not to gather some attention."

I hold the painter's gaze for a fraction of a moment before turning away. As warm as it may be, something about the familiarity in his eyes puts me on edge. I don't know what this young man thinks he recognizes in me, but there's nothing to see. Grandfather spent years teaching me to keep my face illegible. If a man's mind were meant to be public, it would not be hidden away inside him.

"Basil, dear boy!" Papa breaks away from Fabián and claps the painter—Basil, apparently—on the back. "I didn't expect you to grace one of my salons after your prolonged absence. Where have you been these last few years?"

"Away, of course. I hope you haven't spent all this time looking for me, Étienne. An artist needs adventure to find inspiration. You should know that better than anyone."

Papa nods. "Do you mean to imply you have new paintings to exhibit? Simply say the word and I'll get invitations ready. Our patrons have been asking for nearly a year now when you'll have more work ready to show."

"They'll have to wait a little longer, I'm afraid." Basil's eyes dart to me just as I was starting to think I'd faded away from their conversation. "It turns out adventure doesn't agree with me. Sometimes, the best part of coming back home is the things we see in a new light."

I turn my eyes from Basil to Papa and then back. This stranger has a quality to him I can't put my finger on, but it beckons me forward just as well. I've read in novels that some people are meant to leave marks on each other's lives before they've even met, but the concept has always seemed too fanciful even for me.

That doesn't stop the nagging instinct telling me I want to know him. I take a breath and steady myself, shutting out the chaos and distraction of the gallery until my mind is clear and my posture is perfect.

"It appears my father has forgotten to introduce us," I say, sticking out my hand for him to shake. "I'm Dorian Gray, Lord Kelso's grandson. And you are?"

His smile has an earnest surprise to it that I wouldn't have expected from a man who's spent the last few years traveling, even if he doesn't seem much older than myself. "Nobody in particular, but you may call me Basil if you'd like. It's a pleasure to meet you, Lord Gray."

The title sends a shiver down my spine, much like it always

does. It seems too early, too proper, too much like a coat impeccably tailored for someone else. Grandfather would say I haven't earned it yet, but that doesn't ring true, either. Nobody earns such a title, at least not these days. Families hoard them and hand them down like the trinkets left behind in their wills.

"Please, call me Dorian."

"You're being too modest, Basil," Papa corrects before turning back to me. "Mr. Hallward here is something of a prodigy. He exhibited his first series of paintings to mass acclaim at fourteen, then vanished for . . . two years, was it?"

"Three."

"Three years! And still no new collection to show. You wound me, dear boy."

"I expect you won't be waiting much longer," Basil promises. "I've spent much of my absence learning about portraiture. Faces have such an honesty to them, don't you think?"

The question is aimed at Papa, but Basil's eyes lock onto mine. I don't hear my father's answer, and I sense that Basil doesn't, either. Whatever pull that tenses between us is a potent one. It frightens me, and yet the thrills it seems to promise are beyond my wildest imaginings.

"Has anyone ever painted your portrait?" Basil asks me.

"I'm afraid the opportunity has never presented itself, no."

"You must grant me the honor of your first one, then. I'm sure every painter in London will be lining up to paint the future Lord Kelso before long."

His voice is husky in a way that doesn't detract from its smoothness. I think back to the Greek poems my first tutor used to read me, and the sirens that awaited Odysseus on his journey. Basil's words lure me in, beckoning me in directions I never would have thought to travel. I can see nothing but rocks ahead of us, waiting to wreck my ship and leave me at the mercy of the waves—but if destruction is little more than potential, why should I fear it? If I can't make art of my own, perhaps I can be its medium. Would it be enough to *become* a beautiful thing, rather than to create one?

I smile at Basil, and the gravity between us pulls even tighter.

"The honor would be all mine, Mr. Hallward."

2
Canvas White

The first time Basil invited me to sit for him, I thought it was a poor attempt at a joke. The second time must've been pity, designed to pad my ego and reassure me I hadn't been as awful a model as I'd fancied myself. But this being the third time, it's easier to believe Basil Hallward might genuinely enjoy spending time with me.

I haven't figured out why yet—it can't be that he enjoys painting me. Whenever I sit for him, my eyes wander to every corner of the room. I kick my ankles side to side and hope he doesn't notice. I rattle on endlessly about books he probably couldn't care less about and art he must already know far better than I. My cheeks flush red anytime I catch him looking up from his canvas, throwing off any semblance of an even complexion I could have.

Sometimes I even find myself watching him as he paints, losing myself in the gentle ease with which his hand guides his paintbrush along as though leading it in a strange yet beautiful dance.

"Wouldn't you rather have a model who can sit for you patiently?" I ask when Basil guides me toward his sitting room. "It must be easier to work with people who know how to hold a pose. All I do is cause you trouble."

"Perhaps I don't want someone who knows how to pose. If I wanted a still life, I'm sure a bowl of fruits would be much easier to work with than you are."

If I've learned one thing about artists from visiting Papa's gallery, it's that whatever logic they operate on is entirely their own. These last few sessions with Basil have taught me he's no exception. Often, when he looks at me, it feels as though he's in a different world entirely, processing thoughts that don't or even can't exist in the room. He'll say one of them, unprompted, and I'll be left even more unsure which fraction of his mind I've glimpsed into. Wherever he goes when he paints, I imagine it must be a place more wondrous than any London could offer.

"I thought we might picture you differently today," Basil says, somehow warm and detached at the same time. "An imagined scene, drawn from the Greeks."

"What scene is that?"

"I was hoping to paint you as Hyacinthus, if you'll allow me."

A frown grows on my face as I try to remember the name from my lessons. I dig through my mind as I change into the toga Basil gave me. It's colder than I'd expected, and I can't help but be aware of how much of my shoulder is uncovered. It feels strong and vulnerable at the same time.

"I don't remember Hyacinthus," I tell Basil once I've stepped out from behind the screen. "Who was he?"

"A Spartan prince. I thought the flowers would suit you."

The more time I spend with Basil, the less I think I know. I imagine the feeling might frustrate me were the novelty of it not so exciting. Before I can ask any more questions, Basil arranges a crown of flowers atop my head. Petals brush against my hair, tickling at the sides of my forehead; I bite my lip to hold back the laughter. Basil's fingers brush against that same ticklish spot as he tucks a strand of hair behind my ear.

"I believe an old friend of mine might be joining us today," says Basil. "Lord Henry Wotton. I mentioned I'd been painting someone as of late, and he thought you might like some company to keep you occupied while I paint."

"Aren't you worried that might distract me?"

"Frankly, Dorian, you do that well enough on your own." Basil's smile doesn't quite reach his eyes. "Besides . . . once Henry makes up his mind, I'm afraid it's rather impossible to persuade him of anything else."

The idea of another person intruding on Basil and me sits strangely in my chest, though I can't quite fathom why. The two of us sit mostly in silence during our sessions, Basil focused on his painting and me trying my best not to disturb him. If anything, it should be nice to have someone to speak with while I sit, and yet I find myself feeling more protective of this shared time between us the more I think about it. Perhaps it's simply the uncertainty with which Basil is speaking about this potential visitor that's filling me with hesitation.

"Do you *want* him here with us?" I ask.

"I'm accustomed by now to Henry doing as he likes." Basil's eyes dodge mine as he twists around my question. "That being said, if anything he does brings you discomfort, give me a sign and I'll send him on his way. Understood?"

It's strange. There's a protective tone to his words I've never heard before. Papa gets close at times, but the way he speaks about Grandfather is too defeated to bring me the sort of comfort Basil's words do now. I bask in their warmth for a few moments more, imagining how it might feel for this to be a constant in my life rather than a rarity for me to treasure whenever I can.

"Understood. Thank you, Basil."

It takes only three hours of sitting for the tediousness to wear on me—which, in my defense, is about three times better than my last attempt. Lord Wotton sits on a sofa across from me, taking a drag from a pipe to punctuate his latest jab at some Lady Brandon I must have met but whose face I can't place. I vaguely remember Grandfather being fond of her, and as such have been quite happy to snicker at his comments. Even without recalling any details about their subject, Wotton's gibes have such a piercing specificity to them that they paint a scene on their own.

Despite having been in his company for the better part of an afternoon now, I have no clue what to make of Wotton. He speaks and carries himself as though he has no mind for the way others perceive him, but I'd be foolish to think any noble in London cares so little for their reputation. Whatever he might get out of this act is beyond me, but I'd be lying if I said it wasn't entertaining, at least.

"Really, Henry," Basil chides from behind his canvas, "I wish you'd tell me what Lady Brandon has done to earn such ire from you. She's a kind enough woman, and certainly not an outlier within her age and rank."

"I never recall saying otherwise," Wotton argues. "Lady Brandon simply has the distinction of being the member of the Old Guard I've seen most recently. You're welcome to replace her name with Lord Ashby or Lady Agnew if you prefer—although I'd argue it's quite easy to be kind enough, so long as nobody asks you to open your purse."

"I happen to know that Lord Ashby regularly contributes to a local orphanage, and that Lady Brandon still sponsors one of those homes for unwed mothers. Surely, Henry, even *you* must have some respect for charity."

"I can hardly think of anything less private and less generous than charity. The whole thing has become utterly vulgar, if you ask me."

"What about piety, then?" I ask.

Basil sighs. Lord Wotton turns to me, a glint in his eye. Heat rushes to my cheeks, which only seems to amuse Wotton further. I look away, suddenly unable to bear the attention on me. Something about it feels too tantalizing, too much like an invitation to reveal more of myself—more, maybe, than is safe to. If there's one thing Grandfather taught me about London, it's that its people obscure themselves more than the smog ever could. It's much better to hide behind titles and reputations than it is to be real. Disaster and shame cannot be attached to flat, mirrored surfaces.

Though I might struggle with most of Grandfather's lessons, I've always thought myself an expert at this one. It's easy to hide away when nobody has bothered to ask what I might want.

"I like this one," Wotton says, somewhere between a chuckle and an announcement. "I can see why you were so reluctant to invite me, Basil. You haven't been conspiring against me, have you?"

"And what, exactly, would I conspire to do, Henry? I'm an artist, not a politician."

A cloud of smoke puffs out of Wotton's mouth as he exhales, his pipe still balanced between his index and middle fingers. The smell is harsh in a way that shouldn't be pleasant, but there's a strange sort of comfort in the way it pricks my nose. "That depends on who you ask. I'd say art is much more political than something so frivolous as politics."

I frown, my crown's petals brushing against my face. Watching Wotton and Basil talk feels like trying to follow a conversation on the other end of a room. I've never heard anyone talk the way they do: harsh and sharp, but carefully disguised under the guise of playful snobbery, layers of frustration and fatigue hidden through wit and laughter. Listening to them, I hear exhaustion with our world as it is, but also a clear vision for what it could be. What would it be like to see life the way they do, for all the secrets and shadows most fight so hard to keep concealed? It would be richer, if nothing else, than the London I've grown accustomed to.

"I don't understand," I chip in. "Isn't the point of art to make beautiful things?"

Wotton raises an eyebrow. "Would that make you the beautiful thing, then?"

The directness in Wotton's tone pierces me. There's none of the jest he wielded moments ago, no artifice, as if he wants me to know this conversation is no longer a game to him, and yet I don't quite believe him. There's a probing quality to his low, velvety voice that makes it clear he wants to see how far he can push me, how willing I am to let him string me along before I get uncomfortable or bored. I'm not sure what reaction he's expecting out of me, but the way he challenges me is new, at least, fresh and sharp in a way that reminds me of holding those shards of broken window glass. Something in me craves to press my fingers deeper so that I might feel the sharpness of those jagged edges.

It hits me, then, that Wotton is handsome in a way I've never noticed in anyone before. I pride myself on knowing when someone looks respectable, or if they're aware of current fashions (or, for that matter, if they're *too* aware of them), but this is a beast of its own kind. The rich brown of Wotton's hair, the low warmth of his voice, the way he holds himself tall without becoming rigid—they all register not just as pleasant, but interesting. Appealing, even. They make me wonder about him. What does his life look like outside of this studio, and what sort of thrills could he bring into mine?

Grandfather's shadow looms behind me, appearing from nowhere and sending shivers down my neck to let me know I've done something wrong, but refusing to tell me what. If I focus enough, I can hear the perfectly kept rhythm of his breaths ticking away each second I disappoint him. Basil's studio fades away as the shadow grows, and before long it becomes the only presence I'm aware of.

"I'm not much of anything, really," I finally reply.

Bit by bit, the shadow begins to fade as the studio re-forms around me. The river-blue cloth draped at my feet is the first to return, followed by Wotton on his sofa and then Basil at his easel, a careful frown sat gently on his brow. There's a reverence on his face I've seen on many artists whenever they get lost in their own work. It's hard to imagine that anything as simple as a portrait of me could inspire that kind of devotion, but I can't doubt it when the proof is right before me.

"Somehow," Wotton tuts, "I think you truly believe that. The illusions we conjure for ourselves are baffling, don't you think?"

"What I think is that the two of us are being awfully rude," I reply. "I'm here to pose for Basil, yet here I am spending the afternoon distracted by you instead. We ought to apologize for being bad friends."

"Unthinkable. Basil has too many good friends as it is—he'd grow spoiled were I not a bad one. And you, if I might venture a guess, are too in want of friends at all to care whether they be good or bad."

"Frankly, Henry," Basil grumbles from behind his easel, "it's a miracle you have *any* friends, speaking as callously as you do. I don't even know why I let you visit today."

"Don't pretend this isn't exactly what you had in mind, Basil. You set the scene too perfectly for that. A drape for a river, trees out your window as a background, a crown of hyacinth on his head? You wanted Hyacinthus looking past the Artist, and you needed me to be the zephyr."

"I'm sure I have no idea what you mean. You invited yourself so you could meet Dorian, and I simply know better than to try changing your mind."

Despite his protests, Basil grows sullen under Henry's amused eye. I'm not sure what scene Wotton is referring to, or why my looking away from Basil has anything to do with it, but now that he's mentioned it, I can't deny that the studio is too specifically set up not to have some intention behind it. The other two times I've posed for Basil, I merely sat on a stool as he sketched me. Practice, he called it, while he looked for inspiration as to how he wanted to paint me. I assumed this was standard, but the more I think about it, the more I struggle to think up a single portrait with this elaborate of a setting—or, for that matter, one that required costuming. Most portraits I've seen frame from the shoulders upward, and never have I seen one drop lower than the chest.

Acknowledging any of the oddities feels like it would break the enchantment in the studio, so I don't. If Basil wants context to inspire his portrait, I see no reason why he shouldn't have it, and if he needs me to be ignorant of it, then I'm happy to comply. He's given me no reason to doubt him in any of our sessions, and if it means that every now and then he'll glance up to me with the devotion he has for his canvas, I'm more than willing to sit still and play along.

Besides, I'll gladly take the opportunity to try to understand Wotton's game of back-and-forth. I've never thought myself a particularly surprising person, but a voice in the back of my mind insists I'm on the verge of depths neither one of my companions could have fathomed. By the time Henry and I fall back into our conversation, Grandfather's shadow is little more than a flicker in the corner of my eye.

But it never fades entirely from my sight.

3
Yellow-Bellied

I've always been aware of the cold that fills the air in Grandfather's estate, but it's never seemed harsh to me before. Until today, the chill within Barsden Hollow seemed no different from walking around London on a crisp autumn day. Now, however, I realize the underlying bitterness betrays the coming winter. It seeps into my bones and leaves me chilled, even when I'm safe by the fire.

After a day in Basil's studio, the silence I've grown accustomed to feels utterly foreign. Even as my body grew stiff and tired from the hours spent sitting in place, my mind felt a lightness I can't put into words. Somehow, in a scene made up to frame me for Basil's eye, I felt real. *Alive.* As if I weren't some ghost in the shape of a future lord, but a fire crackling in every direction, warming and fascinating those who came near me; an open flame unrestrained by any hearth, free to blaze as bright as it could dream.

Free to burn the world to ashes, if it so desired.

I've come close to that feeling before, in the few times Papa's shop was empty when I visited and I had him and Fabián to myself. When I'm with them, I know I don't need to earn their attention or their care, but I never shake the sense that's in part because they see traces of other people when they look at me. People they love, maybe even more than they could ever love me. After all, for every piece of my mother Papa sees in me, there's a reminder of the man who tore them apart. Sometimes, when Papa looks at me, I see pain strike through his eyes as he remembers that any moments we share are stolen at Grandfather's expense.

When Basil looks at me, however, I am not Dorian Gray, or at least not the version of him I know. I may not have the skills of a painter or sculptor, but in Basil's eyes I see myself as the medium of my own art. I weave Beauty not through a paintbrush or a chisel, but through a tilt of my chin or a shift in my gaze. I can take on whatever form I wish with a shift in my stance. And when Wotton looks at me, I see in the intensity of his stare all the power that art gives me. I could fascinate the world, if I chose to.

Something in me insists the thought should scare me, and yet I can't see it as anything other than an invitation—a purpose, even. I need to know how bright I can burn. Maybe, if my flame grew hot enough, I could burn free from Dorian Gray and all the expectations attached to whoever he may be.

A gust of cold air bursts through my room, snapping me back to my plush quilt and gentle linens. I pull myself from my bed to close the window I must have left open only to find it sealed shut, the broken glass replaced without so much as a question or a care. I wonder whether this one is stronger than the last, or if I could break my way through it again.

I entertain the thought of hitting the window to find out, but decide against it. I wouldn't put it past Grandfather to reinforce the next one with iron bars.

Basil promised the portrait would be finished after our next sitting. He said the shading still needs some work and then mentioned something about it lacking the spirit it needed. It's an ominous phrase to hear, and one I can't begin to understand, but it's hardly the most eccentric thing I've heard an artist say. I'm sure the difference is so minuscule I wouldn't notice it without someone pointing it out.

Whatever the case, I'm happy to oblige if it means another visit to Basil's studio. However uncomfortable it may be to sit so still for hours, it pales in comparison to the freedom that comes with it. It almost feels as though when Basil is painting me, he is hiding away a piece of me in his oils, storing it where I'll never need to compromise it. There's no respectability to be found in shapes and colors, no standards of nobility to enforce on a subject as flat as canvas.

Perhaps that's what Wotton meant when he called art political. Maybe oils and pencils are another form of smoke and mirrors that only the most skilled can use.

If that is the case, I think it's only half the story. Beauty and reputation may be cousins, but where propriety is used to manipulate, art protects. One can hide their hopes and dreams in a painting, tucking away a part of their soul where none can reach it.

I wonder, briefly, what I might find hidden in my portrait once

Basil has finished it. Would it show me some secret part of me I've never seen? Or perhaps a strange mix of Basil and me, each of us concealed by the other so there can be no telling which secrets belong to whom?

The luxury it offers is by far the best part of living in Grandfather's home; even the most wretched of souls would not struggle to sleep bundled in goose down and gentle silks, not to mention the metal springs that have grown in popularity as of late. Luckily, Grandfather's distaste for all manners of fashion does not apply to technologies and domestic improvements. That, he's told me, is a symbol of status, not wantonness. When one is better dressed than their company, it shows them to be vain—but when one feels more tended to in your home than in their own, it shows magnanimity.

Comfort or not, morning finds me weary and frazzled, rocked by an evening spent tossing and turning. My dreams are hazy, but I remember the feeling of a sword hanging over my head, heavy with the weight of some unknown destiny. I remember a mirror, too, more ornate than any I've ever owned. A framer would consider it their masterpiece had they sculpted its rollicking waves and bristling thorns. The reflection, however, I can't recall. Perhaps one isn't meant to see their own face in dreams.

It takes a few knocks at the door for me to notice them in my stupor, but Peter doesn't complain when I finally call him in. My valet enters the room with a heavy silence that startles in contrast with his usually light gait, eyes refusing to meet mine. Looking at him makes me wonder if maybe he'd hoped I wouldn't answer so that he could avoid whatever chore Grandfather sent him in on.

I yawn and stretch, not bothering to worry about any kind of modesty despite the flash of a blush on Peter's face as my nightshirt lifts and exposes my stomach. Despite his being fairly young for a valet, I struggle to think of anything he could see that would shock him after five years in his position. I suppose Grandfather might have thought it good for me to have at least one boy my age in my company, although status and Peter's fear of my grandfather serve to build as thick of a wall between us as any that age could achieve.

"Good morning, Peter," I drawl as my brain struggles to catch up with the morning sun. "It seems early for breakfast, don't you think?"

"Lord Kelso said to wake you no later than nine. If the clock in the hallway is to be trusted, it is quarter past that already."

In that case, it must be half past by now—I set the old grandfather clock back a few weeks ago in a fit of frustration with Grandfather's sharp punctuality. So far it has done little but buy me a few minutes here and there, but at least now it might provide Peter with some excuse for my lateness. Or, if nothing else, it should provide a distraction to help him avoid being reprimanded. If there's one thing that bothers Grandfather more than servants failing at their tasks, it's machines doing the same.

"How disobedient of you," I tut, prompting yet another ghost of a flush across his face. It suits him, warming up his otherwise pallid complexion.

"Who's to say I haven't spent the last fifteen minutes trying to wake you?" Peter counters, though his bold tone is undercut by his continued refusal to meet my eyes. "You're quite the stubborn sleeper, Lord Gray."

"I suppose that's inevitable. Grandfather says the Devil gave me his stubborn temper to match my—"

My teasing stops in its tracks as I straighten in my bed, eyes locking with the shadow behind Peter. It takes a few blinks for my still-foggy mind to process that it isn't a figment of my imagination, nor is it a mere shadow. His features populate one by one, steel-set eyes followed by hollow cheeks, a furrowed brow preceding lips set so tight one might mistake them for a singular line drawn straight across his mouth.

"I wondered why it had taken so long to rouse you," Grandfather says. "How many times must I tell you that lateness is a sign of apathy and disrespect?"

People rarely tell me that Grandfather and I look alike—usually they prioritize my mother, or maybe Papa if I know them from the studio—but I know I get my sharpness from him. The difference lies in how we wear it. While my traits have a pleasant geometry to their precision, Grandfather's have the harshness of a painting made too theoretically. They lack feeling, miss the gentle lift at the end of a paint stroke, leaving a slight uncanniness to the portrait that seems just shy of humanity.

I imagine it's only a matter of time until I inherit that same harshness, the more Grandfather chisels away at me.

Peter stumbles his way through an apology and bows, all but shaking under Grandfather's stare. I want to jump in and take the blame, tell him I set back the clock and spent the last fifteen minutes resisting Peter's best efforts to wake me, but my mouth feels too heavy to move. It's as though there were an anchor attached to my top lip, pulling it down until I can feel my mouth form as tight a line as Grandfather's.

Guilt curdles in my stomach as Peter looks to me for sympathy, then looks away. *I'm a coward.* I've inherited that from Grandfather, too. It's much easier to let others suffer—to cause their suffering, even—than it is to risk confronting our own problems. He'd rather rip a child from its father and watch his daughter be killed by a bullet meant for her husband than face further scandal, and I'd rather let the closest thing I have to a friend face my grandfather's ire than speak back to him.

Mother must have resented him when she drew her last breath. I'm sure she'd resent me, too. I may not remember her, but it's clear from Papa's stories she was braver and bolder than I could ever dream of being.

"I know managing my grandson is a challenging task," Grandfather tells Peter, "but that is why you are well paid to do so. I suggest you remember that."

"Yes, sir."

Peter's posture is so stiff it breaks my heart. There's no hint of his usual ease and lightness, no trace of the way he seems to dance when he moves. He is as frozen as I am, and there's nothing either of us can do to help the other. *You would do well to remember that,* Grandfather's voice echoes in my head. *There is nobody you can count on besides yourself. That is why you must remain beyond reproach.*

"Now"—Grandfather turns his attention back to me—"I believe we have left the barber waiting long enough. Come, before you make yourself look more careless than you already have."

My body rises from its bed, each limb tugged forward by strings

I neither see nor feel. I don't look at Peter when I pass by him, nor does he look at me. Sometimes I wonder whether I really do have more power over my fate in Grandfather's home than Peter does over his, or if even that is an illusion.

My stomach growls, but I hush it before Grandfather can hear. I suppose if I wanted breakfast, I should have followed his schedule more carefully. By now, I'm sure, the table has been cleared and the cooks are busy preparing for whatever luncheon is on today's agenda. Time, after all, is the one thing nobody can get back—not even when I cheat the clock itself.

4

Envy Green

The first time I had my hair cut, I was inconsolable.

I remember shrieking with each snip as if I could feel every individual strand being ripped apart one by one, as piercing and red hot as if someone were cutting through my fingers. The barber reassured me that my hair couldn't feel the scissors slicing through it. Hair can't feel anything, he'd explained. At most, I might feel a pull in my scalp if the scissors got tangled and tugged, but that was rare in the hands of a skilled barber, and of course, Grandfather had hired the best he could find. In fact, this was the same barber who cut his hair—wasn't that exciting?

Grandfather, in the meantime, reminded me how significant it was to finally shed my baby curls. I had turned five a few months prior, and it was well past time I faced this ritual. After all, this was my chance to show I was no longer a child but a young boy of good name, ready to start learning the ways of the world. The appeal to my curiosity had been enough to get me in the chair set up in the room that had once served as Mother's boudoir, but not to keep me still.

I decided that day that I would model myself the same way hair did. If scissors were to cut at me or a candle singe at me like the fashionable ladies often did to their locks, I would not feel it. As long as nobody pulled me too far from my roots, I would remain limp and pliable, as well-behaved as one could reasonably ask. It seems, in hindsight, a grim resolution for a child to make, but I can hardly deny its efficiency. It certainly made life under Grandfather's grasp more pleasant than it might otherwise have been.

I'm not sure when exactly I realized that feeling nothing prevented joy or pleasure as well, but it might explain why I've been so intent on breaking my resolution as of late. Grandfather claims it's some adolescent rebellion I need to purge from my system, but that seems a superficial answer to me. What I feel reminds me less of a ship on a rocky part of its voyage and more like a lion at the zoo thrashing at its cage, begging to be let out.

Is the lion scared of the ferocity it displays? Does it feel overwhelmed by the sheer intensity of its fury, or is it so deep into its desperation that it's lost the ability to notice or care?

Whatever the case, it's been a long time since I've found myself struggling to hold back my winces under the barber's scissors. He has always been gentle, as if some part of him can't help but remember the scared child Grandfather brought him eleven years ago. Perhaps it's the softness of my face that gives him pause. He would not be the first to tell me that, although I may not look younger than my age, I appear as if I have yet to see the world and its realities. I suppose that's to be expected, given the care put into ensuring I'm kept away from anything unseemly or undignified.

"Chin up," Grandfather orders from behind me. "We don't want your neck or shoulders to slump. Posture goes a long way in communicating a young man's character."

"Yes, Grandfather."

"I saw many young men flogged for lazy posture in King George's army, and even held the flog for a few of them myself. Character mattered much more than money back then. No wonder Victoria's England is overrun with dandies and fops."

I bite my tongue. Papa mentioned a few months ago that Grandfather's position as an officer in King George's army was paid for and that he never saw active duty—something my mother would often share when she vented to him about the militaristic authority with which Grandfather raised her. I haven't been able to take his reminiscing as seriously since finding out, but I haven't had the nerve to point out the irony to him, either. Something tells me Grandfather himself might have forgotten those facts.

Still, I oblige, raising my chin and straightening my spine atop the barber's stool. I take a deep breath and steady myself, letting my eyes wander the room without so much as tilting my head. I've become quite practiced at this little exercise—anything to avoid the mirror and the mockeries it likes to whisper.

Mother's old boudoir hasn't changed since the first time I had my hair cut. The furniture is still suited for a young lady's private sitting room, albeit decades behind modern trends. There's not a speck of dust to be seen, each part of the room perfectly curated as though it had been frozen in time. Mother's chambers are the one part of the house Grandfather refuses to open up to guests even though they serve us no purpose. Perhaps he thinks one day they'll belong to my wife, though Grandmother's old rooms are much more suited to a future mistress of this estate.

Sometimes it feels like part of my mother is still in the room. I'm forbidden from entering her quarters without Grandfather, who treats them as a sort of middle ground for when we need to gather, but every now and then I manage to sneak in just to bask in her presence. I'll close my eyes and imagine a girl my age with eyes like mine and a nose like a shard of glass sitting at the desk by the window, watching the sun set.

Imagining her is as close as I get to remembering her, but it does the trick. If nothing else, it at least makes me feel as though someone else has been where I am now. This mother I imagine might be the only person in the world able to understand me.

It's no wonder she was dead by eighteen.

I'm not sure how much time passes before Grandfather's voice calls me back from my wandering, but when it does, the barber is packing up his scissors and the apron he has somehow taken off me without my noticing. "Go on, then, boy. Take a look."

When I force my eyes to face my reflection, I find exactly what I expected. The hint of curls that had begun to grow has been chipped away, leaving hair that frames my face with military precision. It's not unappealing. In fact, I daresay many a young man in London would envy the way the neatness shapes my features, making their sharpness reminiscent of a carefully forged sword one might mount above their mantel. But swords are meant to be used, not hung on display to grow dull.

My face might be framed, but it's also flat. Hollow. A blank canvas waiting to be painted upon, but I have no idea what shapes I'd make or even what colors I might use. Sometimes I'm tempted to scribble on it or even tear the canvas apart. At least then I'd know it's mine and mine alone.

"Thank you," I tell the barber, prompted by Grandfather's silence. "Your work is perfect as always."

As we leave the room and I make my way back to my quarters, I find myself wondering when I got so good at telling people whatever they want to hear. I suppose it was always inevitable; it is, as Grandfather taught me, the way London works. Everyone tells each other what they want to hear, but nobody truly says anything at all. That would require putting one's thoughts on the table, and we're all much too good at concealing ourselves to make such careless mistakes.

Sitting on Basil's stool, I feel more exposed than I ever have in his studio.

He told me I could keep my hat on when he saw my hesitation, but something about that felt too vain for me to do. Getting self-conscious over a haircut is the type of thing even a child would be mocked for, and I can't imagine how Basil might manage to finish shading his portrait if my complexion is covered by the shadow of a top hat. A prickling sensation dances along the back of my ears as a voice suggests Grandfather's insistence on having my hair cut this morning might ruin Basil's painting. Surely, whatever essence of mine that captured the painter's attention is long gone now that I've been turned into a lifeless model of the classic Victorian gentleman.

"You're self-conscious," Wotton notes from his place on Basil's sofa. The pipe he held yesterday has been replaced by a glass of whiskey he nurses between phrases as if its sole point was to punctuate his sentences. His eyes have the same piercing quality they seem to whenever he looks at me. "There is no greater fear than that of change when we're young. It feels as though any shift might forever ruin what it is that makes one special."

"Foolish, I know."

Wotton shakes his head. "Youth is the one treasure anyone ever has. I daresay losing it is the greatest tragedy that befalls every individual."

His words are reassuring and chilling all at once. As much as I like to hear that I'm right to worry, I can't bear the idea that life will inevitably make me into the same mold as all young men. I picture myself, watching as some invisible hand paints my features harsh and bitter until I look the spitting image of Grandfather. The image chills me in a way I can't fully fathom. Fear at the thought of becoming my grandfather is nothing new, but it isn't what strikes me into helplessness. Even if I could be more like Papa than Grandfather, manhood feels like a specter haunting me with its inevitability.

"You speak as though you're an old man," Basil chides. "You're eighteen, Henry. You know as little about the world as the rest of us."

"You forget I've inherited my title already, my friend. Any noble in London can tell you that is all a man needs for his thoughts to matter."

"A notion you've long ridiculed," Basil parries.

Wotton shrugs. "Someone needs to bring truth to the idea. And, given that the folly of youth is no longer an option for me, the folly of age seems as good a replacement as any."

"And what folly would that be, exactly?" I ask.

"Knowledge, of course. There is no folly more worthwhile than believing one has grasped the ways of the world."

Basil waves him off, a gesture he immediately muddies by grumbling to himself as he paints. I venture a look over Wotton, who wears the smug contentedness of a cat who has trapped a mouse in a corner with no intent of killing it yet. His grin only grows when he notices my stare as I try to piece together what to make of him. Everything about Wotton has a certain absurdity to it, but it seems almost purposeful—as though he has found the exact grain of nonsense that feeds the world, and decided he may as well savor it.

"Dorian agrees with me," Wotton calls over to Basil when he sees the painter's irritation fading. "Don't you?"

"It hardly matters whether or not the old and the titled understand the world and its truths," I offer, cursing myself for the way I avoid picking either side in their argument. "They're in a position to dictate what is and isn't real."

Basil sighs. "I suppose I may as well unveil my painting now. I fear if I work any longer, the two of you might drive me to madness."

"You finished some time ago," Wotton accuses. "That brush of yours has been dancing over the canvas this entire conversation without ever touching it."

A scoff of mock indignation is Basil's only response. I'm not sure why he would delay showing us the finished portrait after all the time he spent working on it—unless he's embarrassed by it. Maybe I was right to worry that whatever made me worth painting vanished alongside most of my hair.

I approach the portrait with the begrudging slowness of a man walking up to his execution, bracing myself to see my fears realized before me. Basil shifts uncomfortably as Wotton and I settle next to him. Wotton has never been quiet this long in my presence, and I expect even his best acquaintances would say the same. It feels unnatural for him not to speak, but I suppose the air is so thick with anticipation and my anxiety even he cannot cut through it.

"This is the most exquisite portrait you've ever painted," he finally utters. Only then do I dare look at the canvas before me.

Wotton's choice of words could not be more apt. There's some magic to this painting that goes beyond what is merely beautiful, some force that reaches beyond the senses and echoes throughout my soul itself.

The youth on the canvas looks more like a projection of nature than a mere mortal. Their sunset-tinted locks freely flow beneath a crown of hyacinth blossoms that seem to have sprouted from their skull itself. The pink buds highlight gently pouting lips, while the white ones emphasize the smoothness of the wearer's skin. The carefully placed blue hyacinth brings new shades out of the youth's eyes, which sit slightly to the left of the watcher, narrowly avoiding their gaze as if caught in a daydream. The tender sharpness of their features seems not quite masculine nor feminine, but rather like a nymph or faerie. Even the tilt of their chin communicates an ethereal grace, though the quiet sadness in their eyes is unbearably human.

It feels as though I'm seeing myself for the first time, and I cannot bear it.

I understand, now, the irony of hiding one's self in art. A painting may guard its secrets, but once that fraction of the soul is locked away, there's no recovering it. Time and society continue to chip away outside the canvas until eventually, that secret truth is out of reach. It will only ever remain untainted within its canvas, and so will inevitably become a stranger—even to me.

This portrait of me has been finished for mere minutes, and already it feels as though the version of myself it reflects is lost forever. I was a fool to think I could ever be Art or Beauty or anything but who I am now. Perhaps traces of the youth in the painting reside in me still, but they will leave eventually. Time is not so gentle a painter as Basil is.

Already, I find the shadow in my mind picking apart the youth in the painting. This is the look of a stubborn child, one who refuses to grow into the world around them. That chin bears the elegance of a dancer, not a soldier. What right do their eyes have to be sad? Do they not know everything they have been given, everything they will inherit? The child in the portrait has the world in their hand, but would rather play with flowers in the woods. Silly. Stupid. *Shameful.*

It's good this youth is locked inside a portrait and would not be allowed to live outside it. Given the resentment weighing on me as I watch it, I doubt it could survive me, let alone the world.

The portrait flashes me a knowing smile. Does it see my jealousy? Does it cherish the fact that it will retain the beauty and freedom I'm already losing? I'm sure it does. How could it not, when it spends its life basking in the glories I've never been allowed to even acknowledge?

I look back to it for answers, but its face has returned to its original position.

"Well?" Basil's voice has a timidity it should never wear, when he is capable of such wonders. "What do you think?"

"You have painted me more beautifully than any brush ever could. I will live the rest of my life haunted, knowing it remains as it does while I cannot. I suppose there is some cold comfort in knowing at least one of us will stay this way forever—but know that I would give anything to reverse our fates. I would offer my very soul, if it meant this portrait might age and I might wear its beauty forever."

"You flatter me, Dorian."

"And you have cursed me, Basil."

Wotton sets down his empty glass, then claps the pair of us on the shoulders. "The air is much too serious here, gentlemen. I think we ought to go for a night on the town."

"Not tonight," I reply. "I fear sitting has made me weary, and I'm in dire need of rest."

"This Friday, then? I know just the place to lift your somber moods, and frankly, the sooner, the better. I must say I find you both wholly insufferable at the moment, and must take my leave if you insist on remaining this sullen."

Basil and I look at each other before nodding our agreement, and Henry leaves shortly after assuring us he'll send a coach our ways come Friday. Somehow, the air is even heavier without his presence in the room.

“I will send your portrait to your father’s shop and have Fabián craft the perfect frame for it,” says Basil. “You will keep it, won’t you? Think of it as an homage to our growing friendship.”

I agree with all the enthusiasm of a defendant accepting a life sentence over execution. My thoughts warned me, when Basil and I met, that he would wreck me, but I had no warning how thoroughly he might do so. His portrait has broken something in me I did not know was there, and now I can ignore neither the break nor this presence I’ve kept even from myself until today.

As I leave Basil’s studio, my eyes fly toward the painting for some kind of understanding—and find nothing but the solemn certainty of my fate sealed in canvas.

5
Amber Glow

By the time the clock rings six on Friday, I have spent the better part of an hour pacing my room with the desperate ferocity of an animal trapped on display. Dressing myself proved a challenge in a way it never had before. Wotton, in his rush to leave Basil and me behind, gave us no hint as to where he planned to take us. Given the impression he has left on me—one I suspect he works hard to curate, however true it may or may not be—it seems a fair assumption that whatever awaits us, it's likely far more fashionable and modern than I'm accustomed to.

The suit and vest I settled on could not be assigned either of those qualities even by the most generous of tongues, but they are not so staunch or classic as to be called behind the times, either. They have no fancy patterns or textures, but the blue of their navy is brighter than usual, and the fit is more flattering than most. While I've yet to convince Grandfather to accept today's fashions, he has at least conceded that a more tailored cut allows posture and presence to shine through.

Negotiating with Grandfather is a careful art. If I can convince him modernities can highlight tradition and proper values, I can win him over. If I'm too heavy-handed in my attempts, however, and he sees my manipulations at work, the conversation closes instantly. Whatever decision we come to, I need to make him feel as though it is his, and that I am graciously accepting some compromise.

Getting his leave to go with Basil and Wotton was no different. If anything, it was harder than usual. With no idea of where the night might take us, and Wotton's reputation as something of a darling at many a Whig salon, Grandfather pursed his lips at the mere mention of his name—the same name that, in the end, won me the case I pleaded to him. The Wottons, after all, are a noble family in good standing—better maybe than our own. Even he could not overlook the advantages a friendship with Lord Henry might produce. The reminder that he had a young cousin of marriageable age, one who came with a sizable dowry, certainly didn't hurt my argument, either.

Nonetheless, it isn't until I find myself seated in the coach opposite Basil that I finally let go of the worry that Grandfather might change his mind before I could be driven away from his reach. Knowing he can no longer stop me feels akin to taking off a particularly heavy coat only to find my shoulders and back sore from wearing it. It's certainly a relief, but my body is far more aware of the exertion than it was before I could breathe.

The smile Basil gives when he sees me exhale is no different from the ones he would wear from behind his canvas: small and fleeting, almost apologetic, as though he's worried his attention might somehow embarrass me. He speaks little beyond his original greeting, and I can't help but wonder if the portrait he made weighs as heavily on him as it does me.

What does *he* see in it? The beautiful youth on his canvas does not count down his days like it does mine, but perhaps he, too, has hidden something inside his art that pains him to face.

"I was worried you might not wish to see me now that I have painted you," Basil admits, though his tone has the air of a musing more than a confession. As though it would be perfectly normal if I'd had my fill of his company, and my presence opposite him is a surprise rather than a matter of course. It stings to hear, though I find myself struggling to explain why.

"You will learn, Mr. Hallward, that I'm much less fickle than my youth or face might suggest," I say. "I enjoy your company; I see no reason why I might wish to relieve myself of it."

"I would never think you fickle," Basil replies, wringing his hands as though unsure what to do with them when they are not holding a paintbrush. "Perhaps I simply think myself unworthy of your company. I am no conversationalist like Henry is, nor am I some poet or philosopher. I say what I have to with my brush, and often find myself struggling to speak much beyond that."

There's a certain adoration in his voice that is as welcome as it is foreign. I've never heard a man speak of a friend in such a way, but I find no desire for him to stop, either. The warmth in his tone is not a wildfire but a quietly burning hearth, steady and strong and rich enough to heat a home on its own.

"Wotton is entertaining, certainly," I tell him, "but I daresay I would not depend on him for much. His company is pleasant, but you have the ability to be a much truer friend than anyone I've met."

"It would please me greatly if you thought of me as a friend," he says, "and if you would call me Basil, rather than Mr. Hallward. I want no room for formalities in our friendship."

"Then it would be my pleasure to do so, Basil. So long as you return the favor, of course."

"Of course . . . Dorian."

This time, the silence between us is peaceful rather than weighted. The nagging sense that there's something I'm missing has not left, but I suppose I'll have time to seek out said mystery later. For the moment, I'd much rather bask in a blissful, quiet night and the way lanterns line the roads like the stars that sailors might follow across similarly dark seas.

"Has Wotton given you any indication as to our destination?" I ask once I've savored the moment to my satisfaction.

"Only that the coach is headed toward Covent Garden. But I have my suspicions, and I regret to say you're too well-dressed for all of them. Do you mind if I make some adjustments? It's important we not look too notable if we want to pass through unbothered."

"Do as you wish," I consent as Basil moves across the coach to sit beside me. "I see no reason not to trust you."

The smile on Basil's face is brighter than any I've ever seen, wide and free in a way that feels foreign to me. For an instant, fleeting as it might be, I find myself thinking him beautiful.

When the coach comes to a halt, several items of my clothing have found themselves discarded and neatly placed atop the bench. I am left only with my shirt, vest, and trousers as Basil fusses with what remains of my hair.

I note, somewhere in the back of my mind, that it seems to be regrowing more quickly than it ought to, but the improbability of that statement keeps me from paying it too much attention—especially when it's competing with the gentle scratching of Basil's soft fingers against my scalp. I don't know how I'm going to explain my disheveled state to Grandfather when I return, but that problem seems so far away from Wotton's coach it's hardly worth considering.

I thought the walk to Papa's gallery was dangerous at night, but it pales in comparison to Covent Garden. I've only ever heard the district's name in the harshest of Grandfather's tones; he paints it as the most vile and hedonistic of areas, the type of place that illustrates how far London has fallen from grace, and how much farther it might drop should we not restore order. I met his words with skepticism, but watching my surroundings now, it's hard not to wonder if there might be some truth to them after all.

The buildings that line the street are more worn down than their design implies they should be, brick growing dusty and gray with lack of care, but it's the people who stand out most of all. Loud and boisterous, they walk around dressed in clothes that give the texture and cleanliness of rags to the fashion of the last few years. Most of them stagger from door to door, guided by purposes I can only begin to guess, eyes clouded with drink or worse. I look to Basil, who guides me into the crowd, his gaze refusing to meet mine.

This is no place for me to be—and yet it's the perfect place for me to disappear.

"Do you see Henry?" I ask under my breath as we weave our way through the crowd, careful not to engage with any other passersby. "He did say he'd meet us here, did he not?"

"I believe I know where we'll find him," Basil mutters in response. Each syllable is spat out with such intensity he might as well be cursing Wotton's name under his breath.

Despite my growing discomfort with every passing step, the thought of turning back doesn't cross my mind. The night bears the scent of adventure to it—a scent which admittedly contains more liquor, poppy, and sweat than I had expected—and I will not be deterred by something as petty as nerves. Even Grandfather's shadow doesn't dare show itself, not when everything here is so contrary to the order and structure that give him power. That alone makes it worth delving deeper into Covent Garden, no matter what I might find here.

When Basil and I finally find Wotton by the door of some tavern, I'm nearly out of breath from the pace at which Basil has been driving us forward. He grins wide and smiles at us as though he hadn't abandoned us at the entrance of Covent Garden of all places, which only feeds the irritation I can sense rising from Basil beside me.

"Dorian!" he greets me, pulling me in as he claps my shoulder. "What a sight for sore eyes. It seems even your best efforts cannot prevent you from being too beautiful for a place such as this one."

The effortlessly roguish charm Wotton wears is only heightened by the sight of him in commoner's clothes, and the oddness of his compliment disarms me. I blink, then smile back. There's no point being annoyed with him now that we've all gathered without trouble.

"I agree," says Basil between gritted teeth. "Which is why it was so thoughtless to leave him to navigate this place without you."

"Why should Dorian need me, Basil? Surely you are not so coy as to claim this tavern is a stranger to you."

Though he doesn't respond, Basil's jaw remains clenched. Wotton ushers us into the tavern, guiding us toward a tall, matronly woman with warm features and dark brown skin. She smiles at Basil as if he were an old friend, gives Wotton a curt nod, then turns to me and narrows her gaze.

"I see you brought a new friend today, Mr. Hallward. Do you vouch for him?"

"I do. Dorian couldn't find it in him to hurt a fly, never mind your patrons."

"He had better not," she mutters, though her eyes soften when they meet Basil's. "I don't care how pretty this Dorian of yours is, your friend Henry is all the trouble this house can handle."

"No need to worry there," Wotton chips in. "So long as your other patrons can behave themselves, given how pretty *this Dorian of mine might be*, as you so aptly put it."

The tavern keeper glares at him in response but nonetheless guides us to a door in the back. The smell of tobacco comes flooding out when she opens it, forcing me to hold back my coughing as I follow my companions down a set of creaking wooden steps into what appears to be the tavern's cellar. Somewhere in the back of my mind, I replay the way both Henry and the barkeeper referred to me as pretty. It isn't a word I've often heard used to describe me—Grandfather would certainly be appalled at the concept—and yet I cannot say I dislike it. The way Henry says it, however, as if he were staking some claim on me, leaves behind a nagging sense of discomfort.

What waits at the bottom of the steps is unlike any cellar I've ever seen. There are bottles of port and liquor and various barrels of beer, as one might expect, but also tables where various patrons are gathered and even a makeshift stage where a figure in an elegant golden dress stands, performing some monologue I cannot quite hear from the back of the room.

As we approach, it dawns on me that every figure sat at the tables is a man. They sit with their drinks and their pipes as they chat between themselves, sometimes breaking into high-pitched giggles when one of them says something particularly daring. Some of them wear gowns and some of them do not, and many of them are seated in pairs, hands clutching each other's arms as though they might be wrested away at any time.

It makes for an oddly beautiful sight—and a sad one, too.

"You brought us to a molly house?" I ask.

Wotton shrugs. "Where else would I take the two of you?"

I frown, baffled by Wotton's response. I've heard of molly houses, usually in some of Grandfather's harsher rants when he sees an article in the paper about a raid on some *disorderly house* or another. Typically, places like this one are discussed through codes and implications rather than any open reference to them. Having a name for such a space, after all, would mean acknowledging they are a regular presence in London. Such scandals can only ever be allowed to exist in the shadows, even when we speak of them.

Though Grandfather's words on molly houses have always been few, they've been vicious enough to make it clear even fleeting curiosity about places like this one would be thoroughly punished. There was never any space to consider if I might want to visit such a place, never mind whether I might belong here.

Wotton's eyes grow wide as he looks from Basil to me and back. "The two of you *are* lovers, are you not?"

"Of course not," Basil replies. "Dorian and I have never discussed my proclivities. Why, then, should he be the object of them?"

"You speak as though you would be the first artist to develop a forbidden affair with his beautiful muse. If you ask me, the idea that the two of you might *not* be lovers is far more ridiculous than the contrary, but I suppose it's just as well. The people here are going to cherish you, Dorian. I'm sure you'll have the pick of the lot."

Basil's dismissal stings to hear. I had never considered the possibility of us being lovers—though I realize Wotton is right to assume we would hardly be an unexpected pairing—but to hear him sweep the idea aside so easily is a blow to my pride nonetheless. Strange as it feels, it occurs to me that I *want* to have stirred such feelings within Basil. The moment in the carriage where I caught myself thinking him beautiful flashes across my mind, but I chase it away before I can dwell on it any further.

I brush off Wotton's words. I have no plans to break my new friends' confidence, but I certainly won't join in their antics, either; Grandfather might kill me if he got word of where I am tonight. I turn my gaze back to the stage, eager to convince myself I'm merely at some dingy theater and quiet the stream of bubbling possibilities rushing through me.

It occurs to me, given the nature of this place, that the actress before me could easily be a man as well, but the word feels hollow when referring to her. Dark hair flows freely as she moves across the stage with such ease one might think her feet had never touched the ground, forming the most beautiful contrast with the amber of her gown and the faint blush of her cheeks. I could not say how old she is nor where she comes from; she looks as though someone has plucked her from a fairy tale and placed her here to entertain us mortals, and she has found something worth humoring in our strange, backward way.

She is free, I realize, in a way I have only ever seen in the youth from my portrait. They may as well have been plucked from the same realm, with all the joy and beauty they share. She is proof that whatever dream I locked away in Basil's canvas can live here in London, though its name eludes me still.

"*That was your mistake, my love,*" she recites. "*You saw me dance in the shadows before you, and so you named me woman. But was it not folly to think you could know me, when all the words you have are for shapes on cavern walls? What could you hope to understand, when you have but now caught your first glimpse of the world beyond your cave?*"

On this note she bows, and the room breaks into applause. I watch her glow in black and amber as she steps off the stage and vanishes behind a curtain in the corner of the room. Something in me aches to follow her, to meet her, but I push the urge down. Perhaps she is an illusion projected before me, and meeting her might break me. I want to think of her as real, even if that means we may never speak.

"Who is she?" I ask once the applause has died down. I may not be able to meet her, but at least I can learn her name. I can make her more real, illusion or not.

"Sybil Vane," Wotton answers. "Lovely, is she not?"

"Beyond lovely. Our words dishonor her."

"She performs here every night. Sometimes classics, sometimes works of her own composition. Perhaps we might come back to see her sometime."

"Perhaps," I agree, but the sense of dread in me grows stronger the moment I do. It feels, suddenly, as if I'm being watched, and whatever eyes now sit on me are filled with nothing but judgment.

That night, as I lie in my bed, Sybil Vane and I dance in my dreams. We are shadows one minute, the tides of a river the next, then winds gusting across open moors. Each time we dance together, and each time we are shapeless.

Each time, we are radiant.

6
Crypt Stone

Mother's funeral was a quiet affair.

It must have been quite the scandal for a lady of her rank to be buried without a proper procession. I suppose Grandfather had hoped this last one might be overlooked amidst the controversy she'd already spurred, or that the murmurs about her burial would replace the ones that spoke of the child she birthed out of wedlock or her death in what was presumed to be a duel gone astray. I can't say whether or not he was right—nobody has dared to tell me much beyond that it was, by all accounts, an odd decision—but given the lack of public speculation as to who my father may be and the ease with which I was accepted as heir to the Kelso name, it seems his gambit succeeded in the long term.

Grandfather has always been quick to cover his tracks. Papa told me the news of my birth had barely reached his ears before an emissary had come from Grandfather's household, warning him not to claim me if he cared about my future. I have always wondered if there was more to his threat than Papa shared, but he has kept his mouth stubbornly shut on the matter. It often feels, when I ask him why he lets Grandfather keep us apart, that he's torn between wanting me to know the truth and worrying it would do nothing but hurt me.

He only told me as much as he had, Papa said when I pressed the matter, to explain why he insists on calling me *soleil*—the word for *sun* in his native French, and a play on the one word he must never call me. I asked, once, why he never returned to Paris upon my mother's passing, but he said he'd rather be nearby and rarely see me than sit back home in France, wondering if I was safe and happy.

What the words *safe* or *happy* mean to him escapes me. Perhaps he only means to know that I am alive and healthy, and prays that I'm not beyond repair when Grandfather finally passes.

Sometimes, I wonder whether I've already crossed that line. It seems to me that Grandfather's shadow is stronger with each passing day, growing taller and darker at my feet. In my bleakest times, I worry that I might look behind me to see it reaching toward me, having consumed my own shadow and found it incapable of quelling its hunger.

"I wish I could know if you were watching me," I whisper, my hands clutched together as I kneel beside the stone coffin in which my mother lies. "At times I think I feel you, but my imagination runs wild and I know such things are blasphemous. Perhaps I feel only what I want to, and find comfort in the thought of your presence. I wish, at least, that I knew if you love me."

My words bounce between stone walls, their muffled echo taunting me as the words *love me* ring across the room. It makes a haunting sound, as if some banshee were trapped in here with me, begging to be wanted. The crypt is fairly new, built when Grandfather was a boy amidst fears of pestilence and contamination. One might think it too young to be haunted, but I suppose fate has forced its hand.

I know little about the other bodies buried here. Grandfather speaks nothing of the older brother he once had, and even less about his parents. When I find myself in a generous mood, I imagine they were kind and noble people, too good to live in this world for long. More often, I think a man like Grandfather cannot have come from nowhere, that coldness and cruelty are traits one must cultivate, and that my mother was an exception to our family's curse—that time could not gray her nature like it did the others.

It's comforting to think a wildflower can grow among weeds. It implies, I like to think, that I might follow in her footsteps.

Then again, the shadow in me mutters, *perhaps she simply died too young for time to do its work.*

I push the thought aside, but it doesn't leave entirely. In the end, all Kelsos are buried together; even the scandal of my birth could not protect my mother from her fate. We are but rotting flesh, delving deeper into our decay. Why, then, would our souls not rot along with our bodies? The thought is blasphemy, but I can't bring myself to care. After all, the most outwardly pious people I know are those who have committed the most graceless acts.

"It feels," I confess to whatever ghosts watch me, "that the older

I get, the less I control my own self. Time will chip at my body and duty will tarnish my soul, and I'll be left another hollow shell to wander London. It seems, at times, as though the only true thing in all the city is the fog. It, at least, moves of its own accord and fills whatever space it wishes. The rest of us are little more than appearances maintained for the sake of convenience. How can I live if I can't even *be*?"

My words do not echo cleanly this time. They bundle together, bouncing into each other and then breaking apart in new arrangements. The result is cacophonous as a crowded market, and I find myself lost amidst it, floating in the chaos.

It appears the ghosts around me have no more answers than I do.

I can't remember the last time I saw Papa in daylight.

Normally, leaving the estate means sneaking around Grandfather, a feat that is much easier at night. On the anniversary of Mother's death, however, he shuts himself away in his quarters, and I'm left to my own devices. I assume he thinks I know better than to wander where he doesn't want me, but what I know and what I do are different matters entirely.

Besides, I have an excuse to be here today: Basil told me that Fabián had finished framing my portrait, and while I could send Peter to fetch it for me, it would be awfully rude of me not to personally thank the artisan who made the frame.

The gallery is quieter during business hours. I suppose that shouldn't come as a surprise; sales may be how the gallery makes its profits, but its nighttime showings and salons are how it makes its name. Artists, it turns out, are a rather nocturnal lot, and tend to reserve their daily hours for their work. As such, there's nobody to spread word of my presence here besides a man in worn, paint-splattered trousers who seems too distracted comparing various shades of red to even notice me.

Papa is hard at work when I see him, rearranging various framed paintings along the left flank of the gallery where private showings are occasionally held. His gait lacks the usual, almost dreamlike lightness with which he glides, and when he turns toward me, I notice a pitch-black handkerchief peeking out from his coat pocket—likely the only concession he could make to his mourning without attracting attention. Fabián orbits him along the exhibition, always one step behind, hands at the ready as if waiting to catch him when he collapses. Each move one makes is perfectly matched by the other, so that I wouldn't know which is leading and which is following were it not for the worry on Fabián's face mirroring the one I feel.

It cannot be easy to mourn what you aren't allowed to miss.

Light returns to Papa's face for an instant when he sees me. He walks toward me, arms open in embrace. I look over to his patron, still absorbed in his samples, then give him the most cautious smile I can muster. However comfortable Papa might be amidst his circle, I cannot account for the patrons with whom he does business by day. My heart races as I pass through the possibilities that might befall us should the warmth of his greeting attract any attention, but when he hugs me, I can't help but return it. The hold of Papa's arms around me is a rarity for which I would pay dearly if I had to.

"You'll have to forgive my familiarity," he says in perfect approximation of a sheepishness that does not suit him. "You know how eccentric we Frenchmen are, and how formal the English. But it has been too long, Lord Gray, since I last welcomed your business."

"It's a pleasure to patronize such a vital gallery. I daresay your arrival is one of this century's greatest boons to London's artists."

Papa's smile wears a shade of conspiracy to it. Pretending to be strangers is a game we have played too often, but it is at least an activity we can share. "You flatter me, but I am vain enough to accept it."

"I hear from Mr. Hallward that my portrait is ready? He spoke highly of the frame you crafted," I say, turning to Fabián.

"It's some of the finest work I have done. I hope it suits your needs."

"You are too humble," Papa chides, placing his hand on Fabián's forearm as he does. "It's beautiful, and I'm certain you will agree."

There is a tenderness in the way Papa touches Fabián that I never noticed before—or rather that I had not thought much of until now. Open signs of affection have always been a common part of their friendship, one that I attributed to their being unrestrained by English notions of propriety. It's hardly uncommon, as far as I have heard, for men in France to express their friendship more intimately than they do here, and while Fabián has told me little about the traditions of the Calé, I see no reason for them to share our shortcomings.

Watching them now, however, I can't help but think of the men I saw at the molly house last week, and that same affection I saw in many of their eyes. I know that Papa and Fabián share the lodgings above the gallery, as painting sales and even the frames and art supplies aren't enough to fund individual living spaces, but I can't help but wonder now if they might prefer it that way as well. The truth, I suppose, is none of my concern, but the possibility of secrets hidden in plain sight fascinates me. How many people live entire lives behind closed doors, tucked away from prying eyes?

Fabián walks away to gather the frame, leaving Papa and me to cherish these few moments of solitude. I search my mind for words I might say, be they about Basil or the gallery or even the weather, though it remains as gray as ever, but nothing comes. The two of us stand in silence, smiling and taking each other in. Simply seeing him warms me. It feels, when I'm in his company, as though there's more than one fate that might await me—more than one person I might become.

Being around Papa reminds me there's more than Grandfather's blood in my veins. Papa's flows through me as well, and so does Mother's. Both of them chose each other, and though the consequences were severe, they were theirs to take on nonetheless. I may never live a happy life, but perhaps I might someday live one of my own choosing. One where my father is not a stranger.

By the time Fabián returns with my portrait, Papa has excused himself to assist the gentleman who has finally chosen a shade of red. I pull my purse from my coat, but Fabián stops me.

"Your father won't accept your money. It's the one thing he feels he can still do for you."

"You made the frame," I counter. "I'm paying for your services, not his. If he asks, tell him I insisted. I would much prefer

Grandfather's money go to the two of you than waste away in my purse."

Fabián nods. "I cannot disagree with you on that point. Thank you, Dorian. It truly is a beautiful portrait."

I agree, then ask if I might take a look at it before I go. The frame is as beautiful as promised, with carefully carved rose vines lining its oval edges, but it's not what stands out to me. In the bright light of the gallery, I could swear the youth's mouth sits a little sterner, his eyes somewhat sadder. Even his curls seem less untamed, as if someone had tried to run a brush through them and given up halfway.

But such things are impossible, and by the time I've loaded the portrait into my coach home, any change in the youth's features has already left my mind, easily dismissed as some trick of the light.

7

Rose in Bloom

Vain as it may be, I cannot stop taking in Basil's portrait.

Though the youth it shows is beautiful, it isn't their looks that fascinate me but the same freedom I resented when I first saw it. The deep black of my sitting room's walls seems too plain, too harsh to host the flower-adorned sprite surrounded by wooden vines and roses, trapping them within London's rigid structure and keeping them from the woods they were meant to roam. It feels, looking at the figure frozen on the canvas, as though it would be a kindness to tear the portrait from its frame and let it run free, and yet I couldn't bring myself to do such a thing. Violent as my envy is, I don't have it in me to harm my strange reflection. The mere thought of it sends every instinct I have flying toward outrage.

I've never wanted anything before, I think, the way I wish I could change places with the youth before me—or I haven't *let* myself want anything, at least. There's never been much point to it, knowing how strictly Grandfather has outlined my life for me. Sneaking out to visit Papa is as close as I've come, but I never imagined those visits could be anything more than impulsive acts of short-lived rebellion. I'm all too aware of what happened when Mother ran away to entertain the thought myself, however much I might have craved a different life—living with Papa somewhere near Paris, spending my time surrounded by art and the kind of thinkers that would shock London's high society. I might have liked to see the world, so I could spend each day exposed to new ideas.

Instead, I stand in a room oppressive in its plainness, wishing I could be an image frozen in time and not the walking shadow of someone else's desires.

I don't quite know what makes this portrait so enviable to me. Youth seems so foolish a trait to envy, and yet it often feels like the only barrier between myself and becoming a person I do not wish to be. However new desire may be to me, I'm quite well-versed in what I do not want. I spend my days surrounded by it, coaxed and trained to give myself to it until I fear it might write over me altogether. Perhaps what I envy about the youth before me is simply their obliviousness. They know no expectation, no fear or remorse. Their sole purpose is to *be*.

I struggle to think of a more foreign notion.

The door to my bedchamber opens without a knock. I hurry to throw the nearest sheet over Basil's portrait and rush from my sitting room to the main chamber lest Grandfather see the image of me on its canvas. I'm not sure which part of it he'd despise most; all that matters is that I must keep it from him. I wager I might never see the youth again should his eye fall on them.

Grandfather's gaze is cold and judging as it lands on me, but he nods in approval when he sees me dressed, posture straighter than the most disciplined of cadets. Even my heart is perfectly steady as it thumps louder and louder in my chest. The urge to adjust some flaw bursts through me, but the only thing that might condemn me more than a stray hair or undone button is some break in my unflinching stance. I suffer his assessment as stoically as I can muster, allowing myself only a fraction of reprieve when he nods his approval a final time.

"There may be hope for you yet, boy," he says, his voice gruff even in contentment. The words make me flinch, though they should bring only relief. "I worried I might find you still in bed, stranded in that laziness that seems all too common these days."

"I've been reading accounts of the Napoleonic Wars," I lie. Grandfather's face moves from its typically analytic detachment to an expression I could almost call pride. Somehow, the sight is more unpleasant than even his judgment.

"A man's mind is his most powerful weapon. I'm glad to hear you have not been rusting yours with such wasteful fancies as novels or poetry. There is little in fiction that cannot be better found in our country's histories."

I nod my agreement so instinctively I don't register the action as I perform it. It's but another step in the dance the two of us do, where I pretend to be the grandson he wanted and he walks away, satisfied to have shaped me in his image. I could not say whether the act I put on for him is convincing or if he simply does not care to interrogate it, but it matters little so long as it buys me a few moments' peace. There will be plenty of time to want more than to survive him, so long as he cannot erase what will I have before his death.

"I think you might be ready to get more involved in London society," Grandfather says. "Lady Blackwell is having a salon tomorrow and has been pestering me to meet you. Her tastes have admittedly grown frivolous for my liking, but such failings are inevitable in this age. She will have the sense not to invite anyone too unseemly. I have faith you'll refrain from letting the extravagance of her home sway you?"

"Of course, Grandfather. I know better than to let such superficial matters dull my sense."

"Excellent." He turns away from me, musing contentedly to himself as he does. "I'm glad to see at least *some* good might still come from your mother's careless behavior."

Grandfather closes the door behind him, leaving me standing amidst the shrinking walls and echoing space around me. I fall to my bed and close my eyes, fleeing to some faraway forest I've never seen. The faerie-like twin Basil painted meets me in its brush and guides me to a meadow where we lie in the flowers and bask in the sun.

For a few blissful moments, no harm can reach me.

If Barsden Hollow is a beacon of how tedious minimalism can grow, Lady Blackwell's estate is a testament to its opposite. Loath as I am to agree with Grandfather, his assessment of her taste is more apt than I care to admit.

Antiques line the parlor like a poorly curated museum, each one from a different era than the last, lit by the largest candelabra I've ever seen. My attempts to observe it have left me blinded by the light and the way it reflects between the countless gems surrounding it, strengthening its brightness with each trip between them. The wallpaper, a pesky shade of rose that manages to be saccharine and dull all at once, is coated with abstract swirls that show no purpose beyond filling space, lest observers somehow grow bored of struggling to discern the Louis XIV poufs from the Louis XVI.

Worse than all, however, are the three grandfather clocks in the free corners of the room dueling hourly, each one ever-so-slightly out of sync with the others. How anybody can have a conversation surrounded by this chaos—never mind an interesting one—is the type of mystery Dickens himself couldn't spin.

Grandfather's complaints about the modern age may not be entirely founded, but there's something to be said about our growing obsession with maximalism. Surrounding oneself with beauty may help to cultivate the mind, but doing so without any discretion or sense of taste leaves one no better than a magpie, unable to tell value from a glittering piece of garbage.

I resent my judgment the moment I think it—it's far too close to what Grandfather might say to sit comfortably with me.

"Lord Gray, have you met my nephew?"

The question doesn't register at first, and Lady Blackwell smiles at me for a moment before I pull my head away from that dizzying wallpaper and toward the guest to whom I'm being introduced. It takes all my willpower not to laugh when my eyes land on the nephew in question and I process that not only have I met him, but that I appear unable to go more than a week without seeing him.

"You ought to have told me Lord Gray would be here," says Wotton, taking his hat off in an exaggerated bow. "I might have showed up early."

"Early!" Lady Blackwell scoffs. "I would settle for having you come when intended, but I suppose young men are too busy amusing themselves for such banalities."

The smile on Wotton's face has a boyish sheepishness he wears disarmingly well. Looking at him, it seems impossible to think him capable of the baffling claims that leave his mouth, but that makes them all the more amusing. "Punctuality is in such poor taste, dear aunt. One should always be either early, so that they may entertain their host, or late, so the host need not entertain them. The last thing I would want is to burden you."

"Of course." Lady Blackwell straightens in her chair as if the claim offered her the utmost importance. Henry flashes me a conspiratorial grin, and as much as my reflexes shout to look away, I meet his smile instead. I don't know what it is about him that disarms people so easily, but it feels almost like a challenge, some invitation to match his charm rather than be bowled over by it. "You've always been so attentive to your poor old aunt, Henry, but one day you'll learn that at my age, all one ever wants is the company of others. You may burden me all you like."

A few guests around the table tut their agreement as Wotton kisses his aunt on the cheek and seizes a chair across the table from me, eyes averted as he engages one of the other guests, an older woman whom Lady Blackwell introduced to me only as

Lady Agatha, in conversation about some local controversy I've yet to hear.

As tedious as society salons tend to be, I can at least rely on them to give me any gossip I've missed. While I can always expect to know where a person's reputation stands once trouble has befallen them, there's something exciting about listening in on the speculations as they happen. It feels almost like reading a novel, but the scandals that befall the real England are far more captivating than what anyone might dream up.

"Do you really think poor Dartmoor will marry her?" asks Lady Agatha, her scandalized tone teetering between shock and downright giddiness with all the ease of someone discussing the end of a particularly dramatic opera.

"I believe," Wotton offers, "that the American has in mind to propose to him, and that English men lack the emotional wisdom to respond to anything so vulgar as a proposal."

"Vulgar! It's certainly unseemly for a woman to bring up the question of marriage, but surely you don't think marriage as a whole to be vulgar, Henry?"

"Of course not. Marriage is far too tedious to be vulgar. It is little more than a business agreement between two people who have found it mutually profitable. Proposals, on the other hand, are presumptuous to the point of vulgarity. Every good marriage happens by chance, when two people come to agreement—independently—that it is in their best convenience to see it done. It's much neater that way."

"Nobody has ever accused you of being a romantic, have they, Lord Henry?"

Wotton laughs. "Romance is best reserved for affairs, and I believe we'd both agree the best of those go unspoken."

Listening to Wotton speak, I realize, makes it all but impossible not to be swayed by him. He speaks not only with complete assuredness, but also an easy charm that makes one *wish* to be swayed, as though the secret to a life as easy and carefree as he claims to live were hidden in the paradoxes he peddles as facts. We lock eyes for a moment as he looks away from Lady Agatha, and I find myself staring into my lap, flushed with the realization that I've done nothing but watch him talk since his arrival. Part of me wants to look back up, if only to see if he noticed my staring, but the idea that he has is too mortifying to risk.

"I think," I start, without fully knowing what I want to say as much as that I must say something to chase away this awkward feeling, "that Dartmoor should consider himself lucky. There are worse fates than a beautiful woman asking to marry you, promising a sizable dowry in exchange. I daresay most men want nothing more in a marriage."

"You're far too young to be so cynical," chides a white-bearded man. "But I suppose there's some truth to your claim. A beautiful wife and healthy fortune is nothing to turn away, although I'm sure we can agree the means through which the American woman has orchestrated the situation are nothing short of appalling."

The conversation carries on, and though I hear some thoughts on America and their ways, I cannot follow them. A ringing echoes in my chest, sharp and bright in equal measures so that I find myself unsure whether it's pleasant or painful. Words blur into a rumbling thunder in the distance as I wonder what point there might be in a life so dictated by the arbitrary norms around me. What sort of world might we have, were matters of propriety and respectability considered less worthwhile than comfort or enjoyment? The idea that anyone might prefer our current reality to that one baffles me. Surely it would be better to live in the kind of reality Sybil Vane preached, unrestricted by the shadows we work so hard to project in our steads.

When I look back up, desperate for a distraction, Wotton's eyes are still on me. Probing deeper into them, I feel with sudden certainty they never left.

"I suppose your aunt's taste in decor can be excused if this is how she tends to her garden."

I could only take another quarter hour of half following conversations before excusing myself for some fresh air. Wotton insisted on showing me the gardens, claiming a need to stretch his legs, and I could find no reason—nor, for that matter, desire—to deny him. His company, as mystifying as it is, has the pleasant feeling of eating more sweets than I know I should after a difficult day. It may not serve me, but it's a preferable alternative to the kind of world Grandfather sees for me.

"Oh, there's no taste to be accounted for," Wotton replies, leading me toward a section of rosebushes in full bloom. "Aunt Honoria simply gathers as many interesting items as she can under the assumption one of them must appeal to each of her guests. It's an eclectic approach, but I have to say it has its charms."

The night is unseasonably pleasant for May, so we walk slowly, taking in each bloom as we go. The violets have started to spring, and even the hydrangeas are attempting to crawl their way up from the ground. The stars seem to fade more with every passing year, chased by the smoke that grows its roots through London—I suppose even the sky is not immune to time's natural ravages. Progress has its costs, and it seems England is more than willing to pay them.

"You are turning out to be quite the surprise," Wotton muses as we stroll around the hedges and deeper into the gardens.

"How so?"

"The way you speak when you think what you're offering is a half-formed thought . . . your mind is much sharper than your face lets on. I find it quite like picking up a rose to admire it, only to be reminded of its thorns when I prick myself on them. I've always found the contrast makes the experience far more pleasant, haven't you?"

I sit on his words for a moment, thinking back to the sharpness of broken glass against me when I crawl out to see Papa. There's a certain pleasure to pain, I decide, when it's in service of some other enjoyment. It feels almost like anticipation, as if the sting of the cut serves as a reminder of the end goal approaching.

"You flatter me," I tell him, but my voice bears none of the reprimand I might have intended. I doubt it would have had much impact if it had, when Wotton is so accustomed to earning people's disbelief and—somehow always playful—disapproval. "But I suppose I have read more than my share. There's little else to do at Barsden Hollow."

"Perhaps you might like to read in my sitting room and have some company, then. I would like us to be friends."

"We *are* friends."

"You, Basil, and I certainly are. But I am a selfish man, as I'm sure you know, and I might like to whisk you away from time to time. I find it hard to believe someone is a friend if our company must always be either mediated or accidental, and if they insist on calling me by my surname."

Wotton's eyes bore into mine with an intensity that has started to grow familiar. It occurs to me, as I hold his gaze, that this might look rather like a courtship if our circumstances were different, and I find the thought is more welcome than I might have expected. Wotton is a handsome man—I dare think he wouldn't be afforded half his eccentricities were he not—and he has looked at me in a way nobody has before him from the moment he met me. In his eyes, I find myself feeling like some great romantic figure, safely immortalized in the realm of ideas where even reality cannot reach me. It isn't quite as freeing as the way I felt watching Sybil Vane or even the lightness I see in Basil's portrait, but it's close enough that it might satisfy me.

I briefly wonder what it would be like to kiss him as I saw patrons do in the molly house, but chase away the thought. Even if I *could* want such a thing, I doubt I'm prepared for the consequences such mad cravings would earn me. Some questions are better left unasked, some taboos best unbroken.

I take a step back and let the chirping of crickets in the distance soothe me back to solid ground.

"Someone watching us might get the wrong idea," I finally say. "What if another of your aunt's guests decided they wanted a walk as well?"

"Then they would see one friend extending a social invitation to another. Londoners only ever see what they want to. Besides, nobody overhears less than gossips. It's why they need to gather their scandals secondhand."

Wotton's words make little sense, but I've grown to expect as much. I wouldn't be surprised if that were the way he preferred it, leaving just enough meaning in his sentences for his audience to interpret it however they choose.

"I suppose it couldn't hurt to have one friend more."

"Perfect." Wotton's smile looks the way I imagine a cat might grin if it could. "I have a book I've been dying to loan you."

8
Orange Sunset

It takes two weeks for me to return to Covent Garden, but each day among them might as well have been an eternity.

I told myself I wouldn't go back, that there were some risks I had no reason to take, but each night chipped away at my resolve as questions piled in the back of my mind. The people at the molly house looked happy—as much as possible, anyway—and Sybil looked so free. I still could not say whether Sybil Vane was a man or a woman, but the truth of her seems to matter far less than the fact of her existence. The sight of her in her amber gown lives in my mind with no regard for whether or not I want it there, taunting me with the way it spun as she moved. The longer I go without seeing her, the more convinced I grow that she was nothing but a figment of my imagination.

If Sybil Vane were real, then the sheer possibility of what she represents is unfathomable. I think back to the shadows she spoke of in her monologue, neither men nor women exactly but beings beyond what either of those terms could explain. There'd be no point in the kind of life Grandfather has spent so much time training me for in a world where Sybil Vane is a possibility, not when I could fashion myself into any shape I like instead.

It's this logic that finally convinces me to go. Once I've confirmed for myself that the Sybil Vane that dances in my dreams is an exaggeration of the one I saw, I can know peace. The thought of losing the image I've built in my mind breaks my heart, but that seems a small price to pay for some clarity. I need to remind myself there's no magic tucked away in London's underbelly, no escape from the smoke or the fog or the all-encompassing gray that stains everything it touches. There's nothing I could want sitting at the edge of my reach, waiting for me to be bold enough to claim it.

My attempts at blending in, at least, are more fruitful than they were the first time I came. Hidden as I am under clothes too small and too worn for proper wear, nobody bothers to accost or proposition me. In fact, I've yet to see anyone so much as glance my way. Why should they? I'm no more than any other street urchin. Even the hair that's always made me stand out is tucked away under a newsboy cap I bought on a whim a few days back.

There's some comfort, at least, in knowing I can so drastically change my own appearance. I never realized how much of a nobleman is clothing and posture and artifice that one can don or dismiss as they please. If I wanted to, I could disregard it forever and vanish into London without a trace, but I struggle to think what kind of life I might lead from there. As loath as I am to acknowledge it, the comfort and warmth that come with wealth are second nature to me. The only possibility that frightens me more than life at Barsden Hollow is life outside it.

The walk to the tavern feels longer than it did when I had the comfort of a coat around me and the pleasure of Basil's company, but I do eventually find my destination. Warmth hits me the moment I walk in, quickly followed by the smell of bread and beer. The tavern keeper I met the other day is behind the bar, speaking with a particularly boisterous pair of customers.

This is it, then. All I have to do is take one final leap and I've made my way back to where I've wanted to go for weeks now.

The fact that I *want* to be here, of all places, is more chilling than I care to admit. After spending as long as I can remember training myself to keep my head down and waiting to be in charge of my own life, the sheer act of desiring something as much as I crave the unsettling familiarity of this molly house is downright dizzying. Somewhere between sneaking out to Papa's gallery and spending time with Basil and Wotton, risking Grandfather's anger has become almost commonplace, and I can't bring myself to stop. It feels, almost, as if I'm an explorer treading through undiscovered ruins, on the verge of discovering a treasure the likes of which the world has never seen.

All of a sudden the tavern is too loud, too bright, too small as the walls come closer and closer, threatening to crush me between them. My breath goes shallow and my chest tightens. A certainty grows in the bottom of my heart that I'm being watched from afar, and that whoever is watching knows secrets

I've managed to hide away even from myself. Shadows spin across my vision until the world goes dark and I realize I've closed my eyes.

This is a mistake. I'm not even sure what I'm here to find out exactly, but some secrets are best kept as such. If I open the Pandora's box that sits before me, there will be no going back—but if I don't, the mysteries inside will continue to haunt me until I give in. The way Wotton looked at me the night I thought he might kiss me flashes across my mind, and I take a step forward, sighing as I resolve to let this curious fascination win out yet again.

"You look like you could use a drink, lovey."

I open my eyes to see the tavern keeper standing before me, worry written across her rich brown eyes. Her smile has the gentle comfort I imagine a mother's might, so I steel myself and nod, grabbing a stool by the bar as she pours. Once my breathing starts to steady, I pull off my hat to uncover my face, grabbing the coin purse I'd hidden under it as I do.

"Do you remember me?" I ask.

"With a face like yours?" She hands me a pint, though it's only about a quarter full. "I think it would take more than that disguise to fool most people. You were here with Basil and that friend of his about a fortnight ago. I'm Tamara. It's lovely to see you again."

I pull some coin out of my purse to pay for my beer, then carefully take a sip. Grandfather claims beer is an unsophisticated man's drink, too simple and cheap for anyone with taste, so I've never had the chance to drink it before. It's pleasant enough, and I feel it start to calm my mind almost immediately.

"How old are you, sweetheart?"

"Sixteen." I try to drop my voice as I say it, which only makes Tamara sigh. "I'm here to see Sybil Vane again. Is she performing tonight?"

"I couldn't stop that one if I tried. Sybil performs every night, and I suppose my purse is better off for it. I believe she selected a few speeches from Shakespeare for this evening."

I take a few more sips, finding the bottom of the glass more quickly than I expected. A strange sort of calm seeps over me as I realize the worst of the night is over. Sybil is here, mere moments away, and I have nothing left to do but go to the cellar and see her. The thought makes my heart race again, but this time I don't mind it. The beat reminds me more of a promise than a threat, and I find myself eager to follow its rhythm toward the back of the tavern.

Tamara looks at me as she opens the cellar door, the gentlest hint of a frown on her brow. "My patrons are good people, but I can't know everyone they bring, and you, for better or worse, are very pretty and younger than you think. There's no tolerance for unwelcome advances in my tavern, and I'm more than happy to enforce that. If anyone bothers you when you're down there, excuse yourself and let me know."

I nod, grasping just enough of the tavern keeper's words to understand the gist of her implication. Wotton said something about me attracting attention the last time we were here, but it's hard to imagine anyone turning an eye toward me the way I look tonight. Tamara disappears behind the door and I find myself atop the stairs of her molly house once more, with nothing but a nagging sense of destiny to keep me company.

The table I find this visit is right by the edge of the large crate Sybil uses as a makeshift stage, tucked away from most of the others to make a nice, secluded spot in the corner. I sit in silence as she speaks, taking her in with the quiet wonder of a man hearing the gospel for the first time.

Tonight, Sybil's gown is the burnt orange of a sunset that promises beautiful skies in the morrow. Pearls sit across her neck so perfectly still one might think they were glued there, and yet she remains in constant motion, discarding one name for another as easily as if they were clothing. She is Juliet, then Cordelia, Ophelia, and even Titania. Each time I watch as her face shifts entirely with nothing but the emotions it wears to aid her.

I came here to prove that the goddess onstage is not the magician I remembered, and I suppose I got my wish: She is so much more than I could have imagined.

What would it look like to shed identities and pick up new ones so completely? Who would I be, if I could transform even half as easily as Sybil Vane? The question echoes unanswered in my head, granting me glimpses of a picture I cannot put together.

She morphs once more as if in answer. Her face grows pained and her eyes grow wrathful as she becomes the fiercest Lady Macbeth I've ever seen.

"Come, you spirits that tend on mortal thoughts, unsex me here, and fill me from the crown to the toe top-full of direst cruelty."

Each word leaves her mouth as a growl, yet her voice is low

and clear as church bells. It's the one thing about her that never changes, though it shifts its tones with reckless abandon.

A man stops by my table, two pints in hand. I don't register his face—why would I care to, when my eyes have Sybil to feast on?—but he appears near my age, a year or two older than Wotton at the most. I offer him a seat but refuse the pint. I didn't come to drink, and I want my head as clear as possible. Maybe, if I focus enough, I can find out the secret of Sybil's powers and keep some of her magic for myself.

"Beautiful, isn't she?" he asks.

"Far beyond beautiful," I answer, my eyes fixated on her even as I speak. "I have no idea how she changes the way she does."

"You could do it, I wager. I struggle to imagine a shape your face wouldn't suit."

I turn to him, ready to tell him off for the utter blasphemy that is comparing me to Sybil Vane when I finally see him. He is tall and broad with lush lips and an unbridled hunger in his eyes that clenches my abdomen into a pleasant heat I don't recognize. I've felt seen before, sitting in Basil's studio, and I've felt admired, but I cannot think of a time where I've felt so desired. The thought fills me with power as I realize this stranger is in the palm of my hand, then shame when I realize how much I savor it.

You could shatter him, a voice whispers. It is not unlike my own, yet it has a confidence that mine has never worn. *You have no idea the things you could do, but don't they sound delectable?*

"Perhaps I could," I say, snapping my thoughts away from its grasp. "Unfortunately, my lot is to become a rather different type of person."

"A tragedy," he replies, "but even the most noble man has his secrets—and even the most pious deserves his pleasures."

I turn my attention back to the stage, attempting to channel an air of cold indifference as I do. A few moments later, the stranger stands and makes his way to the back of the room, two pints still in his hands. Sybil transforms again, and this time I study her as she does. Perhaps, if I watch her often enough, I might learn her technique and grow to master it myself.

Come nighttime, I do not dream of Sybil Vane. I see a different figure instead, with hair like blazing sunlight and bright, sparkling eyes. She beckons me forward and I follow as she leads me to the edge of a pond. We lie down in the grass and sit, far from the noise and scrutiny of high society. Her hand is soft to the touch, but cold as well.

"Sit," she says. So I do.

"Look," she orders.

When I look into the pond before us, my reflection rests where hers should be. Pain burns across its eyes as it looks at me, fading, until I'm left sitting by myself, searching the waters for some last trace of her before I fall in.

I wake up shivering and shaking, soaked in tears shed over a person I'll never be.

9
Blush Pink

Though only a few weeks have passed since Basil and I last saw each other, longing aches as though I've spent months without his company.

The speed with which he has become a fixture in my life would likely be nothing short of baffling, had I many other friendships with which to compare it. At some point, sitting in his studio posing as he painted me began to feel more comfortable than my own home, though I suppose Barsden Hollow is an easy standard to beat. Even when Basil is too focused on his art to hold a conversation with me, the warmth of his quiet is more welcoming than most atmospheres. It often feels, when the two of us are alone, that I don't need to perform on his behalf.

Today, however, the silence in his studio is nearly unbearable. Ever since our trip to Covent Garden, I can't help remembering the way Basil sounded when Henry asked if the two of us were lovers. His tone was harsher than I have ever heard it, laced with a coldness so forceful it still sends a chill down my spine. Now, when I look at him, the rejection still stings, no matter how often I remind myself I have no feelings for him.

How fragile my ego must be if the dismissal of a mere hypothetical can leave me feeling so jilted.

"Are you sure you don't wish to sit for me again today?" Basil asks.

"Very much so, yes. I would hate for you to think I can only enjoy your company when I'm taking advantage of your artistic abilities."

"You hardly need worry about that," Basil counters. "Art is a means of connection. I can guarantee you there is nothing I deem more indicative of intimacy and companionship than someone trusting me to paint them."

The portrait's eyes flash across the back of my mind as Basil speaks. No matter how much time I spend looking at it, I can't shake the certainty there lies a sadness in its eyes it did not hold before. The last time Basil painted me, he left me feeling vulnerable in ways I did not know I could be; I can't afford to let him capture me again without knowing what parts of me he might next leave exposed.

"Is that the case, or do you simply find it more comfortable to hide behind the safety of your canvas?"

Basil's teacup collides against its saucer with a harsh clinking sound as he stares at me, eyes bewildered by my accusation. The venom of my words sits bitter and heavy on my tongue, but I can't bring myself to regret them. The anger and frustration that have coiled around my heart since I last saw him have grown so tight it's nearly suffocating, and though some more reasonable part of me knows Basil is not to blame for their presence, I can't help but feel I would not be suffering it had I not fallen into his orbit. The life I had before I met him may have been empty, but at least I was content with it. There were no dismissals to frustrate me or portraits to haunt me.

Isolation and boredom, for all their flaws, also meant safety and peace. Ever since Basil Hallward entered my life, it feels as though each day brings new emotions I could have done without. For every wonder and joy I've experienced since meeting him, there have been fears and uncertainties ready to counter them.

"I don't understand why you're showing such hostility toward me," Basil says once the air has settled. "Did I do something to offend you?"

"Why didn't you tell me you preferred the company of men?"

The question slips past my lips before I can hold it back, leaving me sheepish in my seat across from Basil, avoiding his eyes at all costs. My cheeks feel hot. I know, already, that there are countless reasons why Basil wouldn't share such a thing with me—not least of which being that he might not have known whether it was safe to. Still, I can't help feeling slighted by his omission. When Basil painted me, he uncovered more of me than I ever expected. The idea that he could see so much of me and still hide parts of himself stings in a way I can't quite put into words.

The more time I spend around Basil and Henry, the more feelings arise that I lack the language to understand. It would be infuriating, were so many of these unknowns not as captivating as they are.

"If it's of any comfort to you," Basil dodges, "I enjoy women just as much. People are uniquely delightful creatures—why would I limit myself to half the scope of treasures this world has to offer?"

His answer does little to address my reproach, but I catch myself smiling at him nonetheless. Perhaps it's the show of faith, knowing that he trusts me enough to elaborate on his feelings now that the subject has been broached. Whatever the case, the frustration that has been weighing so heavily on me since our time at the molly house starts to lighten as I melt into the gentle warmth of his company.

Basil smiles back, and I pause long enough to take him in. There's a sincerity to him I haven't seen in anyone else. Observing him a little longer, I realize his smile is slightly lopsided, lending him a disarming air of self-deprecation. His cheeks are rounder than I registered, and I realize that for all his worldliness, the two of us are only a year apart. Perhaps it isn't fair of me to expect him to always be as put together as he is. Every day, it feels as though I'm exposed to new situations and emotions that completely shift how I understand the world around me. Why should Basil have all the answers when I know so little myself?

"When Henry asked if we were lovers," I start, "you responded as though the mere idea were laughable. What about me makes such an unappealing prospect to you?"

The air in the room comes to a standstill, leaving the two of us looking at each other in near-unbreakable silence. Basil stares at me, searching my face for any answer it might offer, then falls into his seat with a sigh. It hits me, watching him surrender, that my question sounds like the words of a jilted lover asking why he doesn't love me, and I realize there may be some kernel of truth to the matter.

Maybe it's the comfort that would come from someone seeing me as thoroughly as he seems to and still finding something worth cherishing. Or maybe I was so drawn to him when we met because I felt some stirring for him I couldn't put into words. Either way, I want Basil to want me, whatever else that might mean.

Basil's eyes still have not left me, nor have any words left his mouth. His cheeks are pinker than usual, and I might think him flustered, had he not already so clearly voiced his disinterest in me. Perhaps it was a mistake to ask, but there's nothing I can do to take it back. I doubt we'll ever return to the way we were before the molly house, now that I've spoken as recklessly as I have.

"No good could come of Henry's question," Basil mutters. "I'm sure that's why he asked. Perhaps it's why he brought us to the molly house in the first place."

"I'm not sure I understand."

"If there's one thing I know about Henry Wotton, it's that he does not like to share the people who intrigue him. He needs to be the apple of every eye, the gem of each collection, and he loves to cause tension. I have no doubt he knew, when he made that comment, the type of rift it would spawn between you and me."

Were Basil speaking about anyone else, I might think it strange to say such heated things about a friend, but it's grown obvious in the time I've spent with the two of them their camaraderie is more contentious than most. I could not say whether their friendship is held together by the secrets they share or by Henry's refusal to leave Basil be, and I doubt either one of them could explain their bond if I asked. I imagine it might be something akin to the rivalry between brothers, but there's a venom to it I can't quite account for.

And, once again, Basil has avoided giving an answer to my question.

I ought to be grateful for his avoidance and the opportunity it gives me to pretend nothing happened. I've pushed the matter enough as it is, and Basil has made it clear he doesn't wish to answer, but the more he evades me, the more the question gnaws at me. How can someone who has seen as much beauty in me as he did be so amused at the thought of being my lover? And what does it say about me that the person who's seen me more clearly than anyone else should be so disinterested by me? What flaw has he seen that has so soured me for him, and how have I not noticed it?

"You keep avoiding my question."

"Tell me, Dorian," Basil surrenders. "Did the thought of us being lovers cross your mind before Henry mentioned it?"

I remember Basil's face that night in the carriage and pause. I'd thought him handsome, certainly—beautiful, even—but is that the same as attraction? Each time I've tried to interrogate the thought since, a wall crashes into me.

The light in Basil's studio suddenly feels too bright, the space too open, as though I were surrounded by a crowd of observers trying to break me apart and examine me. I can only imagine what

Grandfather would say if he knew I was entertaining such thoughts about a man. The insults swirl in the back of my mind, biting at me with each new addition, but I grit my teeth and try to push through it. Considering how opposed he was to my parents' romance, his words should mean little where matters of the heart are concerned. Yet each time I try to ignore his voice cursing at me, it finds a new weak point to hit.

"I don't know," I confess. "Certainly not in such words."

"Of course not; it isn't the type of thing any of us are encouraged to consider, let alone anyone raised by a man as rigid as Lord Kelso. Henry didn't bring you to the molly house because he thought you might find something of value there, but out of a desire to see your reaction. The only reason he asked if we were lovers is because he thought the discomfort it would cause you might entertain him. I thought it kindest, as your friend, to brush off the topic so we could move forward, and I wish you'd let go of it. It pains me to see Henry's antics build tension between us."

I open my mouth to argue, then close it. However dissatisfying Basil's explanation might be, I can't dispute his reasoning. The thought of us being lovers never did cross my mind. I should be grateful to Basil for brushing off the matter and sparing me questions I'm not equipped to consider, but the thought leaves a bitter taste behind it. I want to know if I could think of him that way, however much the thought might frighten me. I want to understand why Sybil Vane has such a hold on me as well, though the answer to that question feels even more shrouded than whatever I feel for Basil—or, for that matter, for Henry.

But the light is still so bright and the whispers still so harsh, and for the moment I need to rid myself of both of them.

"You're right," I tell Basil. "I miss being able to cherish your company without Henry's words weighing on us. Thank you for explaining your thoughts to me."

When I look at him, however, Basil's face still looks as shrouded as my mind feels.

10
Basic Beige

"Is that the book I lent you?"

I look up from my armchair to see Henry sitting across from me, enough amusement on his face to let me know he entered the room some time ago, and I was too caught up in my reading to notice. I roll my eyes and uncross my ankles, lifting the cover for him to see. It might not be the politest response, but he should know better by now than to talk to me when I'm reading.

Somewhere over the course of the last month, reading at Henry's became more comforting than doing so at Barsden Hollow. I had expected Henry's home to be something of a bachelor's house, given how little time he seems to spend there, and was surprised to find how far my expectations found themselves from the truth. In hindsight, I suppose it shouldn't surprise me; if there's one thing I've learned about Henry Wotton, it's that he finds nothing more enjoyable than doing what is least expected of him.

Basil's doubts echo in the back of my mind, but I brush them off. Whatever jealousy he might accuse Henry of holding, it seems to me that both of them want more of my attention than the other. I'm far too short on friends to make myself choose between them, and I'm more than capable of judging their characters for myself. Even if Basil is correct that Henry likes to scandalize me for his own amusement, I could probably benefit from his provocation; Grandfather's constant monitoring has left me far too sheltered for my liking.

Hartwood Heights, as it turns out, is something of a cozy nook amidst the grandeur of London, perfect to hide away in and shut out the spectacles and pressures of the city. The furniture is neither fashionable nor particularly out of date, sitting in various shades of brown and beige that never seem to age nor gather dirt. A constant quiet crackle fills the air as the fireplace rumbles on, warming the room just enough for it to be pleasant without needing to keep my jacket on.

Henry told me, when I asked him how a place of such simplicity could create a man of such excess, that he couldn't have come from anywhere else. An abundance of color, he'd said, could only ever be a reaction to too much beige. His options were either to let it consume him or drown it out with as heavy a contrast as he could. I asked him why he didn't simply renovate if he disliked it so much, but he brushed the matter off with some line he must have thought was clever. I've realized, in the month I've grown to know him, that Henry only makes two types of claims: ones that sound clever, and ones that are. Telling the two apart, however, still proves something of a challenge.

"You know, most proper people would say it's rather rude to ignore your host," Henry chides.

"And most proper people—if I might call you proper at all—would think it's rather strange to invite someone to read in your sitting room and then not expect them to do any actual reading."

"Perhaps I thought this would be more akin to a book club."

"People in a book club," I counter, "tend to read the book before discussing it."

"Should I assume that you have no early impressions to share, then?"

I sigh and tuck the ribbon back into the book to mark my page, surrendering my last hope for a peaceful reading day. The one downside of reading at Hartwood is that Henry will at times get in a mood where he cannot help but talk, and when he does, he will not stop until he's certain he's engaged his captive audience. Still, it's a small price to pay to get away from Grandfather, even if only for a short while.

Besides, Barsden Hollow has taught me not all peace is pleasant. Sometimes it can be tense and fraught, weighted down by the conditions that come attached to it.

"I don't recall saying I had no impressions, although I will admit I don't quite know what to make of it so far. It's a rather decadent book, don't you think?"

"Is it?" Henry asks, painting a look of false surprise onto his face. "I hadn't noticed. Would you care for some scotch?"

"No, thank you."

Henry gets up from his armchair and moves toward the small table in the far corner of his sitting room to pour himself a glass. The table is perhaps the one piece of furniture in the room I've found myself admiring, made of a rich mahogany that must have been imported from America relatively recently. Its reddish tint forms a pleasant contrast against the rest of the room and somehow highlights the bottle of scotch that sits atop it.

"I'm surprised some of the scenes I've read so far made it into publication, to be frank. It seems to me that much of what they depict are matters we don't discuss in good society."

"Perhaps that's the point," Henry says, taking a drink from his scotch as he sits back down. "One might argue it's a window into the pleasures and experiences we miss by restricting ourselves to what we call *good society*."

I sit with the thought for a moment and allow myself to mull it over before rejecting it the way my instinct tells me to. I have my own objections about what we consider proper and admirable in London—I daresay one would struggle to leave Barsden Hollow without them—but the amount of sin and vice sought out in Henry's book baffles me regardless. There are times when the protagonist seems callous for callousness's sake, or the pleasures he seeks appear too hedonistic for any sense of decency, but perhaps it's by pushing one's boundaries that we discover where they lie.

I catch myself weighing Basil's accusations about Henry once again. Could he have recommended this book for the sole sake of provoking me? I struggle to write off the idea as unlikely, but I also find myself unsure whether his motives matter. Taking me to the molly house opened my eyes to possibilities I don't think I would have otherwise considered. If the books he recommends have the same effect, does it matter why he offers them to me? I'm more than capable of making my own judgments, and there are far worse things one could inspire than shock and intrigue.

Whatever eccentricities Henry may have, they're far preferable to Grandfather's insistence on keeping me away from anything that might challenge his teachings. I think I might even prefer them to the way Basil seems to tiptoe around me, worrying he might expose me to something for which I may not be prepared.

"I wish you wouldn't always drink between sentences," I say to Henry, once enough time has passed for him to understand I have no plans to continue discussing our last topic. "It doesn't give you the authority you think it does."

He shrugs. "I don't *always* drink between sentences. Sometimes I smoke."

"You might be the most absurd man in London."

"You flatter me."

The door to the main hall opens behind me, revealing a pretty young woman in a pastel-pink dress with a hat so wide it almost matches her shoulders. She wears a small, pleasant smile with easy grace and carries herself with the pride of a woman who knows her charm. She appears to be looking for some item or another, but lunges forward when she sees Henry on his chair.

"Darling! I hardly expected you to be here in the middle of the day. Lady Thomas thought it would be nice for us to have tea in her garden after mass, but I simply couldn't go without my parasol. The sun is so strong today one would be forgiven for thinking us in Spain! Besides, it really is too beautiful not to show off. Have you seen it anywhere?"

"I can't say that I have," Henry replies without rising from his seat. "Victoria, have I introduced you to my friend Lord Gray here?"

"I don't believe you have, dear. You so rarely introduce me to your friends."

"Only as rarely as I see you. Victoria, this is Dorian Gray. Dorian, meet Mrs. Henry Wotton."

I try to hide my surprise as I notice the ring on the young woman's finger, focusing on keeping my features as even and pleasant as hers. There's no reason why there oughtn't be a Mrs. Henry Wotton, I suppose. Eighteen might be slightly younger than most men tend to marry these days, but it shouldn't be surprising for a young man in full possession of his fortune and title to be wed. His parents might even have made it a stipulation of his inheritance. Marriage has a way of cooling the characters of many young lords, though I'm inclined to say it may not have had the desired effect on Henry.

"Charmed to meet you," I say, rising from my armchair to bow. "I had no idea you were married, Henry."

"Victoria and I spend little time together. I always know where she is, and she never asks what I do. You could say we have the perfect marriage."

"*Henry!*" Victoria chastises, patting his chest. "The truth is that I can't bring my charming husband here anywhere. Have you ever met a man with such little sense of decency?"

"I have a great sense of decency, dearest, and simply no urge to exert it. Pleasantries are so tedious, and I have no desire to repeat the same few conversations all season."

"It's lovely to meet you, Lord Gray," she says, pointedly turning

her attention away from Henry. "Sometimes I struggle to believe my husband has any friends at all. Bless your soul for putting up with him."

I open my mouth to respond, then close it, unable to fathom what to think about the bizarre rapport before me. I've admittedly not had any married friends, but I doubt this is how wedded couples normally behave toward each other. Henry smiles at his wife's teasing, then turns away as if she'd left the room altogether.

Victoria returns to her searching, wandering in and out of the sitting room as she checks the hall and behind various pieces of furniture. Once it becomes clear Henry has no plans of helping her, I start to search alongside her until I've found a parasol a few shades darker than her dress tucked behind the bookshelf near the mahogany table. I call out to her, brandishing the parasol in the air like a hardly won prize.

"Is this the one you wanted?"

"Quite the one!" She takes the parasol from my hands and curtsies. "Thank you for finding it. It can be unbearably difficult to get behind some of our furniture in this dress; I'm afraid I might have been looking for hours without your aid."

"It would have been worth it. The lace alongside the ends has such a beautiful elegance to it."

"Perhaps I ought to let this Lord Gray of yours steal me away, Henry. He seems to know how to appreciate a good woman."

"I know exactly how to appreciate a good woman," Henry calls back, still nested in the comfort of his seat. "I seldom trouble you with the displeasure of my company. What more could you want?"

Victoria leaves the room, parasol in tow, taunting Henry as she goes with her plans of finding a handsome merchant and running away with him. He takes them in good spirits, laughing alongside her and bidding her farewell, but the humor of his words never quite meets his eyes. I find myself looking back and forth between them, mind still working as intently as it can to navigate the relationship between them. I could almost think them friends, if I had seen friends before whose bond depended on never spending time together.

Once I'm sure Victoria is gone, I turn my attention back to Henry. He seems different somehow, now that I know he's married—older, though the years between us have not changed. Perhaps it's the understanding that he sits in a completely different part of his life, with utter mastery of it. The concept is intriguing and unlike the expectations Grandfather gave me of constant responsibility and fatigue. Henry's lordship is not a burden like I've been taught to expect, but rather a permission to do whatever he likes without ever owing an explanation. I try to imagine what I would do if I had Henry's freedom, but the image I conjure stays blank.

"Do all married couples avoid each other as often as you and your wife do?" I ask.

"If they're lucky. Victoria is a delightfully modern woman. Nowadays, man and wife are married in name only, and she loves little more than the independence that gives her. I could not think of a more admirable quality. Mistresses are for keeping, but a wife is best kept at arm's length."

"I don't think I could marry someone I did not wish to see. I might never marry, in fact. I'm far too in love to ever marry someone else."

"Love!" Henry scoffs. "And who could you possibly be in love with? Hearts are fickle things, dear friend. It is far better to follow one's pleasures than one's sentiments."

"You would not say so, if your heart was as enthralled as mine. I cannot think of a more wonderful feeling than gazing upon her—I might never look away from her face, if such an opportunity were afforded me."

"Who is she, then? Surely, you will not be timid with me of all people. It would hurt me greatly."

"Sybil Vane." The name is like a prayer in my mouth after all the times I've whispered it when nobody could hear. "I've taken to seeing her perform every night, and she has fascinated me more each time. I feel, looking upon her, that she is proof of greater potential for mankind. I can think of no charm she does not have, no freedom she does not possess. One could think, watching her onstage, that she is unrestrained by all of humanity's shortcomings. Truly, Henry, I have never seen anyone quite like her."

"So you've met her, then?"

"No," I admit. "I could never do such a thing. I might ruin her with my presence. It seems to me as though she is untainted by shame or lonesomeness or fear, and I possess all those qualities in abundance. I would not forgive myself, were I to bring such demons to her world."

Henry stares at me with a curious look I can only think of as sitting somewhere between annoyance and marvel. He must think I'm being dramatic. How could he not, when his marriage is so far from the kind of love I feel? Perhaps he's envious. I can't imagine what I might think about love if I'd already settled upon the peaceful avoidance with which he has saddled himself.

"Your words could not be more absurd, my friend. I have no fondness for love—frankly, I think of sentimentality as the worst of the curses bestowed upon man—but what I will not tolerate is self-defeat. If you love Sybil Vane, I see no reason you should not meet her. Tomorrow, you, Basil, and I shall go see her, and I will introduce you myself."

"I would much prefer to be defeated than brokenhearted," I start to argue, but Henry cuts me off.

"My mind is made up, Dorian. I will not hear any argument to the contrary. Tomorrow, you will meet this love of yours. I understand you lack the nerve for it, but you could stand to do more things that frighten you. How else do you expect to find the ones that thrill you?"

"Very well," I concede. "Tomorrow it is. But I warn you, Henry, that I will be inconsolable if I lose what little of her I can cherish."

He doesn't push the issue any further. I pick up Henry's book once more and try to fall back into my reading, but fail. I no longer have the mind to read about forbidden pleasures and unimaginable new delights. Whatever sins of the flesh Henry treasures seem trivial compared to a fraction of the freedom I imagine Sybil Vane must feel as she dances between worlds.

11
RAINBOW MIRAGE

I spend the hours before meeting Sybil Vane avoiding my mirror. Perhaps it's foolish of me, when I could be making myself as presentable and desirable for her as is in my power, but it seems to me that spending too much time with my reflection could only make matters worse. Sybil may find me intriguing or she may not, and I'd wager there's little I can do to sway her mind. I would hate to charm her upon our first meeting, only for her to decide when she sees me again that she fell for whatever clumsy artifice I put together. If Sybil is to love me, I would rather she do so without effort, lest I worry time might steal her from me the way it will every other thing I've grown to cherish.

Besides, if I were to look into a mirror in my current mood, I think I might never look away. There will always be some little flaw to criticize—some hair out of place, or a bag under my eyes to give away the sleep I've lost thinking about her. She might think me a madman if she knew the hold she had on me before she even knew my face. If I arrived too well-groomed, too proper, she might dismiss me as a vain fool who loves only her looks, and who will inevitably grow tired of her. I don't know that I could explain it's her art I love, and that I care little for her beauty when she can transform it with such impossible ease.

My portrait hangs in the corner of my sitting room, tempting me to look at it. It sits prettily in its frame, heavy with some sense of urgency I must be imagining. There's nothing it could say to me, no wisdom it might share that could aid me on my quest tonight. Observing it would be worse than approaching a mirror. The beautiful, charming youth locked safely within its canvas would only taunt me with the knowledge that they are a far truer match for Sybil Vane than I could ever dream of being.

If I'm to maintain my composure, I must try to remember my charms. I've come to understand, in my nights at the molly house, that I still wear beauty enough to steal some hearts.

I time my breathing to the steadiness of the grandfather clock in the hall. The process is soothing, flooding me with some sense of control. I may not sway time, but I can regulate myself to fit its cycles, ensure that each tick of the clock is felt to the fullest.

I pass the clock on my way out of Barsden Hollow. Out of the corner of my eye, I could swear its arrows sit perfectly still.

"I must say," Basil tells me over the trotting of the horses, "I've never seen you look so solemn, Dorian. This behavior is wholly unlike you."

"What else should I be, if not solemn? It seems only respectful, when I'm about to meet perfection incarnate."

Henry scoffs from the bench across from us. "There's no use arguing with him, Basil. Thinking one is in love has a dreadful impact on the senses. I'm afraid there will be no reasoning until our friend's feet have returned to solid ground."

"Mock me all you like," I tell him. "I have no need for solid ground, when the view is so beautiful here in the clouds."

Basil and Henry exchange a look I don't care to consider. I cannot remember the last time I made a decision based solely on what I wanted, and the feeling is as exhilarating as it is daunting. There's something special about Sybil Vane—I know there is—and I will not rest until I understand what it is that makes her so captivating. Despite what Henry might believe, I'm not so naive as to think this will be easy. I have simply decided that the answers I might find matter to me more than how I might feel about them. Perhaps they cannot understand why I care, but it doesn't matter. Frankly, I'm unsure I understand it myself.

As the coach continues to make its way through London, I start to feel a growing awareness that this is not the path we took when Basil and I met Henry at the tavern. The buildings I see out the window are too clean, the road too smooth. There are no bumps from untended cobble to injure my back or dizzy me, no crowds in ill-repaired clothing tending to various illicit businesses.

I suppose the matter should not surprise me. It seemed to me, when Henry spoke of introducing me to Sybil Vane, that he might in fact know her, and perhaps he thought to arrange for us to meet in a more private environment than Covent Garden might afford. It might be more fitting for a romantic meeting to occur in a nicer setting, perhaps even a domestic one. It's slightly later than fashionable for an afternoon tea, but the sun is not quite so low as to make our rendezvous feel clandestine.

The coach halts soon enough, and we exit to find ourselves before an estate I can only describe as grand. Hedges line the path we take from the gates with a near-military precision, framing a mansion that looks both classic in style and modern in upkeep. There's a certain timelessness to it, as if we have stumbled our way across a secret pocket into a reality where matters of decades or eras stood little importance. The doors are large enough that one might lead a horse inside them, guarded on either side by statues of lions on two feet, mouths open, mid-roar.

A sturdy, clean-cut woman dressed in the way of a housekeeper greets us at the door, nodding at us before leading us to a well-kept lounge furnished in various tones of turquoise. A man I assume must be the master of the house sits in the armchair in the middle of the room, dressed in a rather smart waistcoat over what appear to be riding clothes. He rises to greet us, then offers us a seat as the butler beside him pours four cups of tea.

"Dorian," says Henry once the servants have left the room, "I'd like you to meet Lord Ernest Cavendish."

"I hear you're a fan," the man says, extending his hand.

I pause for a moment, taking in the gentleman before me. He stands slightly taller than I do, with tidy blond hair and bright gray eyes that gleam with a cunning, foxlike playfulness. His features have a pleasant gentleness to them that, while clearly reminiscent of a man nearing his thirties, might almost be described as dainty under a certain light. There's a confident sense of self-mastery to his smile, however, that I would recognize anywhere. I would be hard-pressed not to, when I've thought of it as many times as I have.

"Are you . . . Sybil Vane?"

"As much as anyone is, I suppose."

Basil stares at me from the love seat by the window, concern written plainly across his face. Henry, on the other hand, is harder to read. He looks as though he may be studying me, waiting to gauge my reaction for some sense of shock. I cannot tell what he expected this discovery to provoke from me, whether he thought I might express some outrage or even laugh at this sudden twist, as if it were all some jest. It could be, I muse, that he doesn't know what to expect, either.

"This was a bad idea, Henry," Basil chides. His tone is sharper than I have ever heard it, reaching a point of trembling fury I had no clue he could muster. "I wish you'd told me your plan early enough that I might have warned Dorian of what he might discover. It was cruel of you to surprise him in such a way."

"I'm not naive, Basil. Surely you do not think so lowly of me as to believe I'd see a beautiful woman at a molly house, of all places, and not entertain the idea she might be a cross-dresser." My voice comes out sturdy and even as I speak, fueled by the truth of my words. I expected that Sybil might be a mirage herself, given the context in which I met her. In fact, I think I might have *hoped* she was, now that I consider the matter. It makes her skill all the greater, that she's capable of materializing herself like Aphrodite from her shell.

And yet despite my efforts to keep up appearances, a sense of dread sinks into me as I look over our host. I thought, when I met Sybil Vane, that I would see some trace of the woman I saw onstage in her; the thought that she could vanish so thoroughly behind Lord Cavendish chills me. Someone as artful as her must have found a way to bridge the gap between fiction and reality and assert some amount of control over the mortal clay that is man's flesh, even in the light of day.

I never loved Sybil Vane, I realize, now that my hopes have crumbled. I simply needed her to be, so that she might show me the secrets of her alchemy. I should have known such things were impossible, instead of imagining some chance for escape.

"There is no Sybil Vane, I gather?" I ask, careful to quell the trembling in my voice. After all, I doubt I could explain my disappointment when I don't quite understand it myself.

"Of course not," Lord Cavendish replies without a care in the world. "Sybil Vane could never be more than a disguise, though I'll admit she brings me great pleasure. The most beautiful things are only ever fleeting. It's part of their charm."

Sybil Vane is dead, then—or perhaps she never lived. Whatever possibility she might have represented, whatever hope she might have inspired has melted away into shadows, mocking me. A cold, cruel surrender scars over the bleeding in my heart as Grandfather's laughter rings through my head, taunting my naivety. *The world*, he says, *is a bitter and gray place, and there is no escaping it. There is little more to life than playing one's part, but you have the privilege of a comfortable one, and there is great relief in enjoying it. Put away your dreams, my boy. They will do nothing but hurt you.*

I sip my tea and smile, nodding along as my company exchanges pleasantries. I should have expected I wouldn't find any escape in Sybil Vane. The only life she can live is a half-one, flitting through the shadows of London's most secret corners, anchored to the feet of a man like any other. Whatever freedom I thought she might represent, it's no reprieve from the whims that restrict us.

Basil and I walk up Covent Garden, moon high above our heads as we discuss Sybil Vane's last performance. The magic she weaves seems less marvelous now that I know it's little more than a mirage, but it still retains most of its charm. Sybil Vane may not have the same untempered freedom as the youth in my portrait, but there remains some hope in the fact I can see her at all. There's more to the world than what lives under daylight. There is, at least, some safety to be found, some places I can escape to and imagine for a night I could be anyone I wish.

The air between us is not as light as it once was, nor is it as heavy as it might be. I have tried, in a few of my bolder moments, to further interrogate my feelings about him, but something still holds me back each time I dwell too long on the matter. Perhaps, in a world where Grandfather's judgment did not weigh so heavily on me, I would be able to know the answer—but that is not the life I live.

"The world would be better," I muse, "were people less quick to cast judgment on each other."

Basil smiles at me, his hand brushing against mine for a fraction of an instant, fleeting and yet more than enough to fill me with panic. The road from the tavern we've grown fond of back to Barsden is dimly lit, but I can't chase the fear someone might see us. I struggle to think who might recognize us in such dim lighting, and yet the thought does little to calm me. I suppose some fears are hard to forget when one has lived their life ruled by them. Still, I would love nothing more than to cherish this moment between us, unburdened by what anyone else might think.

"I like to think that flaw isn't inherent to humanity," Basil says. "There might have been a time we were less prone to such judgments, and there may yet be one where we cast them aside altogether."

"How do you explain the way we treat each other, then?" I ask. "Why are places like that cellar forced to exist where nobody can find them, even those who might need the space they offer?"

"Perhaps we've grown dominated by structures that benefit too few people, and anything that might let people question the norms we've been trained to accept is too threatening for those structures to allow."

The picture Basil paints is a pretty one, though I don't know how much comfort it brings me. The idea of a world less dominated by shallow notions like propriety is intoxicating, but I can't fathom a way such a world might be built. Whether Basil is right or wrong, the realms he imagines are as distant as the ones in his canvas. What good does it do to picture some other future if it does nothing to change the pains of the present?

"I wish I believed we might see these other times of yours," I tell him.

"Me, too." Basil sighs. "For now, it's enough for me to believe in them. If the two of us do, there must be others as well. Perhaps one day there'll be enough of us that we can build those times ourselves."

I let the back of my hand rest against his. It's an innocent enough gesture, but even it is enough to leave me wary of each corner we turn. He does not pull away, and so I settle my mind despite the fear, clinging to the warmth and roughness of his skin against mine as long as I can.

We part ways, as usual, a quarter of an hour's walk from Barsden Hollow. The journey from Covent Garden never seems long until he has left me, but I never tell him I loathe those last minutes without him. The air feels colder the moment we part, and a shiver runs through me as the moonlight grows hollow. I wish I could tell him how deeply I treasure the moments we steal, but I've neither the courage nor the words to do so.

The moment I enter, it's clear something's astray. Grandfather should be asleep this time of night, and yet no sooner is the door shut behind me than I hear his voice call me to the guest lounge. I freeze, mind frantically weighing the merits of ignoring him, but straighten my coat and leave my hat perched by the doorway. If Grandfather's awake, nothing I do will help me avoid him. It's better to answer his call and shake his suspicions than to dodge them and let them fester.

I find Grandfather sitting in his armchair, two cups of tea on the table between him and his guest, an old friend of his. Inspector

Gartens is a narrow man in both features and frame, but with the power in his stance of a man with a remarkable history. His mustache is crisp and gray, and what little hair he has sits perfectly in place despite the fatigue that's clear under his eyes. He looks as though he might have been moments from slumber when something tore him from his bed, but also like this is not an uncommon occurrence for him. Grandfather, in contrast, wears in his eyes the fury of a tempest waiting to strike.

"Lord Gray," the inspector greets me. "Thank you for joining us. I hate to bother your household so late at night, but I was hoping you might answer some questions for me. I'm afraid I received a rather alarming call from an informant of mine, and thought it best to make straight to Barsden as a courtesy to Lord Kelso here. I'm sure all three of us know the importance of solving strange misunderstandings before they reach the domain of public speculation."

Pain twists my stomach in a knot as panic sets in. Whether or not Gartens knows exactly where I've been, I doubt he would have come here had he not heard too much for me to deflect. I force myself to look Grandfather in the eyes and raise my chin, praying to any force willing to help that I might still free myself from the precariousness of my position.

"Please do," I answer, moving to stand before them. The heat of the fireplace is close enough to warm my back, bringing with it some petty comfort. "I have nothing to hide."

"Would you care to explain, then, why you were seen in a part of Covent Garden known for attracting a significant number of criminals? Sodomites, to be precise."

Grandfather's glare could cut through flesh with ease, but

I've become far too familiar with his moods to let myself melt under its intensity. The only way to navigate this disaster is to hold steady and keep a facade of confidence. He will decide my guilt the moment I waver. It takes all my focus to hold strong before the pair's combined gaze, but I will myself to stone. I've gathered too much experience lying to him not to mitigate the situation before me.

"Believe me, Inspector, it was as shocking to me when I learned where I'd been led. In fact, I meant to write you tomorrow and report it myself."

"You mean to tell me you did not know where you were?"

My heart pounds more violently with each passing instant. The skepticism in Gartens's tone makes it clear I won't escape reproach from where I was seen, but so far he has not mentioned my having a companion there with me. There might still be some tale I can weave that keeps Basil as far from this discussion as possible.

Lie, Dorian, a soothing voice whispers. *If he were here to arrest you, he would have done so by now. Gartens wants to know how you ended up in such a place. What can you give him to shield Basil from his suspicion?*

"Of course not. I answered a social call from a young lord I met at a salon recently, thinking we might go to some gentlemen's club. I'll admit I was shocked when he led me to Covent Garden, but it's hardly uncommon these days for young men to find thrills in less tasteful parts of London. I thought he might be prone to drink or rent a girl for the night—distasteful, certainly, but nothing worth alienating a potential friend in good standing. You must understand, Inspector, that the lack of company I'm accustomed to has left me admittedly sheltered to the ways of the world."

"And when did you understand the error in your judgment?"

"When he attempted to make an advance on me."

The words taste like venom in my mouth, thick with a self-victimhood I loathe to wear, yet I see no other escape from this trap. Grandfather's eyes burn into me, and Gartens looks at me with cold, analytical detachment, but I know at least who I am and what defense I can offer. I am the heir of a man with an impeccable reputation with no particular reason to earn his ire and a history of heeding his word. Surely I would not *knowingly* stoop to the depths of which I've been accused. I smooth my face as best I can, letting slip only a hint of embarrassment at the thought I might so easily have been misguided. Being deceived is shameful, certainly, and I expect Grandfather will have his share of reproach when all has been cleared, but it's far preferable to admitting to a crime.

"And who was this young friend of yours?" Gartens asks. I read no suspicion nor conviction in his face, as if he were pushing only to see if I might break. "I know you must be eager to see him face justice after abusing your trusting nature."

My mind races as I try to think of a name I might give him. Whoever saw me might not have recognized Basil in the darkness—his return to London was recent enough I would wager few outside artists' circles have yet met him. Besides, I would rather find myself caught in this lie than turn my back on Basil.

Henry would certainly fit the profile of the sordid young lord who might lead me down such a shameful road, but I can't bring myself to give his name, either. It would be too easy to draw a connection from him to Basil, or maybe even to Tamara and her business. The people I've endangered are real, and so are the consequences that might befall them. There will be time later, when I know they are safe, to think on matters as negligible as my own feelings.

An idea starts to form in my head, wicked and twisted and vile. The voice I heard in Mother's crypt whispers in hushed, icy tones, tempting me with each passing word. *There is one name you could give them*, it tells me. *One who has done nothing to earn your protection and might not remember even meeting you. Surely you would not sacrifice yourself on their altar.*

Grandfather's eyes burn hotter with each moment's hesitation as sweat starts to pool at my forehead. Any further hesitation would delve beyond the natural reluctance to betray another soul, even one who abused my trust. If I stay silent one more moment, I may as well seal my fate.

"Cavendish," I surrender. "The man who tricked me is Lord Ernest Cavendish."

12
Scarlet Shame

When Inspector Gartens takes his leave, the air of judgment I've grown to associate with Barsden Hollow finally feels deserved. After all the time I've spent trying to be different from Grandfather and all the complaints I've thought about the way he sees the world, I retreated into his shadow the moment it offered me the slightest bit of safety. I bumped into one hurdle, faced a singular threat, and ran back into the gray, setting off a chain of events I can never take back.

I won't go unpunished for my cowardice tonight. Somehow, maybe even years from now, the world will pay me in kind for the betrayal I've dealt. I feel, with a grim sense of certainty that settles deep into my bones, that I've changed the path on which the rest of my life will unfurl. The marks of my hypocrisy will find some way to show themselves on me, painting my sins in vivid scarlet on my face for all the world to see.

The thought, for all the sorrow it brings me, settles in with a somber resolve. Whatever consequences my actions bring, I will have earned them, and I will not complain. A glimpse of Lord Cavendish flashes across my mind, sleeping without any notion that the Crown is gathering evidence against him as he does. My testimony, at least, will not be convincing from behind my anonymity. Perhaps if I'm lucky, he might rise from this scandal untouched in any meaningful way. I pray he does. I pray that my mistakes tonight don't bring attention to anyone else, that the worst of their consequences might fall on me and me alone.

The sense of judgment only grows stronger when I find the solace of my chambers. A cold has settled inside them, harsher still than the one that reigns over Barsden. My legs buckle the moment I reach the Louis XV set that furnishes my sitting room, and I all but fall into the plush armchair. Though my bed is but a room away, it feels too far to reach. Whatever strength I have has left my body, leaving me to wallow in the privacy of my own thoughts.

Out of the corner of my eye, Basil's portrait calls to me from beside my vanity. The strange sense of fate I've felt pulling me to it lately has only grown more magnetic in its pull. I may as well be sleepwalking as I drag myself forward to take a closer look, the ache in my body muted by the siren's call beckoning me forward. A strange sense of dread runs through me as I take a candle from the window and light it for a better look.

The youth in the portrait before me is not the same one Basil painted.

The first change I notice is the smirk he now wears, smug and self-important and secretive somehow, the look of a man who has buried the first of many skeletons in his cupboard. His posture has straightened as well, shifted from a graceful ease to a static rigidity, his chin and nose upturned, eyes fixed on me as if looking down on his painter rather than daydreaming away. His features have retained their stained-glass delicacy, but it no longer suits him. Where once it gave him the look of some faerie disguised in our mortal realms, there now seems a sense of deceit in his gentle prettiness. His face reminds me of plants I've heard described in travel journals, whose flowers serve as bait to lure their prey. I feel, studying his features, as though his mouth might unhinge if I reach too close, ready to swallow me whole.

The young man in the portrait, I realize with growing horror, looks like an heir of whom Grandfather might be proud. He wears cruelty and callousness with startling ease, eyes glinting with a pleasure I can only describe as malicious. *Cavendish disappointed you*, he tells me, voice as smooth and twisted as his features. *He was expendable, far more than you or those you call friends. Whatever fate he faces, it will be the outcome of the risks he took. Why should you feel guilt, when any other catastrophe might have found him as easily as you have?*

His words, imagined as they may be, burn colder than even Grandfather's glare did. The thought I might somehow justify myself only deepens my shame. The picture before me cannot be real. Perhaps I truly was sleepwalking when I made my way over to the portrait, and this image is a nightmare conjured up by my own guilty conscience. Portraits, I remind myself, have no life of their own. Even the famed Mona Lisa, for all the discussion of her wandering gaze that follows its viewers, cannot truly move.

I will go to my bed and get some sleep, and when I wake I'll find my portrait as it was. It's far too late for any rational thought, but morning will bring the clarity I'll need to make my amends. For now, all I can do is rest so that my mind doesn't continue playing its tricks on me tomorrow. I pull myself away and blow out the candle, forcing my body toward its bed.

I try not to think, as I walk, of the cruel gaze I feel piercing through me. It does little to stop the fitful dreams where I find myself trapped in an artfully crafted frame, watching as some snakelike reflection of myself slithers out from my prison and coats everything I've ever touched in its venom.

The sun has already started to fall from its zenith when I wake, my bones still heavy with exhaustion. My memories of last night are shrouded in fog, drowning in a sea of the nightmares that plagued me overnight. My head throbs as I pull myself from my bed, heart heavy with the blurry certainty that my life took a turn last night from which there is no coming back.

I look into the mirror while dressing myself, baffled by the lack of fatigue on my face. My skin has the dewy rosiness of someone undisturbed by anything as childish as nightmares, and my eyes are bright and full of a dreamy wondering, unclouded by any redness or dark circles in their vicinity. Even my hair is tidy in its dishevelment. There are no knots or tangles to be seen, and yet it bears no artificial manicure, either. Each strand falls of its own accord, but the effect is rather like a bouquet of wildflowers, every piece in natural harmony.

The thought of Basil's portrait crosses my mind, bringing with it strange memories of a figure in the frame unlike the version of me that sparked such envy. The notion is so fanciful I ought to laugh, but I can't shake the worry it brings me. The memory feels so vivid, the horror I recall so startling it sinks its claws into me. Any common sense I have fades away, refusing to fight the worry that this twisted portrait in my mind might somehow exist.

Each step toward the sitting room is accompanied by a deepening dread, until I might as well be forcing my way through mud and not walking over perfectly laid carpeting. By the time the portrait frame enters my line of sight, I can't bear to look in its direction. Some base instinct freezes me in place, desperately trying to protect me.

Slithering within the rose-vine confines of its frame, a carnivorous serpent in the shape of a haughty nobleman stares at me, mockery in his eyes. The cruelty of his sneer pierces me, taunting my foolishness in thinking such a monster could be a dream. Whatever fiction stands before me, it could only exist in such implausible a place as reality. Some aspect of it is too horrible to invent, too twisted for any other world.

I would offer my very soul, if it meant this portrait might age and I might wear its beauty forever.

My own words repeat themselves to me, reminding me of the foolish wish I made when Basil unveiled his portrait. Could some devil have heard my petty sentiment and seized the opportunity to punish me for my vanity? The notion that my portrait might somehow bear the traces of aging and cruelty in my stead ought to be impossible, and yet it has, at least, some sort of logic to it. The portrait Basil painted has changed, and I have not. These two facts must be connected, else each would need its own plausible explanation.

I pull myself from the portrait's gaze, falling into the Louis XV armchair as I do, finding some solace in its comfort and blush coloring. Grandfather gave me what felt like an endless lecture when I bought the set, claiming it a waste of my fortune to decorate with frivolous antiques. He wouldn't have understood the real value it has, so I never explained it. There's a warmth in the Louis XV set, knowing I have some history of Papa's country with me. It has seen me through many of my darkest moments, and each time I've found comfort in the thought part of him might be with me.

Today, it reminds me of one more person I betrayed last night. The consequences have no reason to reach him, yet I've wronged him nonetheless. He could not look at me, I decide, if he knew how quickly I turned my back on Cavendish. I hurt someone like him—someone like myself—without a moment's hesitation.

It might be for the best, then, that my portrait grows monstrous in my stead. Nobody will have cause to guess the darkness of my deeds if I do not wear it. The secret in my portrait has shifted from my longings to my sins, but they'll be guarded just as safely. My heart remains hidden, and I must become the art concealing it.

A knock at the door pulls me from my self-pity as Peter calls from the other side, notifying me I have company waiting downstairs. I don't remember making plans for today, which suggests whoever is waiting for me has come for some social call. My head is ill-equipped for pleasantries, but it would be stranger for me not to greet my guest, and so I make my way to the parlor, bracing to meet whoever might be there waiting for me.

When I reach the parlor, I find none other than Basil, holding on to his tea as if it were his only anchor. I see no signs of sleeplessness on his face, and yet his body is slumped over with a fatigue that does not suit him. He looks frail despite the sturdiness of his build and the quiet assuredness I've grown to associate with him.

"My apologies for bothering you," he says as he rises to embrace me. "It didn't occur to me when I came to check on you that you might have slept through the day. I suppose there's some small mercy, at least, in knowing you haven't yet heard the rumor."

"What rumor?"

The grimness of Basil's nod tells me all I need to know before his words can. "May I speak freely here, or is there a more private room where we are less likely to be overheard?"

"Grandfather rarely leaves his quarters, and he avoids the parlor even then. Whatever you have to say should fall on our ears only."

Shame pinches at my chest as relief floods Basil's face. At no point does the thought cross his mind that I might be an unsafe audience for his words, and the sheer sense of unbridled trust I read from him pains me more than any self-reproach I could muster. I've grown to think of Basil as someone who could see me—understand me in a way no other has—but he has missed the wickedness I possess. He thinks I am good; knowing he's mistaken might just shatter me.

"Lord Cavendish was arrested. I heard witnesses are being

gathered after anonymous reports of deviance and depravity. I hate to be the bearer of such news, Dorian. I was so afraid I would arrive at Barsden Hollow to find you devastated, and instead it's I who must hurt you."

"Hurt me?" It takes no effort to keep my features even, and I wonder, absently, if the portrait upstairs is shifting expressions for me, betraying the inevitable sense of dread that creeps into me. "Lord Cavendish was a stranger, and Sybil Vane a mirage, albeit a talented one. The news you bring me is grim, certainly, and it saddens me to hear it, but I fail to see how it could be so personal as to cause me pain."

"Perhaps I have misread you, then. I got the sense, the night you first met Sybil Vane, that you saw in her the same thing I did."

"There's nothing to see in her. Lord Cavendish said as much himself. Sybil Vane does not exist."

"Sybil Vane *could not* exist," Basil corrects me. "There lies a world of difference between those claims. Surely you must have grasped as much."

I huff. "I'm growing quite tired of you telling me what I must have grasped or thought, Basil. You ought to tell me what you mean, for once, and give me the chance to respond instead of deciding on my behalf."

Fear bubbles in me that Basil might read deeper than I'd like into my words, that he might glimpse within them my inability to let go of the way he dismissed me that night at the molly house. Perhaps he is in too poor of a state to notice, or perhaps he does not think his response could have frustrated me. Whatever the case, he doesn't seem to consider any deeper meaning in my words.

"It wasn't my intention to insult you," he apologizes. "I simply

meant that some emotions must be hidden away behind layers of deniability. Some realities cannot be acknowledged as such. It would endanger them."

Basil's words settle into me with all the ease of a knife into my ribs. I assumed yesterday that I was acting in some surrender to the truth that the world held no place for me. Faced with the consequences of my exploring some secret, half-hidden realms, it seemed best to direct those same punishments to someone I knew mostly as a fiction. My actions were not made less wicked by my reasoning, but they are surely made more cruel now. Sybil Vane *is* real, whatever illusions she hides in, and I've condemned her to the very fate I wished to avoid. Even if the inquest fails to yield results, I've condemned her to such scrutiny I may as well have killed her myself. However fleeting the shadows in which she hid have been, they too will vanish with London's eyes on her.

"I would like to tell you a secret, Dorian. May I?"

I want nothing more than to say no. Whatever Basil wishes to confide, I don't deserve to hear it. I would never wish him harm—even my actions last night were at least in part fueled by an urge to protect him—but I've proved myself unworthy of his confidence. What little conscience I have urges me to tell him before he entrusts me with information I do not deserve, but my mouth refuses to open. If I tell him, I'll have to explain it was I who turned in Sybil Vane. I couldn't stand to see the look on his face as he realized I'm not the person he thinks I am.

I could not bear to watch myself become a monster in his eyes.

"Of course. The two of us are friends, are we not?"

"I did not spend the last few years traveling to learn new types of art," Basil tells me. "I spent them hidden away from London so that a young lady might be forgotten, assumed to be some long-dead runaway, and I might return in her stead."

I look Basil over, taking him in as I process what he has told me. I had noticed, in the absent-minded way one keeps track of the fashions, that his cheeks bore no sign of either beard or the coarseness of a razor, but thought little of it. Given my own lack of such traits, it was easy to assume a young man my own age might be another late bloomer, and they would appear in due time. He is shorter than me, perhaps, but taller than Henry, and larger than both of us. Certainly, Basil Hallward is not without his eccentricities, but what artist is?

"You are an even better artist than I have credited," I say, "to have sculpted a man of what materials you had available."

"Not a man precisely," Basil clarifies, "though I've yet to find some better word to explain myself. It is more comfortable to navigate the world as one, but I find there is some truth lacking in the word. I am *like* one, certainly, in the way stone is akin to brick for most purposes. And I suppose the differences matter little here, but I find they matter still, if only to me."

"Like the shadows in the cave Sybil spoke of that night."

"Precisely. I have taken on a man's shape, and it suits me, but England lacks the words to understand me. It cannot see outside the cave, so figures and shadows must suffice."

"You say you aren't a poet," I muse, "but every time we speak, you weave your words as masterfully as you do oils."

"You flatter me, Dorian."

"I could flatter you more, but you need rest. You've been the bearer of hard news, and I can see the burden that carrying such weight has exerted."

"Will you manage by yourself?" he asks.

"You need not worry about me," I answer. "Rest, Basil, and know you have a friend in me. I do not wish to see you exhaust yourself for my sake."

"Very well," he agrees, rising with an effort I could only describe as Herculean. I fetch his coat from the rack and wrap it around him as carefully as I can, my hands unworthy to rest too close to him. I could live for a hundred more years and still fail to find a way to forgive myself for how deeply I've betrayed him.

Once I've ensured that Basil has left Barsden, I gather some old drapes from Peter and retreat to the loneliness of my quarters. He does not ask me why I made such a request from him, but the confusion in his eyes is impossible to miss. I throw the sheets over the portrait as soon as I enter, refusing to bear the cruelty of its sight for a single moment longer. In the space of a day, it has transformed into the sole proof of my wicked heart—even as it mocks me, however, there remains some comfort in the knowledge its cruelty exists for me alone.

No one will ever see this portrait again, I resolve as I take one last look at the atrocity before me. No one will know the wickedness of which I am capable, least of all Basil Hallward.

13

Storm Cloud

The attention attracted by Sybil Vane's arrest exceeded any magnitude I might have feared. For days, one could not go to any social event without crossing whispers about the great shame that had befallen Lord Cavendish and how unspeakably *awful* it was to see such potential for depravity in London's aristocracy—unspeakable, of course, except for entertainment's sake. London socialites love nothing more than to discuss the scandals of others. The more sordid, the better.

Even without a verdict or a witness to take the stand, each day that passed brought with it new theories as to what fate might find Cavendish, as well as which mysterious source might have brought about this inquest. Each theory was more outlandish than the last—everything from some jealous cousin hoping to inherit with Cavendish in prison to a former lover somewhere, smitten and spurned into fury enough to make up the accusation.

It took little time for me to stop worrying the matter might somehow fall back upon me. Though discussions of the Cavendish trial still left me plagued with guilt and nervousness on Sybil's behalf, my own fate brought little concern. The more ridiculous the theories, the safer I grew to feel. There remains, after all, no public connection between myself and Cavendish, and no reason to draw one. As a week stretched into a fortnight, interest began to fade and people began to suggest Cavendish would be released at any time. Little was said, however, about any remorse for the way in which his good name had been destroyed.

Scandals, it was determined at most salons, do not come without some cause. Even if the charge itself was proved false, there would remain some misdeed to warrant the hit to Cavendish's reputation. It must simply be one the Crown cannot punish.

After two and a half weeks, when a trial was finally called and a witness announced, the hubbub originated by Cavendish's arrest had fizzled entirely, replaced by talk of some heiress or another who had run away with an American millionaire. The public apathy swayed me to believe I could attend Sybil's trial unnoticed.

Though I can't make out her face from my seat, Sybil's posture does not seem too heavily worn by the last few weeks. She holds herself tall behind the stand, pleading innocent on all counts without so much as a waver. Even in her lord's clothes, the self-mastery and sense of spectacle she wears onstage is easy to recognize. Looking at her, I might almost think the entire trial is little more than a stunt drawn up for her own entertainment, were I not keenly aware of its true cause.

The witness takes the stand after her, but the trial may as well be over the moment he appears. Though it's clear the prosecution has made great pains to make him presentable, tidy clothes and decent grooming do little to cover poor posture and his piercing cockney accent as he claims that Lord Ernest Cavendish, who he recognizes as the man sitting across from him, offered him some coin in exchange for performing various lewd acts.

The Crown, for all the time it spent searching for people who might bear witness to Sybil's depravity, found nobody that might bear any kind of authority in their accusations. They settled for the testimony of an unknown young man plucked off the streets, who, if his testimony is correct, has admitted to prostitution. He may very well be telling the truth—I would wager he has little reason not to, though I'm sure he was paid well for his willingness to testify—but it matters little. The prosecution's witness has no reputation to verify his reliability, and no physical proof to back his claims. Even the money, he says when asked if he could produce it, was spent already, though he remains tight-lipped when asked where.

It should come as no surprise, I realize, that the Crown could find no further evidence to make their case. Anyone whose voice might have carried some authority would have to implicate themselves to testify, and has no motive to do so. Sybil Vane's crimes, if they can be called such to begin with, have no victim. The only person to have suffered on the account of her actions is herself, and the fault for that lies with me, not her.

"The prosecution has brought you no evidence against me," says Sybil when called to respond to the testimony. "The best they could find, despite keeping me in prison awaiting trial for over a fortnight, is the evidence of a poor young man who has clearly suffered greatly in this world, and who offers no proof of his claims. I'm a man of good repute whose family has long lived in London and knows its laws. I have no reason to engage in any kind of indecency, and much to lose by it. Even if I were inclined to such depravity—which, I assure you, I am not—I would know better than to act publicly with such disregard for my own well-being."

Watching Sybil speak, one would think she has no fear of what a guilty verdict might mean. Had I not seen her in the molly house myself, I would have no reason to read her confidence as anything but a sign of innocence. Knowing what I do, it hits me that Sybil Vane understands London in a way even Grandfather fails to. Reputation and one's standing in society bear the utmost importance, yes, but they're nowhere near so frail as Grandfather insists. They are tools, and in the hands of a skillful wielder, they can obscure whatever truth one wishes.

The jury does not huddle for long, exchanging only a few whispers to confirm their agreement before proclaiming Sybil's innocence.

The court empties bit by bit. The scarcity of people in attendance makes slipping out a challenge, but I feel no eyes on me as I leave, hiding behind the building to catch my breath once I've made my escape. But relief does not come. If anything, my chest tightens as I replay the scene in my mind. No further punishment will befall Sybil for my actions, but the harm is already done. Only the legal repercussions have been obstructed; the whispers will still follow.

Smoke fills my nostrils, and I look up to see Sybil beside me, pipe carefully balanced between her fingers. She looks at me, eyebrows pursed. My heart beats as she scans over me, but my face is as even and remorseless as hers. Despite the panic rushing through me, I know Sybil will find nothing when she looks at me. She may know how to wield an illusion, but I am one made manifest. I couldn't show her the truth if I wanted to.

"You came to rescue me," she drawls, her voice as hollow as her words. "How chivalrous. I hope you enjoyed the show."

We stand in silence as I wait for her to leave so I can walk as far from the courts as my legs will take me. Even behind the safety of my mask, I can't shake the certainty I will give myself away. My face might be beyond reproach, but my words are clumsier than hers by far. I will have to learn how to speak lies as easily as I wear them. It's the only way anyone can survive here in London.

The sun has just begun to set when I reach Barsden Hollow, but night feels as though it hangs in the air already. Storm clouds weigh down the sky with a layer of thick, dark gray, replacing what should be the warmth of a late June evening with a grim and heavy breeze. The dark skies above give Barsden an aura that verges on the gothic, filling my imagination with all kinds of grim and shocking secrets one might hide in the estate. It's certainly well-versed with scandals already.

Did Mother ever dread her returns to Barsden? Surely she must not have found great comfort in the estate if she fled it for whatever shack she and Papa shared for a few brief months, but she may not have hated it, either. The building itself isn't without its charms, after all, with its imposing facade and elegant interior, and the living spaces are furnished comfortably enough. Sometimes I think Barsden Hollow could be a pleasant place if Grandfather did not rule over it. I suppose, when I inherit it, I'll have a chance to test that theory.

I find Grandfather seated in the hall when I enter, staring at the door with clouds in his eyes darker and heavier than even those outside. Danger prickles at the back of my neck as the dread I've felt since Gartens's visit reaches a crescendo. There must be some detail I missed in my lies, some telltale sign to give me away. *He knows.*

"How did you meet Lord Cavendish, boy?"

I note, before I've even processed his words, that the sneer of disgust on Grandfather's face is painfully familiar. Though I've kept to my decision to hide away Basil's portrait, the face inside it has made a habit of visiting me unprompted, haunting my thoughts and dreams whenever it sees fit. As such, it's with both resignation and distress that I register the portrait's scowl and Grandfather's are one and the same.

"The answer is as I told Inspector Gartens," I answer. "I met him at a salon. Lady Blackwell's, in fact. I thought anyone whose character you recommended could be trusted not to greet ill company."

Grandfather's grimace deepens until even the wickedness that haunts me pales in comparison. "Do not play smart with me, boy. Did you think I would not ask her if she'd introduced the two of you? You have been a stain on this household from the moment of your conception. I suppose I oughtn't be surprised you would one day decide to dishonor me purposely as well. Now, tell me when and where you began to surround yourself with deviants."

"I don't surround myself with them," I try. My face might be steady, but my voice trembles before Grandfather's fury. I may as well be a child again. "I will admit I've spent time in Covent Garden—dishonorable, certainly, but hardly abnormal for healthy young men to do—and I saw Lord Cavendish there, acting in ways so scandalous I would feel ashamed to say them. I would never dishonor you, whatever you may think of me."

Grandfather slams his cane into the floor with a crack like thunder, and I jump at the sound. I will not talk my way out of judgment when his mind is already made up. Perhaps I deserve whatever fate awaits me, not for the reason Grandfather thinks but for betraying Sybil in the first place. His fury is the natural consequence of my actions.

"I said not to lie to me, boy."

"I am not lying, Grandfather," I try once more. Admitting my guilt will not satisfy him, not until he has wrung out every bit of information I know and I've endangered every person I care for. It might be too late to protect myself, but Basil at least should not suffer for my actions.

"Very well. I see I'll have no success today, when your mind is still stubbornly made up. We will talk again in the morning, after sleep has had some time to show you sense."

He begins to walk away, cane clutched so tightly in his hand I can see his knuckles turn bone white. He pauses, then turns back to face me, eyes grayer still than they were when I entered.

The storm, I see, has not subsided. It will rumble throughout the night, and strike harder still come morning.

"I should warn you," he says, "that there is no room in my home for those who consort with deviants, let alone those who protect them. I would start to think, if I were you, about these friends of yours and whether any of them would take *you* in, should you insist on taking the fall on their behalf."

There's my answer, I suppose: This will be my last night at Barsden Hollow. If I have to leave, then I will do so before Grandfather has the chance to question me again. I may not know whether I'm strong enough to continue hiding the truth from him, but I can avoid the question altogether.

Strange as it may be, the thought of leaving brings some sadness with it. I will not miss Grandfather or the cold, piercing judgment that fills his home, but I can't convince myself I'm glad to leave, either. Never again will I see Mother's coffin in the crypt, nor imagine her at my age in her quarters. My portrait will need to find a new hiding place, and I a new bed on which to rest. What little comfort Barsden Hollows offers, I'll have to do without.

Then again, I suppose I deserve my fate. I'll bear it without complaint, if it means nobody else must suffer the consequences of my actions.

14
Emerald Silk

If I'm to be a scandal, I will at least dictate on which terms I become one. I won't go quietly and let Grandfather decide the details of my shame, framing me as some ungrateful runaway who failed to appreciate the generosity he showed by taking me in despite my mother's shortcomings. He will not get the chance to portray himself as a victim, forever disappointed by his descendants and their refusal to inherit his good graces. By the time I've had my way, Grandfather will not dare to speak of my escape, lest the details of the story bring him greater shame.

Reputation, I've realized, is a double-edged sword. The trick is to know when to exert your own, and when to let that of others influence its will upon them.

The chest of Mother's old affairs was heavy to carry from her abandoned quarters, but that does little to stop me from taking it for myself. By the time I've dragged it to my bedchamber I feel sore and out of breath, and yet any strain or exertion pales in comparison to the sheer satisfaction I feel as I open it. I might spend the rest of my life with my prayers unanswered, unsure whether or not Mother would have loved me or frowned upon me like Grandfather does, but this touch of rebellion, at least, I feel confident she would enjoy. Sneaking out to visit Papa, going to the molly house with Basil and Henry—those feel like such tiny acts of resistance, a way for me to spectate the worlds outside Grandfather's approval while keeping some semblance of deniability should I need it.

This, on the other hand, is a point of no return. I will do whatever I desire, explore wherever I will, and I will not leave myself any room for distance or denial. I turned my back on Sybil far too quickly to trust myself not to do the same should the occasion rise again. Whatever I do from here, I must dive in headfirst. That way, I'll know I cannot turn my back on it.

It takes some time before I find anything in the chest that might suit my plans for the night. While Mother's taste appears to have been quite refined, the fashions have changed significantly in the past twenty years. Many of her old gowns are rather plain, with the narrowness of their skirts and lack of buttons or trim for accent. The fabrics, at least, have the elegance I'd hoped for, full of satin and organdie with lace detailings on a few pieces. I suppose the fashion of the clothes matters little compared to their ability to shock, but some part of me insists I might at least try to find something becoming. I think back to the way Sybil Vane looked each time I saw her onstage. This could be my only chance to feel the freedom I envied her. Whether or not I deserve to, I may as well make the most of it.

Eventually, my eyes settle on a simple gown of emerald green silk, with lace around the wrists and a wide but modest neckline that leaves room to show its wearer's neck and the top of her shoulders without plunging so low as to be unseemly. I even uncover a fan in a similar shade, perfect to hide my face should I pass by anyone on the street. It ought to be quiet out at this time of night, but I'd rather show caution than take my chances. The skirt is rather modest in shape, falling nearly flat toward the floor when I lift it, but I suppose it will at least save me the trouble of managing the more cumbersome shapes that are so popular these days.

Getting dressed without the assistance of a lady's maid, navigating the sheer abundance of fabric as I do, proves to be a bigger challenge still than finding suitable clothing. I have to quiet my mind to keep it from criticizing the looseness of my corset or the crease in my skirt. There's only so much I can do by myself, and my appearance—as foreign as the concept feels—needs only to be adequate, not perfect.

The end result, I confirm in my mirror, is satisfactory enough. The darkness of the green suits the brightness of my hair and the pallor of my complexion, bringing out subtle hints of color in my eyes I hadn't noticed amidst the gray that dominates them. My hair is shorter than I might wish and my jaw square enough to lend me a sharper, sterner look than I'm accustomed to, but the waves that have started to re-form in my locks and the height of my cheekbones give the young lady in the mirror the air of a pixie escaped from Titania's court for a night to explore the mortal realm.

A familiar feeling rumbles in my stomach as I watch my reflection. Envy, the same as I felt when I saw the version of me Basil painted. The girl in front of me is as sacred as that youth, as much me as the cruel beauty taking over my portrait. The realization is as warm as it is sharp, but whatever fleeting joy it might bring is undercut by the fact that this girl, much like Sybil Vane, is cursed to live only in whatever shadows she can find.

At the last minute, I pin a sapphire broach below my collarbone, shaped like a small hummingbird mid-flight. It adds some level of detail to the gown, I suppose, but more important is the calm that washes over me when I pull it from the chest. It feels as though a piece of Mother has been plucked from the past, resting above my heart to lend me some fraction of her nerve.

I close my eyes and take a breath, picturing her phantom hand atop my shoulders, then turn toward the window.

No, I decide moments after breaking the glass, *not the window.* It's difficult enough to climb the trellis in my normal garb, let alone the added difficulty of managing a gown. Besides, if this is to be my last time escaping Barsden Hollow, I want to do it with the confidence I could never muster before. Grandfather must be long asleep by now, the servants retired to their quarters. I will walk out the door, head held high, and leave the scared child who crawled out her window behind. There's no place for her where I'm going.

Before I leave, however, I pull my portrait from my wall and hide it under my bed, still wrapped in the drapes that obstruct it. I doubt it will be safe for long, but with some luck it might stay tucked away until I find a way to retrieve it, wherever I end up. Whatever sense of shame I've chosen to abandon tonight, some piece of it remains with the portrait—I sense that that fragment, at least, will never be far behind me.

I drag the chest of Mother's things next to my open door as I leave, keeping it wide-open and its contents revealed. When Grandfather comes to question me tomorrow, I want him to be plagued by the image of his only heir fleeing into the night, dressed in his mother's old clothes so they might both shame him one last time.

I spend the better part of an hour walking London's streets, unsure where my feet are guiding me.

The possibility of going to Papa's gallery flashes across my mind before I brush it off. Grandfather might know to look for me there, and I can't bear to bring Papa trouble. The last time one of Grandfather's heirs sought refuge with him, after all, resulted in a headhunt that only ended because of Mother's death. If the bullet had struck true—or even if it had missed and simply not hit Mother instead—I have no doubt Papa would be dead by now. I couldn't live with myself if I led Grandfather back to him, especially when it would endanger Fabián as well. Besides, I couldn't face the two of them after turning in Sybil Vane. I don't have it in me to abuse their generosity, knowing the kind of person I truly am.

Basil, sure as I am he would take me in without hesitation, isn't an option for much the same reason. Whenever I've looked at him in the fortnight since Gartens's visit, I haven't been able to shake the certainty that he knows, somehow, the secret my portrait hides. It seems perfectly plausible, given the unfathomable nature of the portrait, that its painter might somehow be privy to its changes as well.

I find myself, after some more time wandering, at the entrance of Covent Garden. It seems strange to think I could be so familiar with its graying buildings and unsavory passersby, when even two months ago I wouldn't have dared step foot in the area, but somehow the chaos and anonymity that clutter its streets have become comforting. I've grown to feel that nothing I say or do could matter here. I could be anyone, and nobody would know.

I suppose it's no surprise, then, that I would seek refuge here when Lord Dorian Gray is the last person I wish to be.

A man staggers in my direction, breath heavy with drink, and I raise my fan over my face as he passes. I've found that anyone passing through Covent Garden pays little mind to the motives of others—all of us are here for reasons we do not wish to share—but I'm not so naive as to forget the way I look or how I'm dressed. There are worse fates on London's streets than simple judgment, and I have no escape nearby should I need it. Tamara's tavern is still several minutes away on foot, and I doubt I could run very quickly with a long skirt to trip over and a half-laced corset restraining my breaths.

I used to feel a sense of adventure walking London at night when I would escape to visit Papa at the gallery. Imagined threats for myself, as though they made my journey more exciting. But there are threats enough here, and now that they're real, I cannot imagine them bringing me any kind of thrill. I couldn't say whether the young man I was three months ago was naive or simply so apathetic toward his own safety he wanted to put himself at risk, but he was a fool either way. I can't help but find, now that the streets of London are an inevitability rather than an escape, that some part of me resents him. There's little I wouldn't give to feel so safe as to invent myself threats.

By the time I reach the tavern, every stranger I pass frightens me, and the fan before my face might as well have become a second skin. Tamara stands behind the bar as she always does, tidying the counter, when I see her. The sight of her soothes me, even when I see the concern written clean across her face when she notices me. It's nice, at least, to know there's now someone in my presence who cares about my safety. Some weight has been lifted, knowing I've reached a harbor from the storm still threatening to break outside.

"I need a drink," I tell her, fetching the coin purse I pinned into the bottom of my skirts. The classlessness of the gesture brings a wry chuckle to my lips, but what little humor I can muster does not last me long. "Something strong, if you have it."

For a moment, I think Tamara might protest as she opens her mouth, then closes it with grim resignation. Running a tavern takes money, after all, and though uncertainty is clear in her gaze, I doubt there's a business in Covent Garden that can afford to turn away a paying customer. She brings me a glass of a clear liquid she tells me is gin and tells me to drink slowly, but her warning goes in one ear and out the other as I turn the corner behind the bar and show myself to the cellar, taking a sip as I walk down the steps.

The gin has a bitter, almost medicinal taste to it, but the sharpness of my feelings dulls ever so slightly with each sip, and so the glass is nearly empty by the time I reach the bottom of the steps.

My face twists into a grimace as the aftertaste lingers; I raise my fan to cover it until the unpleasantness has smoothed over. I take a seat at my usual table, ignoring the stares that follow me as I walk.

I've grown accustomed, by now, to feeling eyes on me when I travel the cellar, but today I feel more than ever before. The molly house is busier at this time of night, certainly, and the people gathered have had more time to drink, and yet I feel with utter certainty that their gazes have little to do with drink. *I* am the one hypnotizing them, and the power I taste in that revelation intoxicates me more than any drink could.

The first boy who approaches me looks to be about my age, though I care little to register his features. They're pleasant enough, if somewhat typical, but the timidity with which he approaches me is thrilling. I can't remember the last time someone felt intimidated by the thought of me. That recognition alone makes him three times as interesting, and I find myself entertaining his conversation even as he struggles to find his footing.

"Your glass is empty," he says once I've moved it near enough for him to understand. "Might I refill it for you?"

"If you bring me something strong enough, I might decide you please me."

A piercing cold seeps into my voice, thickening it with husky, controlled tones I didn't know it could possess. The sound of it reminds me of how Sybil sounded, smoking next to me after her trial, and for a moment I feel as if I hold a fraction of her power rather than being some lost girl playing at adulthood.

It takes little time for the boy to return with another glass full to the brim. He looks as though he's struggling not to spill it over—the careful dedication of his movement flatters me, I decide, as a man in a black coat and a top hat takes the glass from his hands, handing him some coins before starting to turn toward me.

"Poor boy," I say, opening my fan before my face as I speak. "He worked up such courage to talk to me, and you sweep in without a care."

"He'll live. Something tells me he couldn't have kept up with you, if you'd given him the chance."

"And you can?"

"Frankly, Dorian," says Henry, pushing my fan away so that I can see his stare burning into me, "I still have my doubts that *you* can keep up with *me*."

"You recognized me."

"I would know you anywhere, you beautiful, beautiful girl."

The low, smooth tone in which Henry speaks all but overflows from him as he reaches across the table, taking my hand to his lips. There's a roughness to them only heightened by the scratching of his beard against my skin, and the intimacy of the gesture sends shivers down my back. I've seen traces of this Henry before, speaking while Basil painted me or the night we walked in his aunt's gardens, but I realize now that the hunger I caught glimpses of in his eyes has always been restrained until tonight.

I hold his stare with mine, matching it as best I can. "It's been some time since I last saw you. I thought you might be avoiding me."

"I was. I worried Basil might be right, and you thought my introducing you to Cavendish was cruel. I hope you know it was never my intention to hurt or embarrass you."

"Nor did you," I lie. It seems so childish to claim insult or injury over information I always suspected, and I have no desire for Henry to see a child when he looks at me. "Though I am curious what your intention was, if you had none of the ill will Basil assumed of you."

"Perhaps I simply wanted you to see the possibilities the world provides, the pleasures one can find outside what is conventional or approved of."

His breath is hot against my skin, and it isn't until I feel it against my neck that I realize how close he is to me. I remember wondering, hidden behind his aunt's rosebushes, what it might feel like to kiss him, but I lacked the nerve to follow through. This time I move toward him, and when Henry's lips brush mine I let them, soaking in the meaning of his words—but I feel as though I'm only peeking behind the curtain at the pleasures to which he alludes.

"Come," he says, stealing some air from my lungs as he pulls away, "let's get you to my home. I have no clue what has befallen you, but it's late, and even a man as selfish as I am can see you need to rest."

15
Golden Chains

I wake up alone in a room I don't recognize, sun burning through tightly drawn curtains. The bed is soft beneath me, less sturdy than I'm accustomed to, and my ribs ache with the phantom memory of my corset compressing them. Though I didn't drink enough to feel its effects lingering, I still find myself disoriented as my mind stumbles, overwhelmed by my new surroundings, to remember where I am and how I found my way here.

Grandfather's threat comes flashing back into my thoughts, bringing with it the knowledge I have no place to call home. My stomach twists, but I remind myself I have, at least, a roof over my head and a bed in which to sleep. Somehow, over the course of our journey back to Hartwood, I managed to share the core details of my situation with Henry, careful to outline my conversation with Grandfather and his discovery of my association with Sybil Vane without giving away the part I played in her arrest.

Lying to Henry—or omitting some key part of the truth, at least—doesn't bring the same sense of guilt or shame that seeing Basil or even thinking about Papa does. Whatever scruples I have about my behavior, I have no expectation that Henry is in any position to frown upon me or the actions that have led me to his guest apartments. He prides himself too much on his wantonness and speaks too much on the virtues of selfish pleasure to mind my cowardice or duplicity. I can picture him, upon receiving my confession, laughing and reminding me Lord Cavendish got away from the controversy unscathed. *If anything,* I imagine his voice saying, *this whole ordeal ought to show you there are no consequences for people like you and me. We are free to act as we please, as long as we keep our wits about us.*

Nevertheless, I don't intend on sharing the details of my circumstance with Henry. Whatever his thoughts on the matter, I have no desire to dwell any longer on my own shortcomings. It's selfish of me, certainly, but London is overflowing with selfishness and heartless deeds. Whatever I do from here, I do it to survive. There is no greater rebellion, I learned from Henry's book, than embracing pleasure for pleasure's sake, when high society is so fixated on maintaining illusions of morality.

I can't tell if I believe this philosophy entirely, but it's comforting enough I see no reason to reject it. London is full of people who care only for themselves, from Grandfather's obsession with his reputation to the gossips who treat other people's difficulties as a source of entertainment or a chance to call themselves charitable. It's high time I understood the way the world works.

The thought, however freeing, brings with it a certain loneliness. If I've resigned myself to living in a selfish world, then I can rely on no one but myself. There are people, certainly, who try to live good, honest lives—Basil's face flashes in my mind, alongside the way he rushed to my side when Sybil was arrested with little regard for the toll such news had on him—but I've proved already that I am not like them. I will only disappoint him, given the time to do so.

I'd hoped, at least, that Henry might be beside me when I woke. He hadn't yet left my bed by the time I fell asleep, and as foreign a sensation as his company provided, there was a comfort in feeling the warmth of another body next to mine. Letting the rise and fall of his breathing rock me to sleep made the world seem a touch less cold, less uncaring. Sharing my bed turned the room into a pocket cut away from the rest of London, even after the warmth of his touch had left me.

Still, the idea Henry might watch over me as I slept was a foolish one. Victoria, I'm sure, knows better than to cling to any hope of keeping his company after their marital relationship. Who am I to expect more intimacy than he affords his own wife?

The thought of Henry's unfaithfulness brings with it some remnant of shame, but I brush it off. I've seen their marriage in action, and, as Henry once said, Victoria is a delightfully modern woman. She knows the kind of man she married, and enjoys the benefits of that choice. Whatever romantic notions of marriage I have, they do not fit the reality of Hartwood.

The door before me opens without so much as a knock, revealing Henry on the other side. He pauses for a moment, gaze lingering on me as I rush to pull my blankets over my chest. The gesture pries a dry chuckle from his lips, which sparks a flushing heat through me. I suppose I have little reason for modesty around him, but I can't help feeling some need to hide away from his stare. He knows too much—has seen too much—and it leaves me strangely vulnerable, though I doubt he'd feel the same if our roles were reversed.

"I plan to take a trip down to Barsden Hollow this morning," Henry says so matter-of-factly one might think there was nothing unusual in his statement. "I assumed you might want to recover some of your affairs, and I thought you might not wish to see your grandfather, given the lengths you took to avoid him when you left."

"As kind of you as that is, I think I might need to navigate the matter of my lodgings before gathering my affairs. Grateful as I am for your hospitality, I can't monopolize your guest apartments. It would be too great an imposition."

Even as I protest, the reality of my situation undercuts my words. I can't think of anywhere else I might live. Every person I know would either be more inconvenienced by my presence than Henry or would fill me with shame at the mere sight of them. Besides, for all Henry's protests about the tedium of Hartwood and its beige, there's a certain warmth to its simplicity that makes it a rather pleasant place to take sanctuary.

"My guest apartments?" Henry scoffs. "I have no plans of keeping you here. Once we have gathered your affairs, I'll help you settle into my country house, Thornhill. You can stay there until you find alternative lodgings or, if we should be so lucky, until your grandfather passes and Barsden is yours. I so rarely go to the country that it seems wasteful to have an estate there, but with you to visit, I might at least have some reason to make more use of it."

I frown not with displeasure but bafflement as Henry's offer sinks in. "Your country house? That's awfully generous of you."

"Please don't dishonor me by speaking of generosity—I promise you this is an entirely selfish scheme of mine. I can think of little I'd like more than to know where to find you at any moment's notice."

Something about the dry, factual tone of Henry's voice bristles against me. I can't help imagining myself as a songbird, surrounded on all sides by beautiful, gilded bars, but I dismiss the thought. Living in Henry's country home would give me more freedom than I've ever had. I've grown used to relying on the will of others, and Henry—unlike Grandfather—will not hold me to some absurd standard of morality or propriety.

It dawns on me that I might not be sitting in Henry's bed, unwelcome in my own home, had he not brought me to the molly house or pushed me to meet Sybil Vane, but I ignore the discomfort at the bottom of my stomach. I will not give Henry the power to take credit for my decisions, and especially not for my mistakes. Besides, am I truly worse off depending on Henry's favor than living at Barsden? Keeping Henry's interest seems a far easier matter than suffering Grandfather's judgments and the fury I'm sure is awaiting me—and I can't shake the certainty that this dubious arrangement between us is more than I deserve.

I disentangle myself from the sheets, moving toward the pile of clothing on the bedside table. The modesty I clung to when Henry entered seems useless now that I've settled to put myself so directly within his hands. He raises an amused eyebrow as I rise, but I ignore him, focusing instead on changing into more proper garb for the day.

"I should speak with my grandfather," I tell him. "I think I might persuade him to send me some form of an allowance in exchange for my discretion while at Thornhill. That way I wouldn't have to be as heavy a burden on you and your purse."

"It's no burden at all. I'd be more than happy to care for you, Dorian. What else are friends for?"

"Then consider it a boon to a friend. I'd feel much better about our arrangement if I had at least some control over my finances."

A dark sort of heat lights in Henry's eyes, but he doesn't press the matter. I consider, for a moment, the idea of rejecting his offer before he can pull me into his grasp. I can tell from the disappointed twist of his lips that my sole reliance on him is part of the appeal of his plan, but even then I lack the stomach to reject him altogether. Whatever birdcage Henry wants to hold me in is, if nothing else, a step up from the prison Barsden has become.

"Very well," he surrenders. "If that's what you prefer. I suppose I should let you prepare to visit your grandfather so we may settle you away from him as quickly as possible."

So you may settle me away from everyone, my mind whispers, bitter and cold as the first gust of winter. *So I am yours, and yours alone.*

Henry's eyes burn into me as he pulls me in, tucking a strand of my hair behind my ear before kissing me. The hunger with which his lips move against mine and the heat building between us feel far more sinister in the light of day than they did in the cellar of Tamara's tavern. Henry's fire, I realize as he pulls me even deeper into his embrace, isn't here to warm me but to consume me.

I think back to the boy at the molly house last night, and how

completely I held him within my grasp. I'm not so naive as to think he cared about me as more than a pretty face; it was precisely that knowledge that made him so easy to disarm. Why, then, should Henry be any different?

Power, I've learned, is little more than knowing what others want and how to make those desires serve my own—and I've been given a rare gift in this regard. However ugly the truth of the world may be, I have the sole luxury of knowing its hideous face will never reach my own. Henry wants me, and in doing so he has provided me with a powerful bargaining chip. I will not allow myself to be used if I can't have my way first. *He cannot consume me*, I resolve, *if I consume him first.*

I kiss him back as deeply as I can, leaning in until I could not say where his body ends and mine begins. The fire roars between us the more I feed it, yet I refuse to shy away from it. I will forge myself in the flames until they cannot hurt me. I'll be the one thing they cannot burn.

The chains around my ankles rattle for my attention, but I don't heed their call. In my mind, they are long gone already, and my life is finally in nobody's hands but my own.

I must say, the feeling is delectable.

16
Steel Resolve

When I left Barsden Hollow in the dead of night yesterday, I never dreamed I might see it so soon after my departure. Yet here I stand, mere hours after escaping the belly of the beast, ready to throw myself back into its maw.

I remind myself as best as I can that this is but a temporary return, that once I settle the affairs I've left unresolved here, I'll never need to see Grandfather's estate again. The thought does little to comfort me. Negotiating the terms of my departure with Grandfather myself might have been my own idea, but the stakes felt so much lower when I believed, if only for a few moments, that Grandfather's hold on me had finally broken.

It was naive to think I could ever fully escape him, even as I sign myself over to Henry's authority in his stead. Wherever I go, however long passes, I will always be marked by the scars he left on me; the best I can hope is to mold them into a shape that can at least serve me. Perhaps, if I can twist the fear into foresight and the calculation into cunning, I might one day use the wounds he caused me to build a life for myself.

For a moment, as I walk into Barsden's entrance hall, I picture Grandfather waiting for me, Inspector Gartens behind him ready to arrest me. It's an absurd notion—Grandfather would never want to attract such controversy, and I can't think of a single charge either one could leverage against me with the limited information I've given them, but it chills me nonetheless. However much I may have steeled myself for this meeting between us, whatever fragments of a plan I've managed to put together, the truth remains that nothing can protect me should my attempt at negotiations go wrong. Henry might be willing to lodge me if it wins him my favor, but I know better than to expect him to lift a finger to aid me should I become more hassle than I'm worth to him. In my need to shatter Grandfather's hold on me, I've also put myself at the mercy of his pride.

If nothing else, I suppose there's at least some comfort to be found in knowing I look to be in far better condition than I feel. My eyes should be bloodshot with sleeplessness, my hair disheveled, my skin bruised by the marks of Henry's lips, but whatever strange affliction Basil's portrait has bestowed upon me is as much a blessing as it is a curse. I would have no leg to stand on if I showed myself at Barsden looking as though I'd slept in the streets. My clothes are admittedly ill-fitting, considering Henry is both shorter than me and also wider, but all that communicates is that I have a benefactor supplying them for me. Grandfather will see that any threat he makes to eject me from Barsden will be hollow, knowing I already have a place to land. Any power he might have over me in our negotiations will sit in the fear he can inspire, and any authority I might have will sit in my ability to feign indifference.

It is, admittedly, a risky gamble to take, but I can't think of any better option.

"Master Gray," calls a stern voice behind me. "It's a relief to see you. Your grandfather had started to think something had happened to you when Peter reported you were not in your chambers this morning."

I'm sure he was worried sick on my behalf, I almost say, but I push back the urge. However cold and inscrutable Grandfather's butler may be, he has never given me the impression he did not care for me. As much as I could resent Mr. James for overseeing the estate on his behalf, it would be unfair to blame him when I know he is as much at the mercy of Grandfather's whims as anyone else.

"And where is Grandfather now?" I ask.

"His study. Should I send word to him that you've returned safely to Barsden?"

"No, thank you. I'll inform him of my presence myself."

Mr. James opens his mouth to protest, but I push past him before he gets the chance. He stumbles back and I take off running up the stairs, ignoring his reminder of how much Grandfather loathes to be disturbed without warning.

Good, I think, slowing my pace once I confirm Mr. James has given up on following me. If I can take Grandfather by surprise, I might be able to put myself in a commanding position before we've even spoken.

I have plenty of experience running from Grandfather, but this is uncharted territory. When it comes to finally standing up to him, I'll take every advantage I can get.

I could count on one hand the number of times I've been allowed into Grandfather's study. The first time, I'd been three years old and had asked him why I didn't have parents like the servants' children did. The second was on my eighth birthday, when he explained to me the duties I would one day take on as Lord Kelso's sole living heir. The last time I sat in his study was a few years ago, when one of the maids caught me sneaking past their quarters on my way into London.

Grandfather had lectured me on how stupid I was to put his legacy in danger by walking the streets at night, and I left his office trembling, holding back tears I knew he wouldn't deign to see. A few days later, the latch on my window disappeared, and I began to wonder how long it would take for me to grow the nerve to shatter the glass trapping me within Barsden's walls.

The outside of the study, however, is almost painful in its familiarity. When I was a child, I used to spend hours at his door, thinking how happy Grandfather would be when he saw me waiting after he'd spent the day hard at work. Then, once I realized how rarely he left and how little he'd want to see me if he did, it became the one place I could hide in all of Barsden Hollow where the servants would not dare to look for me.

Even now, I can't help feeling small as I stand before the hard oak door. Nerves dance along the nape of my neck, my breaths shortening with each passing moment. My fist shakes as I raise it to knock, but I drop it at the last moment, steadying myself as I do. However vulnerable I might feel, I am not here to ask to be let in. The goal is to announce myself, to demand what I want from Grandfather without giving him the time to find his footing. Knocking would defeat my purpose entirely.

I swing the door open before I can lose my nerve and stride in as boldly as I can manage. If Grandfather is put off by my assertiveness, he does not show it. He rises from his desk slowly and purposefully, pale gray eyes piercing into mine without a moment's hesitation.

"Interrupting me without so much as announcing yourself, boy? Here I was hoping you might have given up on your tantrum by now."

The urge to snap at him boils inside me, but I know better than to let it take over. The moment I lose my temper, he'll dismiss me as a child being ruled by my whims and I'll lose whatever ground I might have gained. Instead, I simply smile at him as I walk toward the seat closest to his desk, my eyes matching his stare even as he towers over me.

"There's no need to worry about any tantrums," I tell him. "I've simply come to negotiate the terms of my departure from Barsden Hollow."

"And what makes you think you have the grounds to negotiate a thing? I could summon Inspector Gartens and turn you in at any moment."

Grandfather walks around his desk, his eyes turning stormy as his face twists into a sneer. The sight of him towering over me might be intimidating, but I am far more accustomed to it by now than he is to my defiance. Seeing me stand up to him has gotten under Grandfather's skin, and while there's no telling where this development might lead, I know without a doubt I have to keep pushing if I want to maintain my momentum.

"Surely you would have done so when you noticed I was missing. I take it the box of Mother's effects on my bed gave you some pause? I'm sure polite society would love to hear that the sole heir to the Kelso name fled Barsden in the dead of night, dressed in women's clothes like some sort of deviant only to wind up in a molly house of all places—and so shortly after the Cavendish scandal at that."

I hear the thunderous crack of Grandfather's hand across my face shortly before I feel its sting, sharp and brutal in its fury. The storm in his eyes has broken now, pouring down hatred and rage upon me, but I raise my chin in response. I cannot let him see me waver. There will be time to cry later, once I've freed myself from him and he can never hurt me again. I hold his stare, wondering as I do if my portrait's lip is bleeding on my behalf.

"Insolent child," he hisses. "After all I've done for you, this is how you repay me? Everything you have, you owe to the kindness I showed in raising you despite your mother's carelessness. I should have drowned you as a babe and let the Kelso name die off rather than let you grow into as much of a liability as your mother was."

I wince at his mention of my mother, but if Grandfather aimed to shock me with his words, they've fallen short. I've long wondered if he might feel this way toward me, and while it may ache to hear it confirmed, it can't compete with the relief I'll feel once

I'm free of him. He has overplayed his hand now; all I've left to do is wait for the pieces to fall into place.

"Don't worry, Grandfather. I have witnesses ready to testify should you try to discredit me. They'll share what they saw the moment I signal them—or, for that matter, if they fail to hear from me at all. I assure you there's nothing you can do that will stop the shame from reaching your good name. Or"—I pause—"we can reach a mutually beneficial arrangement." I brace myself for Grandfather to strike me again, but the sting doesn't come. Instead, a sigh escapes his lips as he walks back behind his desk and collapses into his chair.

"A friend has offered to lodge me," I tell Grandfather, settling deeper into my chair. "You can say I decided to move to the country so I might prepare to inherit your title away from London and its ever-growing list of scandals, and I will avoid bringing any further controversy to your name. In exchange, you will provide me with a monthly allowance so that I might invest it and hone my ability to grow the Kelso fortune—and, of course, cater the occasional event to maintain the social standing you've worked so hard to provide me."

"Is that all?"

The two of us study each other carefully, daring the other to budge. The storm in his eyes has settled, but I don't miss the venom they still hold. I know better than to think he will forgive the affront I've dealt him today. Somehow, he will find a way to take out his resentment—if not on me, then on anyone in his reach he thinks he could use to hurt me.

"Peter," I add. "It wouldn't do for me to go without a valet, and he already has years of experience in the role. The two of us will load my belongings into the coach I took to get here, and then we will both leave for the country, where you will not have to worry about my tarnishing your name. Does that seem suitable to you?"

"I suppose I have little choice in the matter," Grandfather growls.

I nod my agreement and smile at him before taking my leave. For once, I do not leave his office feeling small or frightened. Instead, I stand taller than ever, steady despite the weight of the blows Grandfather dealt me.

For what might be the first time in my life, I feel powerful.

17
Ice Blue

For all the surprise that Hartwood brought me when I first laid eyes on it, Thornhill Hearth is much closer to the type of home I might've pictured Henry living in. The facade itself stands imposingly tall, blending the sentimental shapes of the gothic with the structure of the neoclassical style. The two blend elegantly to create an imposing, extravagant building overflowing both with unmitigated sentimentality and clear-cut elegance.

The interior, however, forms so elaborate a tapestry it might seem precarious were it not so expertly crafted. I've often found, in the days since making my home at Thornhill, that a single shift in its shades or swirls or furnishing might turn the entire house to pandemonium, though that thought only adds to the sense of marvel I feel wandering its halls. Violet and crimson dance on the walls in wide, sprawling circles as statues of crisp white marble line the halls, spacing out enough tapestries and urns to fill the wing of a museum. I can't think of a single person other than Henry who could push so close to the line where extravagance becomes poor taste without crossing it. It feels as if the estate in its entirety was plotted onto the line where art meets atrocity, daring anyone who enters to tip it over the edge.

It was hard to believe an estate that spoke so clearly of his touch could be one he did not visit, given how prone he is to complaining about Hartwood, until he explained that Thornhill needed rebuilding shortly after he inherited his fortune.

"I often wish," he told me when he left me here, "that Hartwood had been the one to burn in Thornhill's stead. The estate is much more to my liking, but I can't stand the country. Nothing of any interest happens here, and so I must choose between a dull home and a dull life."

"Perhaps I might find a way to liven the place, then," I'd replied.

"I doubt there's a single place you could not liven, if you set your mind to it. You could move into a friary and tempt them to excess."

Henry left within a few hours, claiming business in the city he needed to attend. The freedom of having a home to myself grew stale in little time without neighbors nearby to visit or guests to entertain, and so I've spent much of the last few days browsing through the library. It's with some relief that I note that none of its volumes are quite so provocative as the first book he lent me, though enough novels tell stories of vice and sin to distract me from the tedium of my self-imposed isolation and the guilt motivating it—at least for a moment.

By the time my fifth day at Thornhill runs along, I resolve to throw the first of what I can only assume will be many a soiree in my new home. It will be a lavish event, I determine, with only the most traveled and controversial minds in attendance. If I must live away from the city and all its thrills, I will simply import the world to me. I will hear every thought, live all there is to experience, all from the comfort of Thornhill—and, given the remote nature of my exile, no word of what I do will reach Grandfather's ears. Whatever occurs at my soirees will exist only in hushed tones, whispered in secret by people desperate to be included. An invitation to Thornhill will be the most coveted of trophies, a badge of honor bestowed upon only the most fashionable and modern in London society. The allowance I negotiated from Grandfather should more than cover the expenses necessary to bring the city to my doorstep.

I'm seated in the study nearest the grand hall, writing Henry to inform him of my decision, when I hear a knocking at the door. I assume, at first, that Henry must have come to visit me, seeing as I've told no one of my whereabouts, then remind myself I've never heard him knock at a door, let alone the entrance to his own country house.

Curiosity guides my steps to the door, but worry freezes my hand before I can open it. For a moment I can only picture Grandfather behind it, Inspector Gartens behind him as he tells me he has come to drag me back to London, where I'm expected for trial now that I'm no longer under his protection. I can all but hear the whispers behind me, each voice filled with ten times the cruelty and glee they had when discussing Sybil Vane. It occurs to me how easily I could end up in her position, and how I wouldn't stand half the chance she did with Grandfather pressing the charges, and how deserved a fate it would be if I found myself behind bars for the same crimes I tied to her. The irony of it all is as baffling as it is chilling.

I take a breath to steady myself, remembering that Grandfather could easily have stopped my departure from London altogether had he wanted to. He has no reason to come for me now. Without wasting another moment, I open the door, braced for whatever might await me on the other side.

I'd hoped, when I fled Barsden Hollow, that I would not have to cross Basil Hallward's path again—that I wouldn't have to explain the best way to honor our friendship was to remove myself from his life before I could hurt him. I should have known that fate could never be so kind as to give me a clean escape.

If Basil looked tired when I left him, his fatigue was nothing compared to the person I see before me now. His eyes are hollow, his shoulders slumped forward, and he throws himself into my arms the moment he sees me, as if the thought of reaching me had been the only motive animating him. I hold him in my arms, frozen, as I start cursing myself for consoling him when I only plan on hurting him further. It would be kinder of me to turn him away now, but I can't bring myself to let go of him. *He needs the comfort*, I tell myself, ignoring the selfish part of me focused on how good it feels that I'm the one he turned to for it.

Somehow, the desperation coursing through him only endears him more to me. The mere thought of Basil tossing in his bed, wondering where I might be, chips away at the loneliness that has sat so heavily on my shoulders.

If I were the person Basil deserves for me to be, I remind myself, the sight of him in this state would bring me sorrow, not relief.

"I went to call on you Wednesday, but the housekeeper told me she hadn't seen you in two days. Why would you leave London without telling me?"

"How did you find me?" I ask, pushing aside my guilt at the hurt in his voice. The ice with which I try to surround myself cracks at the reminder that I abandoned him without so much as a letter, but I can't question my decision now. What little resolve I feel to keep him at arm's length would shatter if I second-guess myself.

"Did you not want me to?"

"Of course I did, Basil. Come with me, let's find you somewhere to sit."

It would be better if I chose not to reassure him, but I can't bring myself to do it. I can't tell him he'd be better without me or that I'm not the person he thinks I am, no matter how much pain I might spare him by breaking his heart with one clean cut. The basest, most selfish parts of me haven't yet given up the hope he might tire of me if I can simply act distant rather than cruel. I hardly need to consult my portrait to know the type of stain that treating him with cruelty would bear upon my soul; I can feel it in the way the mere thought of hurting him stings like acid.

I guide Basil to the study, all but carrying the weight of his body. His frame has gone limp in my arms, as if what little drive were possessing him has finally abandoned him. I place him in the more comfortable of the two chairs as slowly as I can, taking in the faint smell of fresh canvas and linen that rises from him and cursing myself for my sentimentality all the while. Tears well at the corners of my eyes, but I push them back before he can notice.

"I bumped into Henry outside your father's studio," Basil tells me, voice distant. "At first I thought I might find you there, but he told me you'd been with him since the night you left."

"I ran into him at Covent Garden when I had nowhere to go. Henry was kind enough to take me home with him and to set me up with lodgings after that."

"Nowhere to go?"

Basil's voice cracks with the last word, and though I try to convince myself I'm mistaken, it would be impossible to miss the wetness in his eyes. I know the moment I see it that I've betrayed him in a way I never thought possible. Nothing I could have done would have cut him so deeply as deciding I could not have gone to him when I needed to—except, perhaps, seeking Henry's help instead.

The wall around my heart cracks deeper, but I steel my face. The deed is done. In trying to avoid cruelty, I let cowardice take the reins, and in doing so I've torn us apart already. All I can do now is deal the final blow and hope one day he might recover. Eventually, he'll look at this moment and see me for this wretched thing I am, and the thought of being rid of me will bring him the relief he deserves.

"Basil, you're behaving absurdly. Sentimentality has no place in this."

"You could have come to me for help," he argues. "You could have turned to your *father*. We might not have had a plush country house for you, but either of us would have taken you in. Henry is not to be trusted, Dorian. You should have heard how he spoke when he told me where you were. He made you sound like some trophy he won, not a friend in need of his assistance."

"Is that it, then? Are you jealous I leaned on Henry and not you?" My laugh is cold, methodical, harsh in a way that makes me ill. "Frankly, Basil, your insecurity is laughable. Whatever flaws Henry might have, he at least knows what he has to offer, rather than speaking ill of himself every chance he gets."

If Basil looked wounded before I spoke, I lack the words to describe the expression that crosses his face now. Some hint of resignation seeps into its core, and yet it can't chase away the remnants of hope that cling to him. Even as my cruelty pierces him, I see him fight to justify my actions, to find some way my words might not have the vicious bite I gave them.

"Something about you has changed," he finally says. His voice isn't quite as hollow as it was before, but the observation brings me little joy. "I felt a shift in you when I first showed you the portrait I painted, but I told myself I must have imagined it. Perhaps, if I could see it, I could understand what has caused this rift between us."

My blood runs cold at the thought of Basil seeing the portrait he painted. As desperate as I am for Basil to tire of me, I can't bear imagining the revulsion on his face when he sees the hideous truth of my nature.

"If I hear another mention of that portrait, I shall never speak to you again."

Basil frowns. "What could possibly possess you to make such a threat over something as simple as a portrait?"

"You won't fool me, Basil. Henry told me, once, that you vowed you would never exhibit this portrait despite it being your best work. *If you want to spend a strange quarter of an hour*, he told me, *get Basil to tell you why he won't exhibit your picture.* Clearly, I'm not the only one hiding secrets in your portrait. Perhaps, if you told me what you so wish to hide, I might believe you when you chide me for attaching this much importance to a painting."

Basil opens his mouth as if to respond, then closes it again. For all his art, he lacks the ability to weave his heart away beneath layers of artifice. He wears his feelings as wonderfully as if he had painted them upon himself for all the world to see.

It seems so obvious, now that I let myself acknowledge it, that Basil fancies himself in love with me. Perhaps it was that devotion that granted his portrait life, though I suppose it matters little. Whatever Basil thinks he feels, he's mistaken. He cannot love me without knowing the truth about me, and he could not love the cold and wicked creature he would see if he gazed upon the painting of me now. Leaving him with the ideal he painted for himself is the last kindness I can do him.

"Very well," Basil agrees. "I think I put too much of myself into your portrait and tinted my lens too heavily with the way I perceive you. As I painted you, you became to me an ideal of beauty, of youth, of freedom from the restrictions society so loves to place upon us, and I thought it might be dangerous to attach such idolatry to a person. It revealed too much of me—of you as well, perhaps—and it seemed to me irresponsible to expose such intimate thoughts."

"You have painted me perfectly, Basil, and I cannot bear to see you look at my portrait and change your mind. You must promise to always picture me as perfect as you painted, and never to look at your work for confirmation. It would break my heart to know you could see me as anything but what I am before you."

"I sought to paint *you*, Dorian, precisely as you are. The perfection is incidental, and matters far less than the reality that stands before me. If you wish me not to look at the painting, then I shan't, but it pains me to think you might so treasure it above your own self. It wounds me even more that you might value hiding some secret flaw you've imagined above our friendship."

"Whatever the case," I conclude, "all you have said is that you fear you admire me too much. A pleasant compliment, I suppose, but rather disappointing for a confession."

"Were you expecting me to say something different? Perhaps you saw something in my painting that caught your attention?"

Basil's question hangs in the air, bridging us together with its implications. I would love nothing more than to tell him what I know, to say I wish I believed he could love me or that I can think of little more I would want than to be worthy of that love, but I know what I must do. As long as this bridge stands between us, we'll remain bound, and I will have to carry the fear that he might see some proof of who I am.

"I did not see anything I would care to discuss."

"Very well, then." Basil's words are as hollow as I feel as he lifts himself from his seat. "I suppose I ought to apologize for intruding upon you. I'm glad to see, at least, that you've settled comfortably in your new home."

I don't answer Basil, nor do I walk him to the door. I simply think, as he leaves, that I'll never need to worry about disappointing him again.

18
Crimson Fate

Papa's letter comes mere days after Basil's visit, but it takes most of a week before I can bring myself to open it.

The knowledge of its existence plagues me like a slow, mild burn, never quite hot enough for me to surrender but never numb enough for me to forget it, either. I find myself thinking of it on and off, wondering if Basil might have shared with him some details of his visit, but no matter how much my curiosity builds, I cannot gather the strength to read it. In the loneliness I've grown to associate with Thornhill, it feels as though one comforting word would be enough to break my resolve and have me running to Papa's studio for the warmth of his embrace. There's little I would like more than to live with him and pretend the last sixteen years have been nothing but a bad dream, but I know all too well that was never an option.

Some logical part of my mind insists I could simply tell him what I did to Sybil Vane—much like I could have told Basil, I suppose—and see for myself if Papa would find it in him to make peace with my actions. It seems a perfectly reasonable plan whenever I consider it, but crumbles the moment I entertain the thought of following through. As soon as I try to picture myself standing before him, the version of me in my mind begins to morph until it matches the portrait hidden in my new bedchamber, still buried beneath layers of black curtain.

Even my father, for all the dedication it must have taken for him to stay in London and watch over me from afar, could not look into the face I've seen and find it in him to love it. I couldn't ask him to embrace me, knowing the true depths of my wretchedness are hidden from his sight.

Some wicked part of me thought, when I first saw Basil's portrait change, that with its curse came a certain freedom. Nobody would ever see me in a way I could not control, leaving me untouched by the ravage my body might wreak on itself over time or the rot my actions might leave on my soul. The truth, however, is both more complicated and infinitely simpler.

Whenever I picture myself, I see only the monster trapped away in its elegantly carved frame. No matter what goodness or beauty others might see in me, they're eclipsed by all the parts they cannot know.

I flip the letter opener in my hands, careful not to slice my thumb as I place the blade to the seal. For a moment, I wonder whether I would still bleed if it sliced my flesh, but decide against learning the answer. I'm unsure if it would be worse to learn I cannot bleed or to learn I still do, and that some part of me is still inevitably human.

The blade lingers against the seal, refusing to tear through. I can all but hear Papa's words calling me from the paper, warmth radiating from the *Soleil* written in his neat, cursive script as if the sun itself were contained within the word. It lights up the study, brightening the dramatic shades of red and purple that line the walls of the room where I've dwelled for so much of my time at Thornhill. Despite my best efforts, it hasn't felt like my home until now, when I find myself curled up in the armchair in the corner of the room, readying myself as best I can for news from who might be the last person in the world who could love me unconditionally.

I can't afford to lose that possibility.

That thought, more than any, is what finally guides me to the fireplace at the back of the study, letter clutched in my hand. Whatever comfort Papa's words might bring me, I cannot risk losing him. If I read his words and ignore whatever offer he must have written, I'll know that I turned my back on my last chance at escaping the hole I've dug for myself. If I never learn the contents of his letter, however, I might stand a chance at forgetting it existed at all.

The stones that line the fireplace are harsh and gray, cold despite the fire that roars within them. The closer I approach, the more my resolve begins to fade. Every step brings with it some new reason to change my mind, so I widen my stride and quicken my pace until the heat rushes against my face, warning me of the destruction it can unleash.

The smell of burning paper fills the air as the flames lick at the letter one by one at first, then rush in to devour it all at once. Panic floods through me at the sight of the page crumpling and blackening, startling me forward until the sharpness of fire against flesh forces me to pull my hand back and surrender to the devastation I've already set in motion. A string of curses leaves my mouth as I note with some strange relief that I can, in fact, feel pain, but when I examine my hand for any traces of burns, I find it as pale and smooth as it was moments ago.

"Lord Gray?" Peter calls, standing in the doorframe. "If you wish to have the fire adjusted, I would be happy to do so."

The sight of Peter before me chills me back to reason as the worry he might have seen me toss Papa's letter settles in. I've yet to piece together what he thinks of our sudden exile, whether he's as grateful to have left Barsden as I am, or if perhaps he suspects I'm keeping some strange secret from him, but I dread to dwell on it. Having Peter's company—especially now that we are both free from Grandfather's overseeing—has gone a long way in making Thornhill less cold and unfamiliar to me.

It has also made it much more difficult to shake the sense that I'm being watched, seeing as I no longer have the comfort of knowing I'm alone. A constant worry lurks behind me, reminding me how easy it might be for Peter to see something I would prefer him not to, asking how long I expect it will take for him to notice some inexplicable shift in my behavior.

"How long have you been in that doorway?" I ask, unable to keep the anxious tremor in my voice at bay as I hide the hand that should be burned in my pocket.

"I heard you cursing from the parlor and thought you might have hurt yourself. Did the fire catch you?"

"It simply startled me. No need to worry on my account."

"Did you need me to tend to the fire?"

Peter walks in my direction, creeping closer and closer to the fireplace with every step. A few strands of paper catch my eye as the fire wrestles with the last remnants of Papa's letter, and I adjust my position to obstruct them as best I can. It might be too late for me to pull the paper from the flames and undo the latest in the unending chain of bad decisions I've made, but I can at least avoid attracting any curiosity as to why I might throw a still-sealed letter into the fire.

"That won't be necessary," I tell him. "While you're here, however, I do have an item I've been meaning to move, though I'm afraid it's too heavy for me to carry unassisted."

Peter nods and steps outside the study, waiting for me to guide him. I venture one last look behind me as I leave and watch the letter continue to blacken and crumple. It takes little time for the flames to finish consuming it, crackling with near-morbid pleasure.

* * *

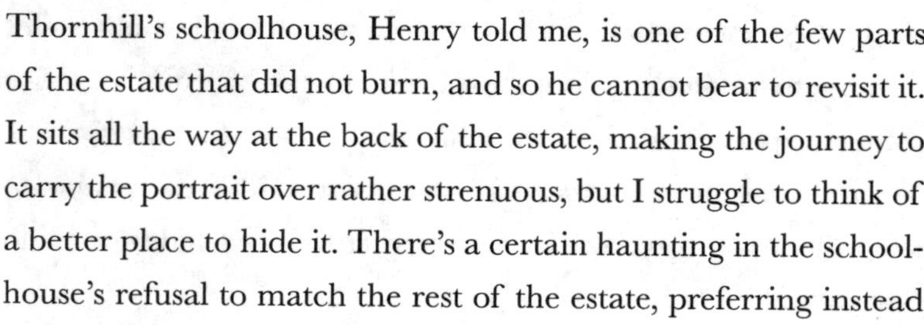

Thornhill's schoolhouse, Henry told me, is one of the few parts of the estate that did not burn, and so he cannot bear to revisit it. It sits all the way at the back of the estate, making the journey to carry the portrait over rather strenuous, but I struggle to think of a better place to hide it. There's a certain haunting in the schoolhouse's refusal to match the rest of the estate, preferring instead light shades of blue and even a few white accents on clean, simple walls. It looks both frozen in time and incomplete, waiting for some trace of life to come back and brighten it as I imagine a young Henry might have. Now it's set to become a tomb of sorts, where I might hide away the cause of my own haunting from the rest of the world.

"This seems like a strange place to display a painting," Peter says as we adjust the frame against the far wall. "I doubt you will host much company in this room."

"I suppose it's for the best that I have no plans to display this painting, then. I simply wish to store it somewhere it might remain out of the way."

Carrying Basil's portrait across Thornhill proved a strenuous task, even with two of us to shoulder its weight. We had to move more slowly than I would have liked, but I couldn't justify the risk of tipping our cargo one way or another and having the curtains slip off to expose it. Peter must have thought my refusal to remove the drapes odd, given how much easier the task would have been had we done so, but the contents of the portrait would have been far more alarming to him.

Besides, I've decided, during our trek to the old schoolhouse, that Peter can't remain at Thornhill with me. He has witnessed too many odd behaviors already and has known me too long not to notice them as they accumulate. It's better to cut ties between us now, when time can help him rationalize my behavior as the struggles of someone experiencing a mass upheaval in their life. The less time I give him to gather evidence, the less likely he is to reach any differing conclusions.

"I think it would do you some good to travel," I tell him once the frame sits firmly fixed on the wall. "A young man of your character deserves the chance to see the world, not waste away in the country."

"The country isn't so bad, especially if we have each other's company. Besides, I doubt I could afford to travel the continent, let alone the world."

"Would you want to? If it was possible, that is."

"I suppose so," Peter answers, "but I see little point daydreaming about impossibilities."

"There's a gold watch on my nightstand next to some rings that have been in our family for some number of generations. Take them. It should be plenty to fund your travels."

"Lord Gray, I—"

"Please, Peter," I interrupt. "Take the jewelry and see the world. Consider it my thanks for your company all these years as well as an apology for the times I left you to bear the brunt of Grandfather's anger."

It takes little more convincing for Peter to accept my offer. Some amount of discomfort bubbles as I frame my need to rid myself of him as generosity, but some comfort lies in knowing that my selfishness can at least bring good to the lives of others. I urge Peter to leave so that he may start preparing for his adventures as soon as possible, then watch him exit the schoolhouse, counting the seconds as they pass.

Only when I'm confident I'm alone do I expose the monster destined to be my sole companion in exile.

Basil's portrait hangs on the wall, drapes pulled aside to reveal cold, empty eyes and a jaw set firm with determination. The sneer I've grown so accustomed to has not changed, and yet the man in the portrait wears it differently. Its glee has shifted to a calculating, self-martyring sort of sorrow that sickens me to gaze upon, but I can't look away. The moment I turn my back, the portrait seems to insist, it will shift again, and I'll find myself even more wretched than I already am.

"As you wish, old friend," I surrender. "I suppose, if the two of us are stuck with each other, we may as well have our fun."

For the fraction of a moment, I could swear the portrait smiles—but when I look again, its face has already settled.

London, 1870

19
BURGUNDY STAIN

It never occurred to me I might one day be older than my mother ever was.

The idea ought to have crossed my mind. Nineteen is hardly an advanced age to reach, barring any dramatic circumstances, but I always pictured myself dying beautiful, young, and tragic, some Ophelia in the river warning the world of how cruel it has become. I suppose I still will, seeing as I haven't aged a day in three years now, though I can't know for sure. All the books I've read on strange, paranormal occurrences have yet to show me any case akin to mine—I've all but surrendered on finding any answer for this strange affliction, though I can't bring myself to give up altogether. It's equally possible the face in my portrait comes rushing back to me with my final breath. Would anyone recognize the old man lying before them if it did? Or would my sudden disappearance spark more gossip and mysteries to swirl around my name long past my death?

I rather like the notion of living on through whispers and rumors. There's something beautiful about a haunting, be it the shimmering mist of a specter or the certainty of a presence behind one's shoulder. The notion is sensual in its truest sense, a sudden abundance of feeling that brings some thrill to it no matter how discomforting or chilling it might be. I can think of few endings more romantic than freeing myself from the limitations of flesh altogether.

Thornhill's schoolhouse, for all the eeriness and foreboding my portrait has brought it, has become something of a refuge over the last three years. The main estate is too big to bring me any warmth when I find myself alone, and the grandeur of its art collections and dramatically contrasting walls leaves me feeling like little more than another piece in the exhibition—a standout one, certainly, maybe even the most captivating part of the collection, but that brings me less comfort with every passing day. Fascinating people is nothing new to me by now, but it pales in comparison to the growing certainty that I've become something not quite human along the way.

I first expected that thought might be freeing, ridding me of all the weakness and cruelty that seems so rooted in humanity. The more time passes, however, the more I worry those worst few traits are all I have left. Every first shift in the portrait brings with it a new whisper in the back of my mind, reminding me that the version of me that hosts grand soirees and charms everyone I meet with my wit and beauty is little more than a facade protecting the beast I keep locked up out of sight.

"Here's to us," I say, raising my glass of sherry to the portrait in a mock toast. "Happy birthday."

The portrait stares at me, unflinching. No matter how many times I wonder if it might respond to me, it never does, and yet I can't shake the certainty that it could answer if it chose to. Every new stain it collects only makes it look more alive, more calculating. It makes me want to tear it apart, to set it on fire, anything that might make me feel like I'm exerting power over it rather than being subject to its vicious judgment.

Some nights, I even bring myself to hold a candle beneath it and watch the flame as it threatens to jump upward, ending the portrait's hold over me once and for all. Even then, however, I can't bring myself to raise my hand even the slightest bit higher and sever our bond.

What would remain of you? the portrait seems to taunt me. *How much of you is yours alone, when you have hidden so much of yourself into me?*

Oftentimes, even the comforts of Thornhill can't chase the question from my mind, and I find myself wandering the halls at night, sleep far from my reach. If there remains an answer to be found, I can say with near certainty it isn't tucked in a corner or hidden passage of Henry's country home. I doubt there's an area in all of Thornhill I have not yet explored, a single secret I haven't discovered.

The sherry I sip is of the highest quality—a gift from the Duchess of Somerset on her last visit, if I remember correctly—but it feels hollow and flat in my mouth under the portrait's mocking gaze. Even drink, these days, does little to dull the way its eyes pierce me and lay bare all my vulnerabilities.

I thought leaving Barsden Hollow would mean I could finally live free from anyone's influence save my own, but I didn't consider that my own whims could be so destructive. It feels as if, far from Papa, Basil, and Fabián, the parts of myself worth cherishing have left me one by one. All I can see these days is the calculated judgment I learned from Grandfather, the cynical selfishness Henry seems to enjoy from me, and the constant paranoid cowardice I keep nourishing under the portrait's gaze—nothing but the shattered remains of a creature ravaged by its own worst aspects. I wonder, at times, if going back to the people I abandoned might give me the space to build myself anew, but there's little purpose in giving myself such hopes. If I couldn't face them three years ago, then I stand no chance at mustering the nerve to show myself to them at my worst.

A sharp, guttural roar of a scream tears its way through me as I hurl my glass at the wall. Shards shatter in every direction, even back toward me, but somehow not one of them makes it to Basil's portrait. Sherry splatters against the wall, filling the air with a heavy sweet scent that makes my head spin and leaves me teetering on the verge of nausea. A few drops land on the portrait beside me, dark red liquor trickling like blood down my tormentor's cheek.

The faintest hint of a smile creeps across my face despite the cuts growing on my fingers from cleaning up the broken glass. If I must bear the portrait's influence on me, there's at least some comfort to be found in the thought that I, too, can make it bleed.

If I'm doomed to this torment, I can at least refuse to suffer alone.

Thornhill, for all its flaws, holds the greatest gift I could think to ask: privacy. Once the servants have withdrawn to their quarters for the night, there are no prying eyes left behind me, judging whether or not my actions fit the picture of Dorian Gray they've created in their minds. The estate has grown something of a reputation for cycling quickly through its staff, attracting many a greener face with its habit of recommending servants for positions that open at loftier, higher-paying households. It's proved a good way to prevent anyone from staying around long enough to notice any eccentricities without adding the repeated firing of employees to my conscience. It is as close to being alone as I can manage without calling attention to myself. I can fashion myself however I wish, try on new shapes and see how they fit, and nobody is around to see it.

Sometimes I'm a young lady of noble rank and fiery conviction, walking the halls of Thornhill without a hint of hesitation written on me, the kind of daughter I imagine my mother might be proud of. Others I'm a waifish figure all in black, gliding without a sound like some faceless specter in these halls. My favorite shape, I think, is that of a barefoot entity with untamed hair, dancing in colorful floral patterns with abandon, but I do not wear it often. It reminds me too much of the faerie-like youth Basil painted to fit me the way it once did.

As absurd a ritual as it may be, dressing myself in the nicest fineries available to me for the most mundane activities has grown comforting, somehow. For a few moments, I belong only to myself, and I can be whoever I please without worrying about who might see me and what they might think. The freedom of it is practically intoxicating, but it rarely lasts as long as I wish. As thrilling as it is to shape myself in my own image, it's inevitably eclipsed by the knowledge I can only ever exist where no one can see me.

Tonight I imagine I'm an artist's muse, preparing herself for an evening at a luxurious gallery in Paris, covered in ruffles and extravagant bustles so I can be as grandiose in the flesh as the paintings of me imply. Though it lacks the unrestricted freedom of my favorite shape, I've grown fond of the way this one feels less fleeting than most. It isn't a person I might once have been, but rather someone I might still one day be. Perhaps this version of me left London with Basil rather than settling into Thornhill, or she could have charmed some other artist with her graces after claiming her inheritance and leaving this place behind. Whenever I try to imagine this mysterious artist, however, all I can picture is the elegant grace with which Basil held a paintbrush and the careful fascination in his eyes when he looked at me.

When I picture Basil, on the other hand, those traits vanish, replaced by the pallor that overtook him when I dismissed him and the trembling in his voice as he excused himself from my company. Even in my daydreams, the pain I caused Basil Hallward continues to plague me until I can't so much as remember him without the cut of my words slicing me as sharply as if he had been the one to say them to me.

When I feel I can't bear the memory any longer, I focus my

attention on my hair instead. Despite all the practice I've had, the elaborate combination of knots and braids that so heavily define modern fashion are hard to execute and even harder to balance on my own head without some lady's maid for assistance, but that's the point of this exercise. Styling myself feels at times like sculpting. I focus my attention into the mirror, watching my fingers as they carefully weave endless strands of fine, gold-orange thread into some semblance of order.

The changes come slowly at first, so subtle I can almost convince myself I've imagined them. Little shifts in the way I hold my head, hints of color draining from my cheeks, eyes growing sharper and more piercing as they lure me in. By the time I can process my own reflection shifting in front of me, I can neither look away nor stop my fingers from their braiding. With every new twist of the strands in my hands, a little more hair vanishes from their grasp until I can't tell for myself if I might be changing alongside my reflection and simply imagining the soft threads twirling between my fingers.

Panic tries to jolt me from my stupor, but even it flows coldly through my body, freezing more and more of me. As my mind shouts at me to leave my seat and run from the mirror, my body remains still. I may as well be made of stone. My fingers continue to twirl around invisible hair, sculpting what must be thirty years onto my face bit by bit. My jaw grows hard as my lips turn cracking and cruel; sleepless bags build heavier and heavier under my eyes, whose callous mischief shifts ever-so-certainly into outright malice.

When the sherry-red bloodstains start to blossom across my neck and face, the figure in my reflection has already twisted beyond recognition—not only past what I can process as myself, but what I can understand as human. No longer satisfied with twisting my features, my hands now chip away at my flesh with their incessant braiding, tearing away fragments of skin to reveal muscles and tissue bubbling beneath them until they too start to melt, dripping down my face like wax down a candle.

When you die, the mirror tells me, *this is what people will find. Whoever you think you can make yourself, however safe you think that portrait of yours makes you, you cannot escape the truth of your flesh.*

The mirror's words finally jolt me from my stupor, letting my mind shout at me to run with all the desperation it can muster. It takes all my willpower to stop my fingers from their braiding and throw myself off my chair, leaving me panting and sobbing on the floor, back turned to the mirror. However much I want to leave this dressing room and its looking glass's warped reflection, I can't bring myself to stand up and leave. If I try, I'll catch some glimpse of the creature behind me, and I doubt I have the strength to escape its gaze a second time.

I stay in a ball on the floor for what feels like an eternity, desperately touching my face and my hair to reassure myself of their presence. All the while, the reflection behind me continues shifting in my imagination as I picture all the ways I could find myself decayed even further should I risk another look, hearing its raspy, withering voice continue to taunt me as I do.

You hold no power over your fate. However much that portrait of yours might decay in your stead, it will not keep me at bay forever. Nothing is eternal, Dorian Gray—certainly not something as wretched as you.

20
Obsidian Petals

Of all the types of events I've hosted during my tenure at Thornhill, none of them hold a candle to my evening parties. Garden parties are lovely, of course, giving everyone an opportunity to show their finest selves in the light of day. My salons are fairly anticipated, known by now for the rich assortment of guests and curious minds that gather to discuss only the most current and unexpected of issues. Even my luncheons are appreciated, though I find myself growing less and less patient with the tedium and decorum that so frequently accompanies them, placing all the work of entertaining on the food and decor rather than any actual personality. It seems, as far as London's most captivating figures are concerned, that no event I host could possibly be unpleasant. I put too much of my charm into every occasion for anyone to dare do something as unseemly as not enjoy themselves.

Nonetheless, masquerades remain my favorite of the obligations on my social calendar. The crowds are smaller, free of the respectable high society names I have to invite to daytime events for the sake of appearances and composed only of people able to appreciate the lush extravagance I've catered to the fullest. Guests come garbed in such opulence that a single piece of jewelry might feed all the hungry in London, eager to steal the attention away from their rivals and even from their closest friends, should the right mood strike them.

I find there's a certain magic to masquerades. I know better than most the boldness that disguises and the illusion of anonymity brings out in people, and there's nothing more delightful than seeing the way London's well-to-do act when they think themselves safe from prying eyes. Vices come out to dance with curiosities, all eased to the extremes by the abundance of drink available. It's easier to blend in with the crowd when everyone is cloaked in the same layers of elegance and temptation, but anybody foolish enough to think themselves truly hidden is due for a rude awakening.

Besides, I've grown quite fond of the freedom that extravagant dress provides. All I have to do is assign a more artistic theme, and suddenly draping myself in a tunic of obsidian petals is admirable rather than scandalous. I couldn't bear to wear a smoking jacket or trousers tonight; I could feel them constricting me with every movement I made, holding me into a shape I couldn't stand to keep. Thankfully, the people here are too eager to win my favor to be bothered by any eccentricity in my dress, so long as I hold the standard of beauty expected of me.

"Dorian!" a familiar voice calls behind me. "I've been looking all over for you. It's awfully cruel of you to invite me only to spend the night ignoring me. One of these days I might grow tired of your apathy and give up on you altogether."

"Perhaps I'm simply waiting for that day to come, Lord Rollins."

Sharp, exaggerated laughter comes sprawling from his lips, oblivious to any possible sincerity in my words. I have learned in my dealings with Rollins that he will always hear exactly what he wishes to, no matter how harshly I speak. It's a tiresome habit, certainly, but it makes interacting with him much easier. I never have to worry about being too cold or too aloof when I know he'll simply interpret it as an act meant to challenge him.

It doesn't hurt that he's pleasant enough to observe, with the crispness of his poise and the rich brown of his eyes. Tonight's garden theme suits him well. The violet petals with which he's adorned his mask, hat, and even the lining of his suiting add a gentleness to him that highlights the carefully curated nobility he works so tirelessly to maintain. If Rollins can avoid wearing on me too heavily, this might be the night I finally grant him the satisfaction of thinking he has won me over.

"You and I both know I could never give up on you," he replies, eyes trailing on my shoulder with such intent it might make me shiver, were I not accustomed to receiving such looks. "You have the makings of an Apollo or Aphrodite tonight. I suppose I should expect by now for you to outshine your own guests by adding some secret theming to your costume."

"I simply love the classics, you know. Perhaps this is a ploy of mine to bring tunics back into London's fashions."

"I believe our weather might be a touch too cold for such garments. Then again, the sight of your neck framed in such dark petals might be enough to heat even the coldest of Londoners."

"Would you believe I dyed each rose petal individually?" I ask. "I wanted them to be the exact same obsidian, lest they pull away from the effect."

"I would. I have never seen you looking anything less than perfect."

I thank him and brush him off, making my way back into the crowd until I can no longer feel his eyes burning into my skin. The image of some ancient deity wandering a hidden garden seemed appealing enough to don, but any power I thought it might bring me has blended with a nagging vulnerability. Eyes land on my skin wherever I turn, and the more I look around, the harder it is for me to tell which stares are real and which ones I've imagined. All I know is the distinct sense of being consumed, though I couldn't say by what or by whom. I wonder if, one day, there might be nothing left of me to devour.

The longer the sensation lasts, the more I crave some way to dull my mind. There's drink available aplenty, and I spot a few glasses darkened with poppy water as I pass through the crowd, but the thought of either turns sour in my mouth as I remember the scene in my dressing room last night. Despite my best efforts to dismiss the changes in my reflection as the effect of too much sherry, I've found myself avoiding mirrors or other glass surfaces all day in fear of learning there might have been something more sinister at play in my mind than mere alcohol.

Whatever the case, I can't risk another episode of the sort when Thornhill is overflowing with witnesses. Vice and sin might be scandals encouraged under the mock-anonymity of our masks, but madness is another matter entirely—and what else could I call the vision plaguing me?

My wanderings come to a stop as I find a pretty young lady with thick copper hair laced with orchids in a myriad of shades, a mask of vines wrapped around her face. Even in a masquerade, the Countess of Tavistock's daughter is hard to miss, though I would wager she prefers it that way. Of all the people I've welcomed at Thornhill, few have seemed to me as well suited to the spotlight as her, though I doubt that satisfies her; I've heard many whispers concerning Evelyn Russell and her radical tendencies. They say her character is as stubborn as her hair, and that the more she's told to avoid certain circles, the less she will be kept out of them.

"I'm so glad I could convince you to attend tonight's party," I tell her after bowing to kiss her hand. "I was concerned you might not want to participate in something as wasteful as a masquerade."

"I cannot help but think how else tonight's luxury might be used," Evelyn confesses, "but curiosity won me over. It isn't every day one gets an invitation to one of Lord Dorian Gray's famous masquerades."

"How does it compare to your expectations? I know firsthand how tedious society events can get, but I would hate for you to find Thornhill as much of a chore."

Evelyn's chuckle is a hearty one, unburdened by any expectations of demureness one might put on a young lady of her age.

"It certainly isn't a surprise to see Londoners are as hypocritical as ever, complaining about impropriety and recklessness while engaging in those same behaviors behind the comfort of their masks, but I do find your party more bearable than most. It's a pleasant change to see extravagance for the sake of making something beautiful, rather than an empty display of wealth. One could call you an artist rather than a host."

"You flatter me."

"You have spent our conversation flattering me," she counters. "I make it a point not to trust any friendships where the flattery is one-sided. It always makes me wonder what my companion wants from me."

The blunt directness that guides every word of Evelyn's is more comforting than I had expected. While it hardly takes much effort to know what people want from me, it's refreshing to hear someone tell me the exact thoughts on their mind without my having to guess at them. It's easy to see how she has charmed her share of people, and easier still to see how she has left a poor impression on even more. Honesty is a rare trait in London, and not one in which many like to see themselves reflected.

"I want company," I tell her, "and find yours to be quite pleasant."

Evelyn raises an eyebrow. "You hardly appear to be lacking in that department. I've heard my share of rumors about you and the company you keep."

"Company that doesn't want anything further from me," I clarify.

"It seems to me that no one is immune to your charms. Why should I be any different?"

"Perhaps you aren't the only one who pays attention to rumors."

Evelyn looks over me with the focused gaze of someone assessing a threat. I know there's nothing in my image for her to find—years of scrutiny have reassured me of that—but I can't help worrying that some part of me might be too poised, too perfect. The neutral expression on her face makes it clear she remains unswayed by any allure I might wield, and yet I see no distaste, either.

"I wouldn't have thought the famous Lord Gray a gossip," she teases, a smile finally breaking through her suspicion.

"You would be surprised how little there is to do in the country besides read and take in whatever news from London comes my way."

"And throw lavish parties."

"Of course."

"In that case," she asks, "have you heard the news regarding Lord Cavendish?"

The name sends a chill coursing through me, but I don't let it show. I haven't let myself think of Sybil Vane in quite some time, drowning any thoughts of her and the shame they bring me in sherry or glitter or whoever might be nearby and willing to tell me how perfect I am as if it were some new discovery.

"The one who had that great public scandal three years ago?" I ask. "I can't say I've heard much news since the trial."

"He left London some months ago. It seems he moved to America, where he performs on their stages in women's clothes under the name Sybil Vane. Quite the fascinating end to that scandal, don't you think?"

"Quite," I agree. "Between you and me, I'm glad to see such

a positive outcome befall Lord Cavendish. That affair was one of the more unpleasant I witnessed during my time in London."

"You and me both," she agrees. "I doubt I'll ever understand how London decides which vices it encourages and which ones it abhors."

"We adore any vice we can pretend not to see in others," I quip, earning a sharp bark of laughter from Evelyn I could almost describe as reproachful. I take her hand to guide her into a waltz as the orchestra changes songs, but find before long that she has taken the lead from me and content myself to follow.

The news Evelyn shared of Sybil Vane nags at me. There's some relief in knowing her life has improved since the scandal I set upon her, but I'm not so foolish as to think it absolves me of blame for the ordeal she faced. Bafflement surfaces to toy at me as I try to fathom why Evelyn decided to share such news with me. Although it seems to be a bridge of sorts between us, I can't help worrying there might be a threat in her words—though what she could threaten I do not know.

Some darker, more sinister part of me resents the news of Sybil Vane's newfound freedom. It's a selfish thought, certainly, but I'm hardly unfamiliar with my capacity for selfishness. It seems she will always be a few steps ahead of me, taunting me with a future outside my reach. There might have been a time where fleeing England was a possibility, but now that everything I have depends either on Henry's generosity or Grandfather's continued satisfaction with my silence, I struggle to think of a way I could build a life outside Thornhill, never mind England. I suppose I could use Grandfather's allowance to establish myself elsewhere, but I'm sure what money he sends me would stop flowing the moment I left his grasp.

"Have you seen Lord Wotton?" I ask Evelyn as she dips me. "His attendance at my parties is sparse, but he's rather fond of my masquerades. The extravagance suits him."

"Is that why you host so many of them?"

"Of course. I throw lavish parties in the hopes that my host deigns to grace me with his presence. That's the secret behind the infamous Dorian Gray."

"I've seen people take on more foolish endeavors for the sake of love."

"I do not love Henry," I tell her, though a darkness I didn't intend slips into my tone. "I am grateful for his friendship and hospitality, but I'm sure I don't know what you might be implying."

I could not say what I feel for Henry, though love is far too simple a term for the matter. I resent the way the roof above me depends on his good graces, and yet I can't pretend I ever feel as seen as when he sees me, as *real* as when he holds me. I thought, when I took up his offer to live at Thornhill, that we might let the fire between us rage until it consumed one or both of us, but it seems he prefers me desperate for his company, eager to do whatever might catch his attention. I've learned that ice burns deeper than heat ever could, but Henry is not so kind as to be cold to me altogether. Instead, he doles out his affection sparingly, keeping me waiting for the next crumbs he deigns to give me. It's enough to drive one mad, but I can't afford to give him even more power over me.

I've tried to replace him more times than I could care to count, but every new person feels too easy, too hollow to matter. I have little need for the desire of others when it comes so readily available.

"If you'll excuse me," I tell Evelyn, "I suppose I ought to find Lord Rollins. I left him without a parting word earlier, and I'm afraid he might feel rather insulted if I abandoned him."

"Of course. Besides, I'd like to enjoy the spectacle that is London society when it thinks nobody is looking. As lovely as it's been to get better acquainted, Lord Gray, I fear you've proved a bit of a distraction in that purpose."

Evelyn curtsies and vanishes into the crowd, leaving me alone in the little bubble we've somehow built amidst the party. Ignoring my earlier trepidation, I find a glass from the tray nearest me and drink it without a care as to what sits inside it as I wait for the next suitor to vie for a scrap of me they might take home with them. Mad as it may be to repeat the same actions in hopes of a different result, it seems to me far preferable to the crushing insanity of isolation.

If I must give away each piece of me in my attempts to finally fill the hole Henry so loves to dig within me, so be it. Maybe one day I'll finally give away whatever fragment has grown so rotten as to leave me all alone.

21
VIBRANT VIOLET

However much I like to complain about the city, I missed London more than I can explain. Even at the most well attended of my parties, I can't find a match for the sheer, unadulterated life that flows through its streets at all times. No matter how much I try to curate my guest lists to include as broad a variety of people in my company as possible, the crowds I host at Thornhill always have a slightly manicured feel to them. I suppose there's no way to create a guest list that fully mirrors the organic quality the city has to it.

Elaborate coaches travel down Piccadilly, the details painted upon them in rich, vibrant hues a greater display of wealth than any finery its passengers could wear. Pedestrians roam next to them, all too engaged in the various tasks that bring them to the area to heed the presence of nobles tucked away in their ornate wooden boxes. Street merchants hawk their wares, calling to anyone who might listen with promises of coffee or muffins or fried fish while people in shabby clothes wander between them to scavenge any discarded items or droppings they might be able to sell for some profit. The contrast has a strangely romantic quality to it, unsettling as it may be.

I pull my cloak tighter over my head as a coach drives by, careful to cover as much of my hair and face as possible. My clandestine visits to London have been admittedly infrequent—only ever when Henry decides he craves my company and calls me to join him at Hartwood—but each one has done little to ease my worries that Grandfather might catch wind of my presence. Instead, every visit further convinces me that my tab has run its end and whatever luck has allowed me to wander unnoticed has gone dry since my last excursion.

Even that worry, however, has done little to stop me from taking detours. Perhaps I'm guided by some self-destructive urge to have Grandfather catch me for once, or maybe London simply finds me too deprived of life and reality to resist its call. Either way, the journey down Piccadilly is impossible to pass up.

The walk to Hartwood is slowed by my need to hide at the edges of the crowds and avoid some of the quieter, more genteel streets where it might be harder to avoid detection, but I don't mind. Even the air around me is refreshing, coarse as it is with the smoke that has only thickened over the years. It stings at my nostrils and scratches my throat, reminding me with each cough that I am alive and real, no matter how little I may feel it. Only in times of discomfort do I ever leave the isolated, manicured haze in which I spend most of my days.

I suppose that must be why I still answer Henry's summons despite their infrequency and his many efforts to cloak suspicions as to why a mysterious coach so often comes to Hartwood the moment Victoria leaves town. He knows me just enough for me to feel present when his fingers graze against me, and has no interest in seeing any more than that. As far as he's concerned, I'm a hollow vessel for him to influence. I'm allowed my flaws and my vices without any scrutiny, since he must be the one to have brought them out in me.

It can be rather calming, at times, to pretend I'm as unmarked by the world as Henry thinks me. It almost feels like traveling outside myself, though I couldn't say where my mind goes when it leaves my body behind.

By the time I've reached Hartwood, the mid-January chill has begun to seep through the several layers of clothing I'm wearing. Rain hangs in the air half-frozen, and the cold doesn't pierce or bite but rather melts into me so gradually I don't notice it until it has burrowed its way beneath my skin. I like to imagine Henry might have a fire ready inside, but I know better. I expect he will have little time to waste on pleasantries, given that he has deprived himself of me for several months. Whatever comfort or warmth I might find at Hartwood, I'll have to wait until he's sated to find it.

The butler lets me in with little ceremony, hurrying to close the door behind me lest anyone pass by Hartwood and notice my arrival. I find Henry in the brown-and-beige sitting room where we once spent so much time reading, absorbed in a book I've already finished. It was pleasant enough, though I often found it tending toward being salacious for no purpose but to shock rather than offering any perspective of interest.

I note the fire crackling behind him and tell myself he had it lit for me before burying myself into its warmth. The armchair next to him is comfortable in its familiarity, though I always find myself sinking too deep into it when I sit. However accustomed I am to the shape of Victoria's frame indented into its plush fabric, I can never quite keep my balance in it.

"How is it," Henry asks, kissing my hand as he does, "that you manage to be the one thing in London that refuses to deteriorate as time wreaks its havoc?"

From anyone else, the question would fill me with a sudden wave of fear at the thought of being discovered, but from Henry it's little more than a greeting. His tone is as lofty and self-congratulating as ever when he says it, making it all too obvious he could not care less about my answer; he simply likes to acknowledge that the most sought-after treasure in London comes at his every call, no matter how degrading such a rapport may be.

"Perhaps you simply choose not to see my decay," I offer.

"In that case, neither does anyone else in this city."

"Why should they? You all seem perfectly content to see me the way you do."

"And I have not seen you in far too long," Henry drawls. "Come, there will be more time to talk once I've reacquainted myself with your wonders."

Henry reaches for the small of my back, pulling me in toward him, but I freeze in his arms. However much I may have longed for his attention, the romance of his company fades the moment his hands land on me. It feels, at times, as though I'm little more than a toy for him to pick up when it suits him. Even the fire in his eyes has lost its warmth, though it never seems to lose its hunger.

"I'm not sure I wish to entertain you today, Henry," I tell him. "It was a cold walk in London, and I've been awfully tired of late. Couldn't we just read together and talk the way we used to?"

For a moment, the look on Henry's face reminds me of the way Grandfather looked before striking me the day I took my leave from him. His eyes grow icy as he frowns, and his nails dig into my skin—but then Henry smiles.

"Don't be silly," he chides me. His voice is as gruff as it is smooth, and I shrink back into myself when I hear it. "Why would you come all the way to Hartwood if not to thank me for my hospitality? It's been so long since I last saw you, pet. Let me show you how much I've missed you. Let me remind you how much you're mine."

This time, when Henry pulls me closer, I let him. My mind travels far from Hartwood, lost in its attempts to ignore the avarice in his tone. I struggle to think what good it could do me to dwell on such matters. The longer I spend in his arms, the closer I feel to breaking.

For all his numerous flaws, Henry has exquisite taste in bedsheets. The cotton that composes them is finer and softer than any I've experienced, and their rich violet coloring provides an oasis of luxuriousness even amidst Hartwood's more restrained decor. If

I close my eyes, I find myself bundled in a warm cocoon where no harm can reach me—not even from the man whose bed I've found myself back in despite the many times I've promised myself I would never return to this exact place.

"Do you remember the first time we met?" I ask him.

"Of course I do," he answers. "I walked into a friend's studio, expecting an admittedly tepid visit where he pretended to be scandalized by anything I might utter, only to find he had plucked a deity directly out of antiquity for me to observe. I knew immediately how immense an opportunity I had been given, to stumble upon so stunning a blank canvas waiting to have every facet of its beauty coaxed to the surface. There was no chance I would have left that day without ensuring I might see you again."

I've noticed, at some point in the last few years, that Henry has made it a habit never to refer to Basil by name, as if the man who introduced us might be no more than a shadow. At first I thought he'd noticed the way I winced whenever I heard Basil's name and wanted to avoid troubling me any further, but the more time passes, the more I struggle to remember when Henry took up this habit of his. On my darker days, I think he might have started the moment I moved into Thornhill, long before the thought of Basil brought anything other than a smile to my face.

The safe little cocoon I've built for myself melts away as Henry pulls himself from the bedsheets, leaving me alone in a slowly deflating bundle of warmth. I reach toward him and feel him freeze as my hand wraps around his wrist to pull him back. The annoyance in his face is so obvious it takes the breath out of my lungs, even if only for a moment. It's enough to leave me winded and trembling, but I hold on to him nonetheless.

"Please," I beg. "Stay and hold me, if only for a moment. Thornhill has been so lonely without you there. You've never missed my masquerades before—not to mention my birthday."

I'm not sure when I started needing to beg for scraps of affection, but it's already starting to feel like routine. I suppose it started when Henry decided he no longer wished to kiss me, or perhaps when he declared he found my touch too forward. I might think that I lost him, if I had any illusions about him being mine. Even Victoria lays no claim to him. I've grown to learn that Henry loves nothing more than to collect people, but will not allow anyone to get so close as to truly believe he is theirs. The best he will do is play along grudgingly so we fools in his web can continue pretending we have any sway over the heart he guards so jealously.

I would resent him for it, did it not remind me so much of myself.

"From what I hear, you have little trouble finding company these days," he accuses.

"Could you remind me, Henry, where your wife is traveling to allow me this latest visit?" I counter. "I do hope she's doing well."

"You know I don't care to discuss Victoria on your visits. I'd rather enjoy our time together without distractions to weave their way between us."

"It seems to me you don't care to spend time with me lately, either. Perhaps I should stop visiting if it troubles you so much."

The fire in Henry's eyes has grown darker over time—deadlier, even, though my mind has always been prone to dramatics. The desire I remember from the night we first kissed still appears from time to time, but it's quickly sated. More often, the heat I see in his gaze is more akin to anger or frustration at my refusal to let him consume me entirely. Every little push against his wishes, any assertion that I, too, might have some agenda for what little time we spend together, only seems to stoke the fire further.

Still, it's so cold these days that I'll gladly take whatever heat I can find.

"Very well, then," Henry huffs. "If you must be so childish as to throw a tantrum about it, I suppose I can spare some time to stay in bed with you, though I'm loath to encourage such behavior. I would hate to give you the impression you can get whatever you wish from me by putting up a fuss whenever you don't get your way."

"And will you visit me at Thornhill sometime?" I ask.

"Perhaps. It has been quite a while since I last attended one of your parties, and I rather hate to miss out on such lavish enjoyment. I heard your latest event was as thrilling as ever."

Henry's words could not possibly make their intended meaning any clearer: He will go to Thornhill when he pleases, but not on my behalf. He slides back into his bed so slowly I imagine him trying to think of excuses to leave me the entire time it takes for him to wrap his arms around me. I try as best I can to quiet my mind and ease into his hold so that I might scavenge whatever warmth I can amidst the blanket of resentment that rests atop us, but it does little to comfort me.

Despite every monstrosity I've seen in Basil's portrait, there's no part of me I despise quite as much as the one pathetic enough to find comfort in so begrudging an embrace.

22
Vicious Granite

However far I flee from Barsden Hollow, it seems I can't escape the part of me that freezes whenever Grandfather's eye rests on me.

I cannot think of a single time he has mentioned visiting Thornhill in our sparse communications, though I'll admit I've long feared he one day might. However little he may wish to associate with me, I'm far too aware of the strings tied around my purse to forget the grasp he still holds over me. Though the feeling of his eyes watching me has somewhat faded with distance, I'm not so foolish as to think I might altogether be free of him. Even in death, I suspect some part of him will always reign in the back of my consciousness, judging me as cruelly as my portrait's vicious whims.

Looking at Grandfather now, I could swear he has not aged a day more than I have. I imagine for a moment he may have made some wish of his own, struck some bargain to outlive me so I might never know life outside his grasp. It should be an absurd notion, but I've seen too much I don't understand to ignore any possibility my mind can conjure. The world is a stranger, darker place than anyone would guess.

I guide him from the entrance to the nearby parlor, calling a servant to prepare tea for us in the meantime. Quietly, I thank the stars I haven't thrown a party since last month, leaving the house in crisp order. One could almost think no soul lives within Thornhill's walls, though I suppose they might be right. Given how little I know about my affliction, it's entirely possible my soul is spoken for, sold unknowingly in some Faustian agreement. It's a dramatic notion, certainly, but there's little to do in Thornhill besides throwing parties and dramatizing my own circumstances.

Grandfather takes a seat across from me, almost comically out of place in the modernity of the parlor room's decor. He does not glare at the lavish furniture nor the patterned china of my tea set, and his eyes wear nothing but an absent sort of detachment as they take in the fashion of my smoking jacket and the tailoring of my trousers. Somehow, the lack of contempt in his expression is more chilling than any scorn he could send me. It feels as though I'm holding my breath, waiting for the moment he casts his judgment and leaves me with little more than a roof over my head—the one thing not in his power to take.

"Thank you for visiting," I say, once I can't bear the silence between us any longer. "What grants me the honor of your company today?"

He does not answer immediately, preferring instead to sit in statuesque stillness, watching me the way I imagine a gargoyle might survey a cathedral's surroundings: unwavering and uncaring, merely monitoring each detail for something out of place. The silence swells as the maid brings the tea, falling to an eerie coldness when she leaves. I take a sip, grateful for the distraction granted by steam burning my tongue, and wait for him to finally speak.

"I wished to see how you live," he says, as if such a sentiment were common between us. "I see your surroundings are as frivolous as most seem to be these days. Did you furnish these lodgings yourself, or is your host to blame for the lavishness of your decor?"

"Thornhill was furnished when I arrived, though I've certainly added to its collection since then. I'll admit the decor is a touch gothic for my tastes—it makes for a rather grim isolation—but I've grown fond of it. It is nice, at least, to have such a space for myself. I feel far more mature than I did when I first arrived in the country."

"It's certainly pleasant to be master of one's domain," Grandfather agrees. "I hear you're quite the accomplished host."

My stomach plummets. I nearly drop my teacup as Grandfather's words strike me, though his tone is strangely void of accusation. He must have heard some story of my parties and the type of vice so common amongst them, and now lies in wait to see what tale I might spin to throw him off my scent or what information

I might surrender under pressure. I remember too well the night he and Gartens confronted me to trust the even measure of his tone.

"We agreed I would not return to London until you sent me word, but I saw no harm in bringing some small part of the city to me. It would be much stranger for me to withdraw altogether than to host gatherings at my country lodgings. Besides, I've found it far easier to control the type of influence to which I might be exposed now that I assemble the guest lists myself."

Grandfather frowns. "You wish me to believe, then, that you have not been entertaining the vice and decadence so ever present of late? Country life must have made you a man of strikingly measured nature."

"You may believe what you wish." I shrug. "I know the truth of my character."

You know it quite intimately, a wicked voice whispers, raising the hairs on the back of my neck with the accusation in its words. Grandfather's visage is unchanged, but it doesn't chip away at me the way it did at Barsden. He may well be stone, but I have sculpted myself into the finest marble. He'll find no flaw in me, whatever angle he might approach. I straighten my back against my chair and hold his eye, daring him to press me.

"Very well," he concedes instead. "I certainly don't believe your claim, but I will confess I've heard no charge against your name. Whatever sins you may keep, it seems you guard them well. There may be hope for you yet."

Though Grandfather's words ought to be a victory, they bring little relief with them. This must be some new ploy of his, some way to disarm me so he may catch me when I least expect him.

"I'm sure I do not understand you, Grandfather. Guarding sins has little to do with the quality of one's character."

"Do you know why I let you live here, boy?" he asks. "Surely you are not so foolish as to think I fund this life of yours from the goodness of my heart."

"We struck up an agreement," I reply. "I would not speak a word regarding Lord Cavendish, nor would I attract any attention to myself with further scandals."

Something, however fleetingly, shifts in Grandfather's eyes. The stone of his expression flickers, the sneer on his face so familiar it sends shivers through my spine. Whatever control I might have had over our exchange, there remains something I can't see—some lesson I've yet to learn.

"Why would I believe such a promise, knowing you'd already attempted to deceive me? What reason would I have to put any faith in your words?"

"What other reason could you have had?"

"Power," he answers. "To be beyond reproach takes many shapes, boy, and though your character may be beyond saving, your mind showed promise. You did not sway me with your silence; you threatened me with the possibility of your speech. I doubt I will ever approve of your person, but it appears I can at least credit your upbringing with the man you've become. Your reputation is impressive, and, while we both know it to be untrue, I will not label it unearned. You guard it viciously, and I knew when you threatened me you'd let no other unmake you."

Grandfather's praise cuts deeper than his scorn ever did. I knew, when he looked at me with icy hatred, that I did not regret my actions. Hearing his approval, mitigated as it may be, only brings to mind the portrait I once envied, and how I can't look at it without seeing his face melded with mine. I wish I felt some outrage at his words, some belief his praise might be unfounded, but I find only the knowledge I've earned every bit of it. I've grown as cold and calculating as he believes—more so, even.

Whoever Grandfather believes me to be, I cannot think of a more hateful truth to face.

I retreat to my study the moment Grandfather's coach pulls away, locking myself in with nothing but paper and my desk for company. The fireplace roars before me, feasting on various letters drafted and abandoned as I attempt to gather the words I wish to say. My eyes grow heavy and my mind turns weary as I try time and time again to explain myself. I may be too exhausted for the task at hand, but I can't bring myself to stop. If I do, I doubt I'll have the courage to try again tomorrow.

I wish words existed that might right the wrongs I've done you, but I could not begin to find them. I wish I had not left you, or that I'd come back when you wrote to me. I wish, at least, I'd read your letter when it came. I knew I could not stay away if you asked me to meet you, and I could not bear to put you in the same danger Mother did.

I crumple the paper and throw it in the fire, pulling a new page before me. The idea of telling him I never read his letter chills me. It seems too cruel to admit, too callous to forgive—and yet each of my regrets stems from my decisions not to trust my secrets to those I loved the most. Perhaps, if I'd confessed them sooner, I might not find myself where I now stand, without a single shoulder to lean on.

There was a version of me I once loved, flawed as she may have been, but I left her behind with all the souls who might have seen her. If I want to make amends to her as well as them, I need to trust them with even the most wretched of my truths. I scrawl the words back on the page, resolving as I do not to burn another draft. Whatever letter Papa gets, I will at least know it is more honest than anything I've said these last three years.

> I wish we could have had a life together, far from London and its curses. I wish we'd gone away to France or any place you and Fabián might wish to see. I should not hope such things might still one day be possible, but I'm sure you've gathered I'm more than selfish enough to do so. There are many explanations I owe you, and even more apologies, but they seem better suited to be spoken than written. If you might find it in you to hear them, I would love nothing more than to see you, so I might try to right the many ways I've wronged you. I hope you are well, and I hope more than anything else you know I never once stopped loving you.
>
> Yours (despite everything),
> Soleil

I seal the letter as soon as it is dried, calling a hallboy to deliver it before I can change my mind. For one blissful moment, as the letter leaves my hands, I think to myself that all might yet be righted. I may still be past saving, but perhaps I can at least help to heal some of the wounds I've caused.

23
Raven of Omen

"Do you ever wonder what it might be like to see the world?"

Evelyn frowns at my question, sipping at her tea as she mulls it over. Though her visiting Thornhill is still a new development, she looks at ease amidst its imposing decor—more so, at least, than she did at my masquerade. I hadn't noticed how discomforting the scope of such an event was to her until I saw her in a simpler, one-to-one setting and understood what it was like to see her relaxed. Our afternoons are often quieter than I expected they would be when she accepted my first invitation to have tea with me, but what conversations we have had left me feeling wide awake and stimulated. Befriending her, I'm starting to see more signs in myself of the person I want to be, sharp and jagged still but balanced by a layer of care for those who've earned it. It's been a long time since I've allowed myself to call someone a friend.

"I suppose that depends on how you define seeing the world," she answers. "There are plenty of ways to see the world without traveling it, and even more ways to travel the world without ever seeing it. If you ask me, the modern obsession with grand excursions to other continents is less about gaining any sense of worldliness than it is about status."

"I'm afraid I don't quite follow what you mean. Surely one can't see the world without traveling it, and I struggle to see how one could wander around the globe without gaining some sense of experience from such an adventure."

I've seen few people smile with as much exasperation as Evelyn can muster, and yet she always makes me feel as though her fatigue is one we share, even if I don't understand how. It always leaves me feeling as though the two of us are on some shared side of an invisible battle against the world itself.

"I'm sure many people gain the sense of having developed some meaningful insight in their travels," Evelyn agrees, "but I'd wager in most cases it's a shallow experience. I think that in order to truly see the world, we must observe it with eyes unclouded by our own perspectives. Worldliness, I think, can only come from stepping outside one's position in the world. I doubt most of the people I've heard speak of their travels have even entertained the idea that other perspectives could have any value to them. Why else would we in England vest such interest in spreading our own ideals without stopping to consider what we might wish to bring back with us?"

"You're being rather unfair, I think."

"Am I?"

"Of course. We care plenty about bringing back all the riches we can. How else could we sugar our tea?"

Evelyn's laughter is as sharp and biting as ever, and it always brings me great satisfaction when I manage to provoke it. The sheer cynicism of our conversations reminds me of early days in Basil's studio when Henry would try to keep me entertained as I sat, but the way Evelyn and I speak feels so much more cathartic than Henry's words ever did. Whenever he let out some remark about the state of London's high society, I found myself wondering whether or not I could agree with words he didn't mean, or whether such sentiments could possibly be anything more than novelty. When Evelyn makes similar statements, however, there's a camaraderie—like I might not be losing my mind for feeling the frustrations I do if someone in the room shares them.

I've spent so much of the last three years seeking out whatever scraps of affection I could find, it never occurred to me that what I might have needed was a friend. Even Thornhill feels less grim during Evelyn's visits. The shadows that lurk behind me retreat, and my portrait's whispers quiet when we speak.

"And how, then, would one see the world without traveling it?" I ask, eagerness tentatively creeping into me at the possibility of some life I might live from my confines here at Thornhill. I can't remember the last time I let myself feel anything resembling hope, but it's far more thrilling than I remembered.

"I suppose one would have to find ways to step outside their perspective during their daily life. It certainly sounds more difficult than traveling the world, but perhaps the challenge is part of its value. If nothing else, having to go out of one's way to expose themselves to other positions might open the mind to better receive them."

The thought is certainly a romantic one, though it doesn't bring the comfort I wish it did. There's some beauty to imagining the world to be a rich tapestry of experiences to appreciate, and there's a sense of potential in the notion that the everyday is rich with opportunities to learn and grow, but I can't help feeling as though every time I try to find answers, I end up being given more questions to unpack instead.

I've spent the last three years gathering novels and other texts from all over the globe, broadening Thornhill's art collection to include pieces from as far away as possible, even explored a few instruments and dances I never knew existed, but none of them have been a suitable replacement for people. Whatever I study in my search to understand the world, I'm always left with the sense that I cannot appreciate them to the fullest without learning about the histories that developed them.

"Would you believe me," I ask, "if I told you I once thought the point of art was simply to make beautiful things?"

"That depends. How old were you at the time?"

"Sixteen, and I'll be the first to say I was a rather sheltered sixteen at that."

Evelyn shrugs. "Plenty of people see no higher meaning in beauty far later than that. I'd argue most don't, especially where other people are concerned."

I pause to take in Evelyn's words properly. I've become all too familiar with the sheer depth of ideals art has to offer, and I certainly know better than most how much a person can disguise behind a beautiful mask, but I never stopped to consider all those qualities that give art meaning might be anything more than vulnerabilities for people to hide and protect.

"Is that why you've been so willing to spend so much time with me lately? Have you been looking for what secret virtue I might be hiding behind all the loveliness and extravagance?"

Evelyn stills for a moment, stirring her tea as she does. There's a rhythmic sort of pensiveness to the sounds her spoon makes against the porcelain of her cup that leaves my mind racing to try and anticipate what she might be pondering. I've had the pleasure of Evelyn's company often enough in the few months since my masquerade ball to know she rarely holds her tongue, and yet the creasing of her brows makes it clear she isn't sure how much to say. I catch her eyes wandering across my shirt and taking in how the ruffles I sewed onto my collar match her own before nodding with the exaggerated certainty of someone convincing themself of their decision.

"I've found it incredibly pleasant to make a friend who understands how it feels not to be quite what people want from you," she answers. "I couldn't begin to tell you how many times I've overheard people discussing what a shame it is for me to ruin any chance such a pretty young lady could have at a good marriage without asking if I've ever wanted the life of some society wife."

"Do you?" I ask.

"It's hard to say when it's pushed so heavily onto me. Would you?"

"Sometimes I think it might be nice to have such a clearly outlined life," I admit. "It would certainly be simpler. I think I was likely meant to be some artist's muse and travel wherever inspiration and adventure might take us, but it seems I've ended up stuck somewhere between the scandalous heiress and the country mistress."

"Can I say something that might be presumptuous of me?"

Evelyn's words come out even more direct and rushed than is typical for her, as though if she did not hurry to say them she would lose the nerve to. The urgency of her tone prompts the faintest of laughter.

"Of course. In fact, I'd be delighted if you did."

"I know we've been friends for a rather short time," she begins, much slower and more deliberate than I'm used to, "but I think we might understand each other better than most people. It seems to me you've decided anything that isn't beautiful about you must, by default, be a flaw. Have you considered that whatever you've deemed so hideous and shameful about you might in fact be the very histories and sense of perspective you would treasure in a work of art?"

I spend what feels like the better part of an hour trying to think of some response I might offer, opening my mouth to speak every now and then only to decide against it and close it back. Evelyn's theory has such a weight to it when it hits my ears that I struggle to convince myself it might not, at some point, have been true, but by now I doubt it could apply. Evelyn might be able to see through some of the glamour I've crafted to hide the scared young girl clinging to whatever parts of her made her feel like herself, but she hasn't seen the portrait of who that scared girl has become. She can't fathom the people I've used or endangered or hurt in my desperation.

I've seen my character reflected before my very eyes; there's no room left for me to believe it might be anything other than wretched.

A quiet knock sounds against the door a few moments before the newest hallboy enters the sitting room, eyes pointing so stubbornly toward the ground I might think him afraid of me were I not already familiar with the nervous look most servants get on their first posting.

"A letter came from you, Master Gray," he stutters, "from a Mr. Basil Hallward."

The mention of Basil's name sends a jolt through me, prompting a sudden stiffening across my posture as memories of his face flash across my mind. There was a time when, in my isolation, I ached to hear from him again, but I've long since abandoned that hope. I pluck the letter from the hallboy's hand and open it with an enthusiasm I didn't know I could still muster, overwhelmed by the clean yet ornate nature of Basil's script on the page, as vivid in my mind as if he had written me every day for the last three years.

Dearest Dorian,
I always knew I would one day write you again, though I'll admit I could not have expected the circumstances that would prompt me to. I wish I had found the courage long ago, but I worried perhaps you might not wish to hear from me.

The more of the letter I read, the further my stomach twists into a vicious mixture of guilt and regret until I can feel tears welling at the corners of my eyes. I can't remember the last time

I cried—I had begun to think, in fact, that I'd lost the ability to—but I blink back the tears before they can fall, all too aware of Evelyn's worried gaze. I read the rest as stoically as I can, though I must do a pretty poor job of it. It's all I can do not to rip up the page and let out such an ungodly shriek any birds outside Thornhill might take flight and never return.

"I have to go back to London," I say, once I can't bear the weight of Evelyn's eyes on me any longer. "I have to bury my father."

24
Mourning Black

I spent years convinced I would never bury my father.

No matter which one of us died first—and I'll admit there were many times where I thought it might be me—I assumed Grandfather would never allow me to attend the funeral procession, lest anyone of note see me and recognize a bit too much of him in me.

It seems strange, in hindsight, that it never occurred to me Grandfather might die before either one of us. It should be the most logical conclusion for me to draw, but I think his mark on me would have kept me under his grasp long after his passing. Even now, despite all I've done to rid myself of his influence, I can't quite rid myself of his shadow lurking behind me, watching and judging my every action.

The cravat around my neck is almost unbearably tight. The formal, traditionally masculine garb I've made myself tolerate is a small price to pay if it means keeping a low profile, though it's not without its discomforts. I can't say what Grandfather would think if word of my presence at the procession reached his ears, but I doubt my attendance should capture the attention of too many onlookers. Papa and his gallery were a key staple of the arts scene in London, so it's hardly surprising that nobles known to have a particular appreciation for art might wish to pay their respects. It might even be stranger for the two of us not to have crossed paths at one point or another, in which case any gossips in attendance might have speculated about the reasons for my absence.

Perhaps this is little more than a lie I tell myself to justify doing as I please, but it's convincing enough I don't waste time debating its merit. If nothing else, it should be enough to convince Grandfather, should he hear word I was in London for the funeral, that there's at least some logic to my presence at the procession.

The pallbearers march his coffin to the cemetery, unbothered by the weight of the elm resting above their shoulders. With no known family to claim Papa, Fabián leads the group of friends and acquaintances ferrying his body to its final resting place. Seeing his usual joy drained from his features makes my heart sink, but seeing Basil carry the back end of the coffin is what breaks it altogether. I cannot cry—I shouldn't know him enough to—but it takes everything I have not to show the way my chest tightens so thoroughly that mere breathing feels like a struggle. He looks older than he ought to, as if the last few years have weighed so heavily upon him he aged twice as fast for every year I stayed still.

The longer I spend staring at Basil and Fabián, the stronger the urge to join them and help shoulder the load grows. It feels wrong, somehow, for me to be at this funeral with them when I went to such lengths to distance myself from both them and Papa, yet I can't help but want to support them. Perhaps, if I were especially lucky, we might even manage to all find comfort within each other's presence, sharing the burden of Papa's loss until it feels closer to a weight we could manage.

I don't think I realized, when I decided to keep everyone at an arm's length from myself, what that might resemble in practice. I pictured gaps, of course, absences in the shape of people who meant more to me than I could ever tell them, but I never considered the passage of time: the rifts that grow as years erode what we knew about each other, the way that the people before me now feel like old friends and strangers all at once. However much I planned not to see them, it didn't occur to me I might *never* see them again.

As the pallbearers walk by, I could swear Basil's eyes meet mine for a moment, though I see no acknowledgment in his look. I tell myself he doesn't recognize me, that he expects me to look older than I do or that his eyes simply failed to process who stood before him in his focus on keeping his emotions in check, but I can't shake the worry that his invitation was a matter of mere formality and that he and Fabián neither expected nor wanted my presence here. The letters Papa sent me burn in my mind as Thornhill's fireplace blackens them one by one—what right do I have to mourn someone I chose to keep out of my life? Would he have even answered the apology I sent, had he lived to receive it?

The flames continue to burn in my mind as the procession passes the gathered crowd, taking with it all the people I've worked to push as far from me as possible. Whatever desires I might have to join them, they hold little power over the marble I've sculpted myself into. I stand frozen in a prison of my own making.

Papa's grave lacks any of the art or flair I associate with his life. It's a simple gray headstone decorated only with his name and his life entombed between the year of his birth and his death, likely the best that could be afforded by a gallery owner more focused on patronizing the artists that roamed its hall than accumulating profit. It seems too plain a resting place for him, no matter how much he would have loathed any kind of spectacle. He deserved a rest as artful as his life, but all I can do is sit by his headstone and try to find the words I wish I could say to him.

Despite spring's best efforts at making an appearance, the early April cold has begun to settle into my bones. I had to wait for the better part of an hour before I felt confident I could steal a moment at Papa's grave, and though night hasn't fallen yet, the sun provides little help in warming the air. The scents of the various flowers left by his tombstone merge into what ought to be an overwhelming bouquet, but instead the aroma soothes me, telling me of the cacophony of people who cared enough about my father to leave a trinket behind with him. Even something as simple as a flower, it appears, can grow imposing when there are enough of them to fill the air.

I don't need to turn to recognize the hand that places itself on mine. Even if the light bronze of its tint was not enough for me to guess its owner, the woodworker's calluses I feel brushing against my skin would be more than enough to recognize Fabián's touch.

Warmth and reassurance flood into me as I remember the various times I felt him and Papa pull me into their embrace, though the relief brings with it more guilt for me to shoulder. I was all too happy to let him and Basil mourn without me, worried as I was that my presence might only cause them further distress; I should have known neither of them would think to reciprocate my distance. If nothing else, I should at least have risked their rejection. Bringing them even a shred of comfort would have been worth any pain their turning me away might have caused me.

"Thank you for making the trip to London. It would have meant a lot to Étienne that you came."

"What a shame he isn't here to appreciate it."

The callousness of my words hits me long before I see the wince it prompts from Fabián or the grimace Basil makes from a few steps behind us, as if he was scared he might disturb me with his presence. The urge hits me to explain I didn't mean for my words to lash out at them—any pain they might have caused was only ever intended for myself—but instinct tells me neither of them would find much comfort in that statement, so I bite it back. Whatever violence I might wish upon myself, I can keep it in check until they're no longer here to witness it.

This is who you are, the portrait's voice returns to my mind, hollow and gravelly as a grave. *You hurt people, not because you can't help it, but because you don't care to. They were better off without you around to bite at them.*

"I'm sorry," I say for what feels like the first time in years. "I let my emotions take control. That was thoughtless of me."

"It's an emotional time for all of us," Basil answers. He hasn't moved any nearer, and I start wondering if he might fear my hurting him rather than the contrary. It certainly would be a logical assumption for him to make, given the last time the two of us were alone. If I study him long enough, I can still see remnants of the shattered look in his eyes I put there the day I dismissed him from Thornhill.

"I'm sorry for your loss." I turn from Fabián to Basil. "Both of you."

Fabián nods. "And I yours."

I force down the instinct to say I lost him years ago by my own design. Even as I burned his letters, some part of me thought there might come a day, after Grandfather's passing, where I would return to London in full possession of my affairs and walk into his gallery to find him smiling, ready for us to finally be a family, no matter how strangely the word might fit. I thought, when I sent him my letter, that we still had some chance at a relationship; it would be a lie to pretend that hadn't been ripped from me as surely as he was from them.

"It's strange to think of his body resting in London when this city has been so cruel to him," I say instead. "It took my mother away from him and did everything it could to keep us apart. If I'd written and told him to go back to France, he would have at least been buried where he belonged."

"I won't pretend to understand the reasons for your distance," Fabián begins, "nor will I pretend to approve of them. What I will say is that your father would not have left London simply because you told him to. He built a life here as best as he could, and he was determined to watch over you. You wield his stubbornness as surely as you wear his hair, and I can say without hesitation that nothing you might have said would have dissuaded him."

I wish, at least, that I had read Papa's letters so I might have some last words of his to remember, but I keep that thought to myself as well. I doubt I could explain how frightened I was that his words might break my resolve without sharing why I determined to keep my distance, and I couldn't begin to put such a strange set of circumstances into words. I've grown so used to guarding myself that I've lost the language with which to express my thoughts.

"What about you?" I ask. "Surely you couldn't have been happy to stay in London."

"Which is why I didn't stay in London," Fabián replies. "You may not have seen us often enough to know, but I left the city regularly for weeks on end—months on occasion—to visit my family or to see new places and discover what sources of inspiration I might find. I knew when your father told me about the child taken from him back in England that he wouldn't rest until he saw you happy, and I knew I wanted to see his journey unfold, even if it brought me somewhere I never felt an urge to go. It might surprise you to hear this, but your father and I have always based our decisions according to what felt right to us. He didn't make some noble sacrifice to watch over you, and I didn't abandon my life to follow his. The world is not that simple."

The air in the cemetery feels heavier than ever as I stand in silence and try to process Fabián's words. I look to Basil, who meets my eyes for little more than a moment before turning away, then back to Fabián again as I take in the unwavering certainty in his face. I see no reason to think he doesn't believe what he is saying, but that makes it no easier to accept his words. The idea that pushing the people I care for most robbed them of the chance to make their own decisions rather than protect them is too harrowing to let myself consider.

"I plan on leaving London once the funeral is over," adds Fabián when it has become clear I don't have it in me to answer him. "While I may not regret my travels here, it'll be nice not to be pulled back and forth between here and the South of France. I know it might be somewhat strenuous to call the two of us family, but you're welcome to come with me if you'd like."

"I see no reason to undercut what Papa meant to either one of us; you might be the last family I have left. But I cannot accept your invitation. You have a life to go on with, and I doubt that carrying my father's unfinished business with you would do you any good. The joy you brought my father is more than I could ever ask of you."

Fabián opens his mouth to protest, then closes it, deciding not to push the matter. However much I know he'd insist otherwise if I voiced my objection, I cannot bring myself to be more of a burden on him than I've already been. He smiles at me, muttering to himself about Papa's and my stubborn natures, then turns to face Basil.

"I have much to do before I leave," he says. "Should either of you decide to take up my offer, you know where to find me. I think I ought to take my leave for the time being and give the two of you a chance to talk."

Neither Basil nor I have time to protest before Fabián turns and walks away, leaving the two of us alone beside my father's headstone. We look at each other in parallel silence, too anxious to take on the burden of breaking the ice I built between us. I remember a time when we could sit for hours without a single word as Basil painted me. It seems impossible I could rupture our friendship so thoroughly that we now must tiptoe around the other, yet here I stand facing the proof.

I finally surrender. "I should never have spoken to you the way I did that day. I thought you'd be better off without me and knew you would not abandon me for such a simple reason, but I hope you believe me when I say that hurting you remains my deepest regret."

"Why would you think such a thing?"

I can't help being aware of the proximity between Basil and me as he closes the gap between us. It's been so long since we stood near each other, but already a sense of familiarity has begun to return. I could crumple into his arms were I not worried about burdening him with my woes after what I've done to him—I wish he would collapse into mine so I might begin to heal the pain I caused him.

"I wish I could tell you, but I'm afraid I don't know how."

"One day, perhaps?"

I nod.

"I saw the letter you wrote him," Basil adds. "I wish he could have read it."

"Thank you. I wanted to write you one, but I thought you might not want to hear from me."

"I see you've yet to learn not to make decisions on my account."

We stand in silence a few moments longer, though the air between us no longer weighs as heavily as it did. Instead, it feels as if neither one of us is quite ready to leave the other, nor do we know how to move forward from our position. I remember thinking, when we first met, that Basil would lead me to my destruction, only to see the portrait he made of me and let it break me time and time again. I suppose I shattered him in return, once I decided I couldn't risk being seen as clearly as Basil once saw me. Perhaps we were never meant to do more than wreck each other, but when I look at him, I can't help but wonder what art we might make of all our broken pieces.

"I see no reason why you would agree to this," I begin, "and between you and me, I feel rather foolish asking, but . . . would you care to join me at Thornhill for tea sometime? There seems so much we need to say to each other, and I must admit I'd rather have that conversation on a day we did not bury my father."

Seeing Basil smile warms my heart, however faintly he may do it. It makes him look closer to my age rather than giving him the appearance of an old man weighed down by the world. Perhaps some things can recover after they shatter.

"I'd like that. Thank you for asking."

I pull Basil into the most tentative embrace we've shared, though neither one of us complains. I don't tell him how much I've missed him—I can't yet bring myself to give him that much power over me—but I'm sure some part of him knows it. His embrace is too tender, his head too gentle on my chest, for me to think he doesn't know how much I've felt his absence.

If I were a more optimistic person, or perhaps a more foolish one, I might even let myself believe he'd felt my absence as well.

25
Poppy Haze

I don't think I've ever seen the sun rise over London before.

The sight is so beautiful I find myself stunned it can occur in so cold and gray a place. Light glistens atop the smoke and the fog, briefly giving them the appearance of a spell flowing through the city to bring it to life. Shades of orange and yellow peer through the gray, however fleetingly, promising a fresh start for whoever dares grab it. I could swear the air itself fills with a dewy shimmering as each sunray dances with the nearest tendril of the toxic beast that has sunk its claws so deeply into the city. There's some sort of peace in the air between nature and the ravage of man, though it only lasts as long as their dance.

Even Covent Garden is beautiful this time of day, trading its bustle for a pleasant stillness as a few errant stragglers wander after a night on the town. Their laughter is vibrant and loud, unfiltered by any notions of decency as they call jokes to each other that could make the most raucous of sailors blush. They look weary, certainly, but even their fatigue has a certain energy to it. Watching them is enough to imagine the kinds of stories they might take home with them, the memories they made when the sun's light could not reflect so harshly upon them.

I left Basil shortly after sunset with the intention to find my coach and return to Thornhill as I ought to, but the closer I grew to my destination, the more restless my steps became until I knew I couldn't yet leave London. The isolation that waited for me in the country seemed ready to swallow me whole, taking with it any opportunity for solace or joy despite the promise of visits from Basil or Evelyn for me to cling to. The idea of being alone in such a big house with no company but the portrait chilled me, and I felt a growing certainty that something terrible would happen if I went back to Thornhill. Even hours later, now that the thought has entered my mind, I find myself plagued by the portrait's glacial eyes burning into me, assessing my every action from afar and plotting how it might twist them to best haunt me.

Eventually my steps brought me to the district I roamed so freely at sixteen, guided by the promise of a drink, some way to pass the time, and maybe even a bed to spend the night should luck come my way. It hadn't occurred to me when I dismissed the coach for the evening that I was losing the means to get back to Thornhill without arranging for any lodging in London. I don't think I expected, at the time, to get much rest. Papa's grave, my encounter with Basil, and the eyes I felt on me all weighed too heavily on my mind for sleep to hold any weight in my thoughts.

One of the perks of being young and beautiful, I've discovered, is that there will always be someone eager to buy whatever I desire at that time. Drink, jewels, art—there's nothing people have not shown themselves willing to spend if it means earning my favor, no matter how briefly. Even a smile, on occasion, has been enough to grant me entry into the most exclusive of gatherings. However tiresome it might be to learn how to think of myself as currency, I'll be the first to admit it's not without its advantages.

Poppy, however, is something I've had offered to me quite rarely. I suppose one has to be in the right place at the right time, where it's present enough for one to offer but still rare enough to covet. With the weight of Papa's funeral on my shoulders and my mind falling into spirals wondering what might happen when Basil and I next see each other, a few kisses seemed a small price to pay for artificial bliss. The world can be such a beautiful place when one looks at it under the right light.

The shadows threaten to seep into reality, daring me to face them, but I focus on the sunrise and the way light shimmers atop layers of dust until they're little more than a nagging sensation behind me. The whispers, however, are far more insidious. First they take Grandfather's voice to remind me how low I've fallen, though this trick of theirs grew tiresome a long time ago. They mirror Henry's smooth tones to tell me how little I'm worth, but he's all but told me that already. It isn't until they twist into the bouncing, musical way Papa talks—*talked*—and tell me how disappointed he is to know I turned my back on him only to destroy myself that I feel their claws deep inside me, dragging me further from the growing sunlight with every passing step.

The man at the den said this would lift my spirits. Why is it, then, that I feel myself sinking lower with each passing hour?

I barely recognize Tamara's pub when I pass it, though it hasn't changed a bit in the past three years. The building is as run-down and nondescript as ever, perfectly cloaking the wonderland I discovered in its depths. Part of me had hoped that, when I next saw it, I would find it renovated and thriving so I could know that Tamara and the patrons she hosts are well, but I suppose getting too much attention or success might endanger the place. I don't think I realized how worried I was that Sybil leaving might have hurt the business until now, standing outside the tavern and wondering in what state I might find it.

I open the door as quietly as I can muster, hiding away in the corner a few steps from the entrance. I cannot see the cellar from here, but the main floor, at least, is busier than I remember, packed with the boisterous energy of a crowd united in forgetting their troubles. Tamara stands behind the bar, her smile as rich and warm as I remember. A few wrinkles have started to gather by the corners of her eyes and mouth, adorning her face with the echoes of laughter even when her features are perfectly still. I envy her, though I'm equally relieved to see the last few years have treated her as decently as I could hope.

I consider walking to the bar and striking up a conversation, but I can't bring myself to venture any closer to the door. However nice it would be to speak with her again, I don't think I could bring myself to look her in the eyes knowing I endangered the space she's worked so hard to keep safe. I hardly need the whispers to remind me how callous I can be when I can look at a place that feels so sacred and know it's standing despite me.

Tamara and her tavern have survived me once already—what right do I have to jeopardize them again? However badly I want to think I've taken a turn for the better, there's no reason to risk being wrong. Perhaps improving means knowing there are some people who are better off without me.

What about Basil, then? I wonder. Is it selfish of me to pull him back into my orbit when I've hurt him as much as I have? What right do I have to hope for his forgiveness when I've done so little to deserve it?

No. None of the questions I'm asking myself are serving any real purpose besides giving me a weapon with which to beat myself. I remember, before I pushed Basil out of my life, how much it frustrated me to see him walk on eggshells and decide what topics to avoid around me. Our situations may be different, but I will not do him the disservice of deciding what he can or cannot forgive. Perhaps it would even be good for me to give Tamara the same choice. In order to do that, however, I'd first need to explain how I wronged her, and I lack the strength to make such a confession.

Tamara looks toward the doorway and, for a moment, I think she might have seen me, but then a patron pulls her attention away and I remind myself that even I can hardly recognize myself at the moment. I've pulled off the tie that was constricting my neck and freed my hair from the careful bun tucked away beneath a hat for the sake of respectability, yet I still can't shake the feeling that I've got some essence of myself locked away. Sometimes I catch myself wondering if the person I remember being is trapped inside Basil's canvas as surely as the atrocities I've taken such pains to hide. I want to tell myself such things are impossible, or that even if it was true, it would be worth it, but I find that claim harder and harder to make with each passing day.

Then again, perhaps that feeling has nothing to do with my portrait. Perhaps getting older means becoming a new person bit by bit, so gradually that by the time anyone can notice it, their memories of who they ought to be are long gone already.

I could not say whether it's the drink, the sleeplessness, the poppy, or simply my mind buckling under the weight that plagues it, but the shadows with which I've become so familiar grow bigger and louder than ever. They taunt me with memories of the person I once was, frighten me with visions of who I've become, and leave me shivering as the world around me goes darker with each quickening breath. I stumble out the door, tripping over my own feet and landing in the street, then pull myself up and race down the street like someone chased by the hounds of Hell.

I have no clue where to go, but if I stay here any longer, I might lose my mind. I need something—*someone*—to tell me I haven't yet crossed a bridge from which I cannot still return.

26
Gentle Arsenic

If someone had told me how lonely it would be to live frozen behind a wall of perfection, I might have reconsidered the wish I made before my portrait. If I'd known that Sybil Vane's story would not be one of tragedy, or if Basil had told me more about his life earlier, I might have known I wasn't nearly so trapped as I doomed myself to become. There would have been other ways for me to be, other people who would have seen me. I could have found a way to leave London with Papa and Fabián, maybe even with Basil if I'd built up the nerve to ask him. I would not be watching myself rot away in a luxury prison, waiting for Henry to decide he wants me to entertain him.

Basil did not make the bargain you did, the whispers remind me. *Sybil Vane did not make the bargain you did. How long will you reach for excuses before accepting that you are simply a worse person than they are? Why should you deserve the happiness they found, when you took the first shortcut you could find?*

The fear they might be right sinks into me as I remember the pain in Basil's eyes when I pushed him away, the simple grave Papa might never know I visited. It seems beyond foolish to think I deserve any kind of solace when I've gone to such lengths to deny it to myself. The buildings around me blur into each other as my steps grow faster and more frantic. I could not say where I'm going, only that it must be better than the swirling storm of accusations surrounding me.

You are selfish, the shadows chant, weaving into one another until I find myself standing in my portrait's mouth, waiting for it to consume me. *You are vain and cowardly and shallow. Even if you had known Basil's and Sybil's fates, do you truly think you could have followed down their paths? How would you have risked being judged in the world's cruel eye when you can't bear to be seen as anything less than some imagined ideal?*

The whispers do not fall behind when my pace picks up into a run, but I continue nonetheless. Purpose finds me as I turn a corner, and I begin to recognize the streets outside Hartwood Heights. The sun sits sleepily in the sky, not quite awake, but decency is the last thing on my mind as I knock at the gate. If anything, propriety would only make matters worse. I need someone who will look at me and listen as I ramble about how awful I am, and tell me none of it matters.

There must be some truth in the whispers plaguing me. After all, what decent person would be so desperate for the sweet venom of a lie, they would rather turn to their jailer for comfort than face their own failings?

Henry's footman doesn't look particularly eager to let me in, but he must understand that shutting me out would only cause a scene. However put together I might look, there's a feral sort of determination to my knocking I know must at least somewhat betray my state. Once it's apparent I will not stop until I've seen Henry, he guides me into what I recognize as the sitting room farthest from Hartwood's sleeping quarters, stuck between the kitchen and the servants' quarters. Being greeted as a shameful, unwanted guest ought to put some sense of embarrassment in me, but such sentiments are far behind me. If being treated as Henry's guilty pleasure could hurt my pride, I would have stopped seeing him a long time ago.

I resign myself to looking as dignified as I can, sitting upright in the stiff, mildewy armchair by the curtained-shut window, and stare at the door, putting my best efforts into ignoring the whispering wisps of shadow still dancing behind me. If Henry is determined to keep up appearances at my expense, I see no reason not to do the same. My attempt at holding on to any sort of power in our relationship—arrangement? No word seems quite suitable to describe how much the rapport between us has rotted—is admittedly pitiable, but at least it's something to do as I wait.

It takes little time for Henry to storm into the sitting room in his nightclothes, sleeping cap half-perched atop his head. I've rarely seen outright anger in his eyes, yet the expression doesn't quite seem foreign, either.

"Are you out of your mind?" he spits. "Victoria could—"

"Victoria knows! You talk so often about how smart and how modern she is. Do you truly imagine she has no notion of what you do when she leaves?"

Henry's lips narrow into a thin, straight line. "Of course not. It simply makes it more thrilling to pretend."

Henry's response should disgust me or at the very least prompt some kind of shame, but his words bounce off me as soon as they leave his mouth. As absurd as Henry's attitude toward his wife may be, he told me the way their marriage works the moment I met her. There's no trust between them to break, only convenience and a mutual agreement not to pry into his affairs. At the time it seemed an absurd outlook on marriage, but after three years with Henry I can say I'd much rather have his wife's freedom than the captivity of being his mistress.

The few remaining tendrils of shadow recoil away from the tender poison of his hand brushing my cheek, leaving the two of us alone in the dimly lit sitting room. Henry sighs before smiling at me, his fingers fiddling with my hair as he does. The anger I saw in his face has withdrawn into its hiding spot, but now that I know where to look, it's all too easy to see. His smile is stretched a hint too wide, his eyes too bright through the veil of fatigue that clouds them. His expression reminds me of an exasperated parent trying to reassure a child after scolding them; gentle enough to be comforting yet ready to break the moment it's tested.

"I'm sorry," he says, brushing a thumb against my cheekbone as he does. "I slept poorly, but I suppose you must have as well if you're here visiting me at such an early hour. What's troubling you?"

There are so many answers I could give him, I don't know where to begin. The constant nightmares keeping me up seem too mundane to bother him with, the shadows taunting me and my ever-mocking portrait too fantastical. Reminding him I buried my father yesterday seems too accusatory, but bringing up Basil would only invite jealousy. Whatever sin I try to admit to, there seems to be a reason Henry's ears are the wrong ones for my confession—but I can't think of another person who might be callous or selfish enough to understand them.

"I turned in Sybil Vane. I'm the reason they arrested her. I was stupid and selfish and shallow and—"

"I know."

I scrutinize Henry's face for any sign of jest, but his expression sits completely still. Even the forced gentleness he put on mere moments ago has faded away, leaving a bored look as he tilts his head to the side as if waiting for me to clue in, but surely he couldn't have known. I spent years tormenting myself with the insistence I could not let anyone know what I did that night. Even if Henry suspected I caused the trial that killed her reputation, it should not be so mundane a confession as to bore him.

"I've known you turned in Sybil Vane for years. It always seemed a reasonable guess, considering you left town so shortly after her trial, but the way you'd squirm and change the subject whenever I suggested returning to the molly house all but gave it away. I'd hoped you might have gotten over it by now, but clearly I was mistaken."

"Gotten over it?" I ask. "It was thoughtless of me. It was hypocritical, cowardly, and petty. I put someone in danger—an entire establishment, even—because I thought myself more deserving of safety than they were. I resented Sybil Vane because she didn't fit some imagined ideal of her I'd dreamed up for myself, and I threw her to the wolves for disappointing me. How can that not bother you?"

"You were sublime," he answers. "A wrathful goddess ready to smite whoever caught your ire. It was a drama the Greeks would have envied. You cannot imagine how disappointed I was to see you shy away from such a perfect tapestry."

Whatever relief I wanted to find in confession sits far out of reach. My visit to Hartwood was fueled by someone to see me in my wickedness and tell me I was perfect regardless, but Henry's approval feels as much like poison corroding me as Grandfather's did. I'm not some mighty deity for poets to write about; I'm little more than a child, vulnerable and frightened, begging for someone to love me without having to prove myself worthy of them.

"I'm a person, Henry, not some work of art."

"Don't disparage yourself. Matters of humanity and morality are so petty and common, but Beauty? One would be hard-pressed to find a higher ideal."

"Is that why you care for me?" I ask.

"You know the answer to that already," he answers. "When I met you, you were little more than a blank canvas—a waste, really, when such infinite potential was written into your features. Lesser men speak of their angel in the house, but London is in abundance of angels these days. I discovered a goddess lost in some artist's studio and domesticated her, cared for her so that she could depend on me. Can you think of anything more grand than to have Beauty incarnate begging for the scraps of my company?"

Henry's words burn so viciously that I think, for a moment, there might truly be fire coursing through my veins. If I could shed my skin the way a serpent might, I would do so in a heartbeat if it meant never feeling his eyes on me again. Even the vision of my reflection melting before me seems like a mercy compared to the fate Henry wants for me. Basil was right; for as long as I've known him, Henry has never cared about me. All that has ever mattered to him was the idea of grooming me into whatever might best amuse him. Whatever uncertainties might lie ahead, I can't stay at Hartwood a moment longer—nor Thornhill, for that matter. I will never be more than some possession of his, waiting for him to pull me from my cage to amuse him.

"You flatter me," I lie, smiling as gently as I can muster. "Beauty incarnate . . . You see the world with such a poetic eye. I apologize for acting so strangely. Papa's funeral left me rather emotional. Could you arrange a coach to bring me back home?"

"Of course." Henry kisses my hand. "I'm glad to see you're feeling more yourself, pet."

I force the smile to hold until he leaves the room, cursing the sight of him all the while. Hopefully, once I've finally fled his custody, there might still be some semblance of a life left for me to piece together. Even as I dream about the other lives I might still live, however, I struggle to imagine the day Henry finally allows his precious pet out of his grasp.

27
Scarlet Sins

When I was a child, there was a game Grandfather and I would play. We would sit before the mirror and I would stand as still as I could, pointing out any flaw in my posture until he decided I'd identified all of them. I don't remember ever being particularly amused by it, but the warmth in his congratulations whenever I won felt like a worthy trade at the time.

Finding goodness hidden in my portrait has proved itself much harder than finding flaws in my reflection. I've grown so used to thinking of it as little more than a devil plaguing me that the mere thought of seeing anything worth celebrating on its twisted canvas seems laughable if not outright blasphemous. Here I stand, staring at my own wretched image, wondering what rare quality

I might find worth treasuring. Ever since I returned from London yesterday, Evelyn's suggestion that there might still be something to treasure in my flaws has run through my mind incessantly. Clearly, the way I've let my portrait determine the terms of my life has only led me astray. What harm could there be in trying to redefine our relationship, impossible as it may feel?

I stare at the canvas before me, taking in every detail as though I don't already know it by heart. I've grown unbothered by the way its chin has shaped as stern as Grandfather's—*her chin*, I chide myself. If I'm to find any kind of agreement with this portrait, the first thing I have to do is think of her as a reflection of myself and not some creature mocking me. The frowning creases that have started to form on her forehead are unwelcome, certainly, but hardly horrific. The way her skin has grown pallid and gaunt from lack of sun and sleep gives me pause as I remember the corpse in my mirror and my breath comes to a halt. I turn away, unable to bear the sight of her a moment longer. I struggle to think of any exercise more futile than looking for goodness in her haunting face.

Stop that whining, Grandfather's voice echoes in my ears. *How do you expect anyone to bother noticing you if you cannot even look at yourself?*

When the two of us played our game, nothing would frustrate Grandfather more than when I would turn away from the mirror, though I wonder now if what bothered him was my disobedience and not my lack of commitment to bettering myself. His words were never meant to have any meaning beyond the surface of my manners and poise; anything unsavory about my character was better left ignored and hidden away. It seems foolish not to wonder now if that might not be another flaw in his teachings. After all, how can I expect anyone to truly see me if I spend my time running from myself?

Twisting Grandfather's game for a purpose he would despise might be petty relief, but it does at least give me some sense of power as I clutch my fists and force my gaze back toward the portrait. However big of an impact he's had on me, I've grown tired of letting his shadow haunt me when I have so many of my own. The dagger I've started concealing on me in case Henry visits without warning burns against my calf, begging me to cut the canvas to shreds regardless of what consequences such violence might bear upon me.

You must be losing your mind, whispers one of the shadows with which I've grown so familiar as of late. *What delusions have you built for yourself, that you now carry a blade for the man who keeps a roof above your head?*

The voice's words leave me shivering and clutching my dagger tighter than ever. Henry may never have hurt me, but I've also never denied him what he wants. I cannot say for how long I can keep surrendering to his whims, nor what he might do the day I no longer entertain him. These days, when I think of Henry, all I can picture is the ice in his eyes and the bottomless hunger growing more voracious with each passing day. The memory of his nails tears at my wrists, though the lack of a mark in their wake leaves me wondering whether I might not have imagined that particular detail.

I don't know yet when or how I might go, but my days at Thornhill are numbered. If I stay around much longer, I fear there'll be nothing left of me to salvage.

I pull a glass and the bottle of port from the fireplace beneath the portrait and pour myself a glass to steady my nerves. Drinking this early in the morning might not be the best decision to make, especially when I'm expecting Basil to visit for tea this afternoon, but it certainly beats the alternative. Unlike slashing through my portrait, this act of self-destruction is one from which I know I can recover.

The first time I saw it appear on the portrait, I assumed the messy scarlet of her lips was meant to look cracked and bloodied, though I can't think of a reason why they would be now that I pause to consider it. I suppose it could be a rouge of some sort, so heavy-handed any decent lady would shudder to be seen wearing it, but the wantonness of such a shade hardly bothers me. If anything, I can see in it a refusal to care what society has deemed appropriate or acceptable that I can respect. The proud tilt of her chin despite the roughness of her appearance could be similarly admirable, were it not for the viciousness of her sneer. As it is, I find myself struggling to determine whether she's trying to maintain some semblance of dignity or if she's somehow convinced, despite all her failings, that she's still superior to those around her, as if there were some virtue in her self-imposed suffering.

Whatever the case, I suppose a few ambiguous outlooks on my portrait are better than outright repulsion. There remains much to despise—far more than any decent person ought to have—and yet I find myself thinking as I sip my port that the picture before me might not be beyond salvaging. Though the morbidity of the portrait's complexion makes it easy to forget, the young woman it depicts might still have a long life ahead of her. Surely, if I have spent three years painting with selfishness, cruelty, and vanity, I could just as well pick a different palette with which to work.

I remember thinking on the day I met Basil that destruction is yet another medium from which one might make art. If that's true, I fail to see why I shouldn't be able to sculpt something new from the wreckage I've made of my life and character. I have no idea how I might do such a thing, but if I can get away from Thornhill, I'll have a lifetime to find an answer to that question.

It's a nice thought, if nothing else.

By the time Basil's coach approaches Thornhill, I'm on my third glass of port for the day.

I drank the first hours ago, and so its effects would've been long gone had I left the bottle when I finished it. I poured the second half an hour before he was meant to reach Thornhill, hoping it would quell the nerves flaring at the thought of his arrival. However well our last encounter went, having him come to Thornhill seems an entirely different beast. I'd hardly expect him to cause a scene by Papa's grave or to scold me in my mourning, but it seems absurd to invite Basil back to the place I broke his heart without expecting him to hold some kind of resentment. Even if he's somehow found it in him to forgive me, I struggle to think how he could wander Thornhill's halls and not be reminded of the kind of person I've been.

I poured the third glass roughly fifteen minutes after the time Basil was meant to reach Thornhill, once I'd decided he must have changed his mind. It might admittedly have been a premature conclusion to draw, but it seemed reasonable enough at the time. If our situations were reversed, I would have strongly considered leaving him to wait for me, if only so I could have the last victory between us—though I suppose that reflects more on my character than it does his.

I jump when the bell by the door rings, startled by its sharp, piercing sound. As I rush to the entrance hall, I wipe off the drop of port I spilled on my shirt in my hurry as best as I can. Luckily, the deep burgundy of the fabric masks the stain fairly well already, and the garment is plain enough that I won't miss it if it can't be cleaned. The last thing I want to do is greet Basil overdressed or, even worse, underdressed, and so I settled for modest clothing without any particular style or occasion. Finding anything so common in my wardrobe proved more of a challenge than I'd expected, but eventually I decided this would do.

"Dorian!" Basil starts as I open the door. "I didn't expect you to get the door."

"I dismissed the servants for the day. I thought perhaps you might appreciate a little privacy, given how long it's been since the two of us last saw each other properly."

He hands me his coat to hang when I reach out for it, but keeps his hat. I wait for him to speak only to end up watching him stare at me, hesitation written so clearly on his face it feels like a blow to mine. I think I might have preferred to see the anger or resentment I expected over his current expression. I deserve his doubt as much as I would his hatred, if not more, but seeing him keep a careful distance between us reminds me how capable I am of hurting him. Somehow, Basil must have decided seeing me is worth the risk of repeating his last visit to Thornhill.

To love someone, I decide as we walk to the nicest sitting room, is to give them the tools with which they might break you, and to trust they will not use them. That honor, more than any, is one I know I haven't earned.

The thought is enough to make me wish I'd poured another glass of port, though the idea of drinking in front of Basil is off-putting. However nervous I might be, I don't want him thinking me any more volatile than he already must.

"I'd hoped we could have tea in the gardens," I explain, "but the weather refused to comply. I suppose I should expect as much from England."

"This is perfect. Did you decorate the room yourself?"

"You'd be surprised how little there is to do in these parts beyond party planning and decorating. I daresay I've mastered both by now."

As tedious as I find organizing garden parties and afternoon teas, hosting only one friend solves any frustrations they cause me. Whenever I put together an afternoon party, it devolves into a society event whether I intend it to be or not. Every aspect of the day must be generic enough to appeal to each person in attendance, becoming hollow in the process. Hosting Basil or even Evelyn, on the other hand, means I can dedicate the day to them as personally as I wish, leaving me far more room to tinker.

The table itself is simple, places set precisely but not with any ornate dishes, replacing the fuss of floral-patterned porcelain with curled-up scripts of paper by every plate and saucer, each one inscribed with a line or two from a poem I think Basil might like. The tea is a fragrant jasmine rather than the popular black tea usually served, and the typical finger foods find themselves replaced with various sweets and even a rum cake spruced up with cardamom. Every part of the service was planned to favor substance over fuss in the hopes Basil might gather what I hope it implies about his character. If the careful smile on his face is any indicator, I might have found at least some success in that endeavor.

Moving all my favorite paintings and tapestries into this particular sitting room might admittedly have been a bigger task than I should have taken on, but it was a welcome distraction on my return to Thornhill. Carrying large frames across the estate—and the ensuing fatigue—proved an efficient way of keeping myself too busy to let the shadows sink their claws into me.

"I've heard more than a fair share of praise for your hosting," Basil says as he takes in the room, "but I didn't expect this. It seems so subdued, though even that falls short of what words I might wish to use."

"I'd be curious to know what you've heard."

"I'm sure you know. Your parties are rather famous, after all."

"Humor me. Please."

For a moment I think Basil is about to push back against my request, but he looks at me and sighs instead. "They say any event you host is certain to be a success, and that each one is more successful than the last. I've heard people insist London has never seen an eye for style as discerning and coherent as yours, that you put together lavish assortments of people and music and themes nobody in their right mind would combine, and yet they blend together effortlessly. Have I flattered you enough?"

I can tell from the way his smile has grown stiff and his eyes tense that pushing any further would be a mistake, but I can't help the urge. It could be the port making me bold, or that hearing Basil speak of me makes me crave to know what he thinks rather than what he has heard, but some part of me finds both answers far too simple to satisfy me. Twisted as it might be, I want to know if Basil still sees me as the naive young girl he painted.

"Enough about my parties, then. What about me?"

Basil's eyes turn to the table as he pours a cup of tea and sips it. The silence grows so heavy it's nearly suffocating, but I don't budge. I need him to know how wretched I can be, if only so I can stop worrying about him learning the truth. I destroyed us once trying to hide it; if I'm to have any chance of keeping him in my life, there cannot be any secrets between us.

"Please," I beg him. "I don't ask so you can flatter me. I want to know where to begin."

"I've heard strange rumors about you, Dorian. London is full of young men who claim you once favored them, all lamenting the way you discarded them once you had your fill. They say they were righteous until you tempted them into vices they'd never pictured, and that you tossed them aside as soon as you'd dragged them into your orbit of depravity. But when I look at you, I struggle to believe them."

"Perhaps you should."

"I couldn't," he says, taking another sip of his tea. I mirror him, if only to stop myself from pressing any further. "I know you—have known you longer than almost anyone, I'd wager. You have your flaws, but you aren't a monster. Whatever hurt you've caused me, you never aimed to tempt or seduce me, though I'll admit I sympathize with the men who feel you discarded them. I have no desire to defend you from their claims, but I can't ignore the feeling there's more to the story than they say. Nor can I shake the thought that whatever these men won't say might help me understand why you left me behind when you fled London."

An idea begins to form in my head as he speaks, as twisted as it is tempting. Even now, for all the trouble I've caused him, it's clear Basil cannot look at me without seeing the lost, faerie-like youth that posed for him in his studio. I could tell him every piece of my story and he still would not believe me. Whatever fresh start I want for us, it won't happen so long as he clings to the perfect picture of me that I've fought so long to maintain.

"Basil," I start, leaning across the table until our faces are a mere breath away from each other. "Would you like to know why I keep your portrait hidden away?"

28
SINISTER SHADOW

I regret my words as soon as they've left my mouth.

Basil winces the moment he hears them, any reservation I've managed to disarm flying back to his face as he remounts his guard. The icy wall I built between us suddenly seems unbreakable now that I see how quickly it can return. A single sentence out of place brings every fracture between us back to the surface, pushing us away from each other so quickly I can't understand it until it's happened and the near-absent space between us feels insurmountable. I crash back into my chair with all the weight of a body dropped from a rooftop, almost knocking it over in the process.

"Why would you ask such a question?" Basil hisses as he pulls himself from his chair. "Did you ask me to visit only to toy with me and insult me again? However little you might think of me, I have better ways to spend my day than to sit around and be a mannequin for you to spar with."

I want to snap my arm out and take Basil's wrist to keep him in the room, but freeze. Henry flashes through my mind, reminding me of all the times he's touched my cheek or pulled me close to him without ever bothering to ask my thoughts on the matter, and I drop my hand. I refuse to make Basil feel the fear and powerlessness Henry brings out in me. However little I want him to leave, I can't be his tormentor or his jailer. I don't know whether he'll agree to stay if I ask, but any potential for friendship between us needs me to give him the power to abandon me.

"Please," I ask in a voice so quiet I mistake it for one of the whispers I've grown so accustomed to. "Stay. Allow me to explain myself before you decide to leave, for old times' sake. I didn't mean to startle you. I only want to give you the choice I denied you—do you want to understand what happened that day?"

Basil freezes for a moment, then turns his head to look at me. His stare is distant and almost analytic, as if I were a painting he found himself unsure he wanted to buy. The look is so different from the warm, pensive quality I associate with his eyes that it makes me think he's determined to turn his back on me, but he sits at the table and picks a scone off the tray.

I watch him eat the scone in silence, eyeing me with an exasperation that reminds me of the times I sat for him in his studio. However patiently he acted toward me, I could tell my inability to stop talking or adjusting myself frustrated him, yet he decided I was worth painting nonetheless. I struggle to think what he sees in me that makes me worth tolerating the frustration he feels for me now, but I want to. If there's one person I can trust to see me, it's Basil.

"Do you remember what you said to me the day I turned you away?" I ask.

"I said many things, as did you. I hope you don't expect me to remember all of them."

"You said you felt you had put too much worship of me into your painting, and that it was dangerous to turn a person into an ideal the way you had. At the time, I thought it little more than pretty words and a hidden way of saying how much you adored me. It was shallow of me not to take your words as anything more than a love confession, but I think we can both agree the whole speech was rather abstract. I doubt I could have deciphered anything else, given how sheltered I was. I'd barely lived anything worth considering."

"I hope you didn't ask me to stay so you could insult my skill for rhetoric," Basil replies, though the twist of his lips implies a cautious amusement that sends hope surging through me. "What do you make of those words now?"

It takes some time for me to weigh my words, so I sip my tea as I do. The third glass of port is starting to sink in, muddying my thoughts and making it all the harder to find the right way of phrasing my response, but I don't hurry the process. This temporary peace between Basil and me feels too brittle to risk, especially when what I need to express is so precarious already.

"The way you pictured me in your portrait seemed so perfect, I couldn't bear to disappoint you. Even outside the portrait, it felt as though the reason you never told me how you felt was that you decided it would only disturb me or cause me pointless strife—as if I were too clean to sully with your thoughts. I told myself it was kinder to break your heart than to shatter the ideal of me you saw, but the truth is that I was afraid you might see me as anything less than how you painted me. I felt you could not possibly care for me if I didn't live up to your idea of me, and that there was no way for us to know each other that did not end in my disappointing you."

"I fail to see how that has anything to do with your refusal to let me see the portrait," Basil says. His voice isn't as cold as his answer, nor does it carry any sense of hurt or betrayal. I can hear him piece my words together as he speaks, as though his response is less of an accusation and more a natural interruption in his train of thought, waiting for me to fill the gap.

"I could try to tell you," I start, "but the explanation is far too fantastical for you to believe. Could I show you instead?"

Basil blinks at me, pausing as if waiting for me to change my mind. Our tea has barely been drunk, our pastries nearly uneaten, but such things seem laughably unimportant. If I don't act now, I doubt I'll ever have the courage to. I stand from the table and reach a hand toward him, waiting for him to accept the invitation.

He takes it moments later. For all the comfort the warmth of our interlaced fingers ought to bring, it does little to stop the fear growing deeper within me each passing moment.

Now that I know to look for it, the bridge where the reconstructed Thornhill meets the part of it that survived the fire is all too easy to see. The groundskeeper has done commendable work of making sure both parts of the estate are in equal condition, pushing any signs of mildew and age aside whenever they appear, but little can mask the shift in style between the two. Where Henry's Thornhill is dramatic and grand, dominated by overwhelming spectacle, Old Thornhill has a certain simplicity that should by all accounts be comforting. The walls are a deep, earthy brown decorated with what I assume to be family portraits. Where most of Thornhill feels like an art piece, the few corridors and quarters nearest to the old schoolhouse resemble a home. It's easy to picture a family living here—a happy one, even.

Somehow, the domesticity of the space makes it feel all the more harrowing. Walking the elaborate tapestry of Henry's design makes forgetting the estate's history all too easy, but the sheer sentimentality of these older halls grants some haunted feel to them, as though Thornhill itself were living and grieving all it has lost. Its refusal to blend with the parts that have been rebuilt feels like some desperate grasp at remaining a family home, if only for the ghosts raised within its midst.

It's no wonder, then, that the shadows' grip always feels strongest when I cross the invisible border into the schoolhouse's domain. Their eyes burn into me, disarming every illusion I keep woven around myself.

Fool, they whisper as we step ever closer to the schoolhouse. *Why would you want anyone to see you the way we do, let alone one you claim to care for?*

I squeeze Basil's hand, pulling as much courage as I can from the warmth of his calloused fingers. As much as I want to think that Basil of all people might see the portrait and not think me a monster, I know there's no reason to believe such a thing. At best, he might be convinced not to share what I'm about to show him, but even that seems worth the risk. Keeping my portrait secret is dominating every part of my life, driving me mad as it does. Once he has seen it and spurned me, there will be nobody whose opinion of it matters to me. With Papa dead and Fabián leaving, I have only one last thread loose before I can move forward and start my life anew.

"Are you all right?" Basil asks. "Your silence is frightening me."

"Talk to me," I plead. "Keep me from thinking about myself too long. I want to know everything happening in your life."

He does. Much to his credit, Basil asks no further questions before launching into a report of the paintings he has just finished and the gallery in Paris that plans to exhibit them, nor does he spare any detail on the beautiful little apartment he has found near it or the view it gives him of the Seine. He tells me of the books he has read, his opinion on them, and the argument he recently entered at one of Lady Brandon's salons when Sir Thomas insisted on singing the virtues of missionary charity. I listen as best as I can despite my awareness of the shadows growing tighter around us with each passing step, grabbing at my ankles to pull us back. Their warnings grow more and more insistent, peppered with insults so vicious it takes all I have to shut them out.

By the time we reach the door to the old schoolhouse, Basil is out of breath from his monologue and I stand at my wit's end. My fingers tremble as I twist the key in the lock, anticipation burrowing deeper and deeper into me. The door opens with a piercing creak, and suddenly there's nothing left for us to do but walk inside.

I see the portrait before we've even entered the room, staring at me with its hollow, sunken eyes. This morning's attempt at seeing it through any kind of positive light feels so misguided, I could scream.

The portrait's sneer snaps into a terrifying grin when I step in. However awful her expression was before, the sheer contentment of it freezes me in place. The glint of her teeth makes her look manic and ready to strike, as if she were seconds from ripping my throat out with nothing but her teeth. The dagger in my boot burns even hotter than it did this morning, begging me to unsheathe it and defend myself, but I can't bring myself to move. Her face decays with each step, protesting her canvas prison. Bone peers through pieces of her flesh, holding uncannily steady even without the muscle and tissue meant to keep it in place.

"Welcome," she says, lips stretched so wide I can see her gums. "Thank you for bringing an audience. I'd started to think you were ashamed of me."

I move to squeeze Basil's hand, only to find it has vanished in the shadows that surround me. They crawl throughout the old schoolhouse, covering every inch of it until I find myself standing in a nightmare fog, alone but for the portrait's fiendish subject and her frame behind her. Her smile is chilling in its calmness, as if she knew this day would come. My heart beats so loudly I can barely hear her voice taunting me above it.

The careless, selfish part of me I've let dictate my life for the last three years begs me to turn and run, but I don't move. However much I might dread seeing Basil's reaction to his portrait, I didn't lead him to this schoolhouse only to abandon him again. The portrait he painted has hurt him too much already. *I've* hurt him too much already.

"Do you truly think he could understand me?" the portrait asks. "How could he ever look at you again, now that he has seen our true face? Basil Hallward will tell the world what he saw today, and he will doom you as surely as he did the day he painted me. The world will see you as a monster, like it always should have, but me? *I'm not real.* The only harm Basil will cause is to you—if you let him."

No. Whatever harm comes of Basil's portrait, it will be harm I've caused myself. My sins are mine to bear, and I can't afford to let them control me any longer. I pull the dagger from my boot and launch myself toward the portrait, blade raised and ready to slash the twisted mirror before me, even if it means I might end myself in the process. I close my eyes, take a deep breath, and—

"Dorian?" a voice that's not my own shouts over the maddening thump of my own heartbeat. "I don't understand. Whatever it is that's troubling you so much, talk to me."

And I freeze, arm still high, clutching a dagger over my own wretched image.

29
Fresh Snow

The dagger falls to the ground with an earth-shattering clink.

I shuffle away from the portrait with the frenzy of a deer fleeing its hunter. My breath hitches in my throat, ragged and sharp, pulling teardrops to the corners of my eyes. My chest tightens as I fix my eyes into the wall before me, desperately trying to chase the portrait's twisted sneer from my mind.

The shadows peel away one by one, revealing faded wood flooring beneath me, covered in dust from disuse. I keep shuffling away until my back hits the handle of one of the cupboards behind me, knocking the air out of my lungs and pushing me into stillness. It isn't until I finally stop moving that I realize every part of me is trembling, threatening to fall apart if I lose what little concentration I have left on keeping myself in one piece. Basil looks at the dagger on the ground, then back up to me, curled in a ball in the opposite corner of the room. The mixture of emotions on his face is too complex for me to decipher, but the fear among them is easy to read. He should be running from me, but the scene before him is too baffling to process.

"The—the portrait," I try to explain, panting between each word in a voice that crackles with the unpredictability of a wildfire. "She was taunting me, telling me to get rid of you, and I thought if I stabbed it she'd finally stop. I'm sorry for frightening you. I just . . . I just wanted her to stop."

"The portrait?"

Basil's eyes trail away from me and move toward the wall on my right. When he turns away from me, I expect the shadows to come creeping back, urging me to finish him before he can process the ghastly sight before him. Somehow, the silence is worse.

"I'm not well, Basil," I whisper, teeth chattering as I do. "I haven't been well in a long time. I see things that can't possibly be, hear whispers when no one has spoken. I live in constant fear someone might see the monster I made myself into. Please, look at the portrait. I need to know if you see it, too."

There's some mercy in Basil's face being hidden from me as I watch him, unable to see his reaction to the portrait. However awful the expressions I'm picturing on his face might be, I at least have the comfort of knowing they're imagined. The anticipation building in my stomach wrenches my heart until I feel I might be sick, but I much prefer it to having Basil look at me as though I were something vile and degraded. He raises his hand to touch the frame, feeling at the vines carved along its edges. His finger pricks against one of the thorns, and he pulls it away to remove a splinter. His face remains turned toward the portrait all the while.

"This is the frame Fabián made," he says, distant and pensive as he pieces together the twisted miracle before him. "I saw it at the shop. He asked if I thought you would like it. And those hyacinths in the painting . . . it took me days to find the perfect ones, and hours after that to weave them together. This looks too much like the portrait I painted of you not to be, and yet . . ."

"It is."

The words leave my lips so quietly I could mistake them for one of the whispers that have now abandoned me, but Basil turns around nonetheless. He takes a step toward me, pauses to look at the portrait again, then turns back to face me. I fight the urge to shuffle farther away as he moves closer, staring at me so intently it feels as though he can read each detail of my life on my face. Fear turns to worry in his eyes, and by the time we're close enough for me to smell the jasmine and sugar on his breath, I realize I've stopped trembling. Instead, I find myself looking him in the eyes, praying that somehow I haven't imagined the hint of compassion in his frightened gaze.

"That freckle on your left cheekbone is as pronounced as the day I painted it. The bottom of your hair curls in the same way—even that one cowlick at the top of your head points in the exact same direction. I heard people wonder how you still looked as young as you do, but you haven't changed a day, have you?"

I shake my head.

"How is this possible?" he asks, turning between the portrait and me as if wondering which one of us held the answer. "Did I do this to you?"

The absurdity of our situation hits me so bluntly that laughter hiccups in my throat, startling me in the process. Basil frowns in confusion, and I realize I must look mad to him, though I suppose that showing him a cursed portrait that ages for me and carries the weight of my sins has likely made him think I've lost my mind already. Compared to that, I doubt there's much I could do to make myself look any less sane to him. There's no humor to our situation, but I feel as though I could break into hysterics at any moment. Perhaps I already have.

"I don't understand," says Basil.

"Neither do I. I tried to find some explanation, if only so I could convince myself I hadn't lost my mind, but none of my reading helped. All I know is that every trace of my sins has written itself on your portrait so I might never forget them. It's why I couldn't bear for you to see it. I never wanted to hurt you, but I couldn't imagine showing you the monster hiding in the portrait you painted me. Breaking your heart seemed kinder at the time than telling the truth—but that's a lousy excuse. I was frightened. I still am."

"Is that what you see when you look at the portrait? A monster?"

"I've tried finding goodness in it," I admit, "but it seems so futile an exercise. Look at the calculation in her eyes, the smugness of her grimace, the self-superiority of her chin. Look at the port and poppy staining her teeth and lips like blood and ichor, and tell me what good I should somehow find. You must be able to tell the portrait doesn't only age for me, Basil. Every awful thing I've done is written on this canvas. Do you see her right eye and the cold glimmer of malice it holds? That one appeared the day we parted, as soon as I spurned you. I often come to look at it, specifically, and remind myself why you're better off without me. Consider it, and see how hateful I can be."

"You don't need to find goodness in it. People are not so simple as to be good or evil, barring perhaps a few exceptions."

"You are."

"I introduced you to Henry," he counters. "I spent too much time entertaining him so that I could feel I belonged in his circles, and now he thinks he can do no wrong. I was too scared to see you again to check on you, though I doubted you could be well in his grasp, and I failed to share my concerns with your father or Fabián because I didn't wish for them to think poorly of me. I care far too much what people think of me to ever consider myself good."

"That's kind of you to say, but there's a world of difference between cowardice and cruelty. You don't know the things I've done."

"Then tell me," he says.

Though I hesitate at first, eventually I do. I start with Sybil, as much as it frightens me to, and spare no detail about her arrest or even the way I tried to speak with her after the trial as though nothing had happened. I tell him the jealousy I felt for her and the way it turned to hatred when it seemed she built a world for herself only to deny the possibility of its existence when asked. I share the way breaking his heart seemed better to me than telling him the truth, and tell stories of men I invited to worship me, only to toss them aside when they no longer made me feel that I was more beautiful than wretched.

And he listens the entire time without so much as moving.

By the time I've finished weaving my tale, the heaviness that's grown so familiar on my shoulders has faded, and the sensation of eyes watching me has dimmed enough for me to feel with some certainty that the two of us are in fact alone. Basil looks at me not like an angel or a monster but something closer to a wounded animal: in need of care but to be approached with caution.

"It seems to me," he answers when he's sure I've finished, "that everyone you've wronged turned out better off than you did."

"Papa died thinking I wanted nothing to do with him. You spent years thinking I despised you."

"Your father died thinking you felt you might burden him, surrounded by people who loved him. I thought I forced my affections onto you, and ended up with a broken heart as a result. I have no desire to tell you what you did was noble or right—it was cowardly and cruel, as you've already said—but I won't pretend your actions were more vindictive than they were self-destructive when they left you alone with someone we both know has had nothing but sinister intentions for you."

"What about the men I used, then?" I counter.

"Frankly," says Basil, "I've seen enough of your taste in men to have my share of doubts regarding their character."

I start to argue with Basil's assessment, then decide better of it. I can't say with any certainty whether or not the other men wished to trap me the way Henry has, but I can't pretend they did not use me as much as I used them. They never spoke of love or affection or anything beyond desire, and I never asked anything of them but to want me. Perhaps it was petty to tire of them when they couldn't reassure me, but the terms of our agreements were never secret.

"You didn't trust us to decide how to feel about you," Basil adds, "and you're trying to make that choice for me now, still. Have enough faith in me to let me make my own judgment of your actions, even if it isn't as harsh as you think you deserve. You said it yourself: You aren't well. Why should your judgment be any less clouded than mine?"

I nod, carefully unfurling myself from the ball I've rolled into, looking up at him with careful, terrified eyes. I must look a wreck, or as close to it as I can, frenzied and shaking and ready to flee at a moment's notice, but I give Basil the smallest, most tentative smile as he pulls me to my feet and leads me toward the portrait.

Instinct urges me to look away as though I might turn to stone should I meet its gaze, but I grip Basil's hand and face it head-on. Even the portrait cannot hurt me, I tell myself, now that I am not alone in the shadows. If I deny it the power to affect me, there's little it can do in response.

"Do you see that line there?" he says, pointing to her—*my*—forehead. "When I look at it, I see the sign of someone who has faced hardships they oughtn't have had to, but bore them as best they could. When I see the cold, sunken eyes on this canvas, I see their refusal to shut no matter how much weight is piled atop them. Neither of those observations are particularly virtuous, but they exist nonetheless. What do you see?"

I look at the portrait before me, thinking on the game I played in this very room this morning. It feels so different from what I'm trying to do now, yet I find myself wondering if this might be what I should have attempted all along. It reminds me of walking outside after the season's first snow; the landscape itself is the same, but the way it appears is infinitely different. Even the most shameful of changes my portrait has undergone don't seem so sinister if I look at them as features of my existence rather than reminders of my sins.

"I see pain," I answer, once the words start coming together. "I see eyes looking three steps ahead out of fear that disaster might lie before them, stains brought on from desperate efforts at dulling feelings too big to bear. I see a mouth twisted into a shape as close to a smile as it can muster, lest people see it and find some cause for concern. It's a moving portrait, if not a beautiful one."

"Do you still wonder, now, why I don't see a monster in it?" Basil asks.

"Take it."

It might not be the answer Basil expected, but it's as close as I can muster. He looks at me, eyes wide with something caught between confusion and wonder, but I don't give him the chance to question me. I need to seize this opportunity while I have it, or I might lose the nerve to follow through.

"Take it," I repeat. "It's yours. Bring it to Paris, store it, burn it for all I care, though I can't say what will happen to me if you do. I want the way we're seeing it now to be the way I remember it. I'm scared that, should it stay with me, I'll only grow to resent it again."

Basil considers the offer for a moment, then gives a tentative nod. "If you want me to have it, I'll accept it on one condition."

"What is it?"

He smiles and squeezes my hand. However long I hold it, the warmth neither fades nor burns me. It holds as steady and comforting as it can, as familiar as his smile.

"Come with me," he says. "We deserve a fresh start."

30
Fiery Red

Dear Henry,

I'm leaving

I shouldn't have written him a letter. I know I shouldn't have. No matter what Henry would say, I owe him nothing. Any gifts he gave me were given of his own free will, and we both know he asked for plenty in return: three years living somewhere caught between a dollhouse and a prison, ready and willing to entertain or visit him whenever he asked, anticipating his every whim. I've given him far more than he has given me, considering how little I've had to spare. For all its grandeur, Thornhill would have stood in place whether I needed it or not, and I doubt Henry would have bothered to maintain it without me there to oversee its operations. The longer I think on the matter, the clearer it becomes. I never depended on him the way he insisted I did. Whatever debt he imagined me in was little more than another chain shackling me to his domain.

At the very least, I shouldn't have sent it. All it did was invite him to try and stop me, and I'd far rather leave under cover of night than invite some kind of confrontation, but I couldn't help myself. Perhaps it was little more than self-sabotage, the newest in my attempts at punishing the crimes for which I've already served my sentence. Tomorrow night, I'll be dead—to the world, at least. Someone will find the ashes of Thornhill, and my disappearance will be chalked up to a tragic, early death. Henry will have no reason to chase after me when there is no me to chase. That cursed letter can only put me further at risk of his anger, but it's too late now to berate myself for writing it.

He would have known, whispers one of the voices that have grown so familiar. *He would have wondered, at least. Burning down your cage won't free you from Henry Wotton's grasp. Every day will be wasted looking behind your shoulder, wondering whether the shadow you see is a monster you've imagined or his figure around the corner, plotting to dig its claws back into you.* Shivers run down my neck at the smooth, low tone in which the voice speaks, reminding me with each word that I'm still the frightened, wretched creature I've always been. Even the freshest snow lands tainted when the ground that greets it is as soiled as I've become.

If he does come to Thornhill, on the other hand . . . I've worn my dagger tucked in my boot the entire week since Basil's visit. The thought of keeping it on me chilled me, knowing how little control I felt the last time I held it, but the thought of facing Henry without some way to protect myself is scarier still. I don't know if

I could use it, if I needed to. If fortune favors me, I'll never need to know.

My worrying is all hypothetical, I remind myself as I finish packing what few affairs I have. The portrait left with Basil, leaving me with only a handful of clothes to toss into a trunk—nothing particularly elaborate or sophisticated, and certainly none of my party clothes, but enough to get me started on the new life ahead of me. Henry hasn't come yet, and some optimistic part of me insists he might not. Victoria ought to be at Hartwood, and he's always gone to great lengths to pretend she's unaware of his infidelity. Besides, I'm little more than a pet to amuse him. Losing me might be a blow to his ego, but that hardly seems worth a trip down to the country on my behalf.

A door slams from the direction of the entrance hall, and I curse my own naivety. Of course he was going to come. Henry Wotton does not lose, especially when he fancies himself the only person aware of the games he plays.

I shut my trunk as quickly as I can, sliding it under the bed once I do. I dismissed the servants yesterday, knowing I would not be here much longer, and so I don't have the time to find a better place to hide it. If I can't outsneak Henry, I'll need to outdeceive him instead. Whatever pretty shapes he can twist his words into, I have the advantage of knowing them all. I know, too, what he thinks of me. A lost goddess in his hands, earnest and easily manipulated. The best way to defeat a serpent, I hope, is to hide your own venom long enough to take him by surprise.

I meet him at the staircase on the way to my chambers. The scene has a canny sort of grandeur to it, the lady of the house come down to greet her lover in her best robe, plotting her escape from him all the while. Dressing in the nicest of my fineries seemed silly when I was packing, but it gave me a certain confidence and dignity I needed to keep my nerve. I may not want to be the goddess Henry fancies me, but playing the part feels delectably powerful.

"Dorian!" he roars, charging toward the stairs when he sees me. "Enough with your tantrums. I never thought you'd be so childish as to threaten to run away if I didn't visit."

"I made no threats. I didn't ask you to visit. All I did was tell you I'm leaving."

The fire I remember seeing in Henry's eyes when we first met is back in full force, raging into an inferno. Despite the anger he claims, what I see in his face more than anything is desire—ravenous and hot in a way it hasn't been since he decided I'd been domesticated. His gaze singes the shoulder slipping out of my gown's red velvet sleeve, eager to devour it. To devour *me*. I suppose all I needed to do to reignite his interest was make myself a challenge once more, another game his pride insists he win.

What a shame I no longer care to keep his interest.

"You aren't hard to read," he tells me, "however clever you fancy yourself. You write to say you're leaving, but have nowhere to go and give no date you plan on making your exit. If you truly planned to leave, why tell me, knowing I might come to convince you otherwise? We both know you're nothing without me, pet."

Because my pride is as vicious as yours, I say to myself. *Because I'm twisted enough to put myself in your grasp if it means I might leave here without feeling like wounded prey. Because I will not be able to live my life if you become another shadow lurking behind me, threatening me with the specter of your presence.*

I hold his gaze and step toward him until I'm near enough for him to reach out and touch me. Henry's fire crackles and roars around me, threatening me with every flicker. Whatever the outcome of this last meeting between us, it was a mistake. It gives me nothing but another reason to think the fresh start Basil promised me is impossible, that I'm nothing but the frightened, dangerous animal he saw in the attic. But I cannot undo it, and so I have no choice left but to face the inferno head-on and hope I might still start over once I've walked through it.

"Why come, then? If you're so sure I have nowhere to go, why not ignore my threat and leave me to try and find new ways of catching your interest?"

"Because you have it." His words come out low and rough, grating against me like his beard against my skin when he leans in to whisper in my ears. "And I see no reason to punish you for finally showing some initiative."

Henry Wotton is a heavy sleeper.

I cannot say whether I would have risked my plan if I didn't know how difficult it would be to wake him. I'd like to think it would have deterred me, but if the possibility of a simple, certain escape couldn't put some sense into me, I'm not sure an added layer of risk could have succeeded. Then again, if the care I take to tiptoe around his bed as I try to leave his quarters is any indication, I might not be entirely without self-preservation. Each step I take is slow and deliberate, so muted even I fail to hear them. The dagger I kept tucked in my boot is now clutched in my hand, just in case. Henry might be broader than me, but he's not so much bigger that the grogginess of his slumber couldn't give me the advantage should I need it. My hand grips the blade's handle so tightly I can feel its edges indenting themselves into my palm. Would I see its mark if I looked, or would even so simple a change find the portrait instead?

I keep an eye on Henry as I twist open the door, but even it stays quiet. I suppose I should consider myself lucky he moved his chambers to the freshly rebuilt wing of Thornhill, where age and rust have not yet come to turn the hinges and floorboards into a sprawling labyrinth of noises. Disarmed as he is in his sleep, I can almost remember how I ever let myself trust him. He looks so boyish—cheeky, almost, even in his dreams—I wager it could disarm more people than not. It isn't until the flames of his tempest have already surrounded its prey that they reveal the violence of their heat.

Not long ago, walking Thornhill at night with no light but a candle would have terrified me. Shadows lurk around every corner, waiting to talk to me should I listen to them, but I don't give them the chance. I've grown all too familiar with the words they would say, and I've no time to entertain them. I doubt Henry will wake for hours still, but I don't plan on staying around long enough to know.

Despite my best efforts to ignore it, doubt seeps into my mind the moment I gather my trunk from under my bed. Paris seems so far when I've spent my whole life within proximity of London, and however trapped I've been at Thornhill, I've never had to find a way to live without wealth before. The coin I've had might never have been mine, but it was always available when I needed it, and I knew eventually I'd be able to inherit a fortune of my own when Grandfather passed. Leaving now means not only escaping my present, but also abandoning any potential future I might have had.

Still, I tell myself, *you've done far riskier than leaving the country with someone you know cares for you, and with far less potential for reward.* It's a refreshing change to hear a voice in my mind speaking positively rather than the shadowy whispers I've grown accustomed to or, worse yet, Grandfather's voice. It's warm and comforting, and though I'm still walking a shadowy estate at night, I feel less alone than I did moments ago.

It's lucky, too, that my own quarters are so near the entrance hall. It takes little time for me to reach the front of the estate, and a quick look out the window confirms the coach Basil arranged for me is waiting outside to take me to the train. I didn't tell him why I needed to leave at such a late hour. If he knew I'd hoped to see Henry one last time before I left him, he would have tried to talk me out of it. My need to claim some sort of victory as I left would've seemed petty and small, and I would have left the way I should have: as quickly and subtly as possible, without any unnecessary risks.

Hatred bubbles in my stomach as I take one final look at Thornhill's interior. The grandeur of the place suddenly seems unbearable, and when I look at it, all I can see is the coldness of an empty cage, waiting to lure its captive into a false sense of security. The inhospitality of Henry's design suddenly feels like a mockery of the old, muted hallways I've roamed and the ghosts that haunt their walls. The estate, in all its beauty, seems cruel and hateful, calculated and vicious, and the mere fact of its existence sparks a fury in me I can't bring myself to sweep aside.

If Henry fancies me some vengeful goddess, I may as well oblige him.

I place my candle and trunk to the ground and pull the nearest tapestry off the wall, turning it on its side to bar the entrance hall. Some small, logical part of me insists I should walk out the door and flee into the night as quickly as I can, but what harm can a few more moments bring? Even if Henry should wake, it would take time for him to find me, and he'd have to crawl over the tapestry to reach me, giving me plenty of time to grab my dagger. I want him to feel the violence of his inferno and know in his final moments he could never have consumed me—that the suffering he's about to feel is what he sought out in me all along. And I want to know, deep in my heart, that he can never return me to the prison in which he kept me. Maybe then I'll finally stop feeling this wounded.

I put my candle to the edge of the tapestry and watch as it lights, then drop it to spread across the new rug he sent some months ago from his travels.

Night embraces me as I slam the door behind me, cold and humid air greeting me as the fire spreads inside. I must be a sight to behold, fleeing such an imposing estate in fine red velvet, tossing my trunk on the seat beside me and laughing with frenzied abandon. The coach pulls away onto the shadowy road, and I take one look behind me to see the flames have reached the window now, devouring Thornhill with such ferocity I catch myself wondering if the fire begrudges the estate for having the nerve to survive its blazes the first time, however partially.

What a shame, they'll say when they find the ashes of my cage in the morning. *So young and so lovely—but such things are never meant to last.*

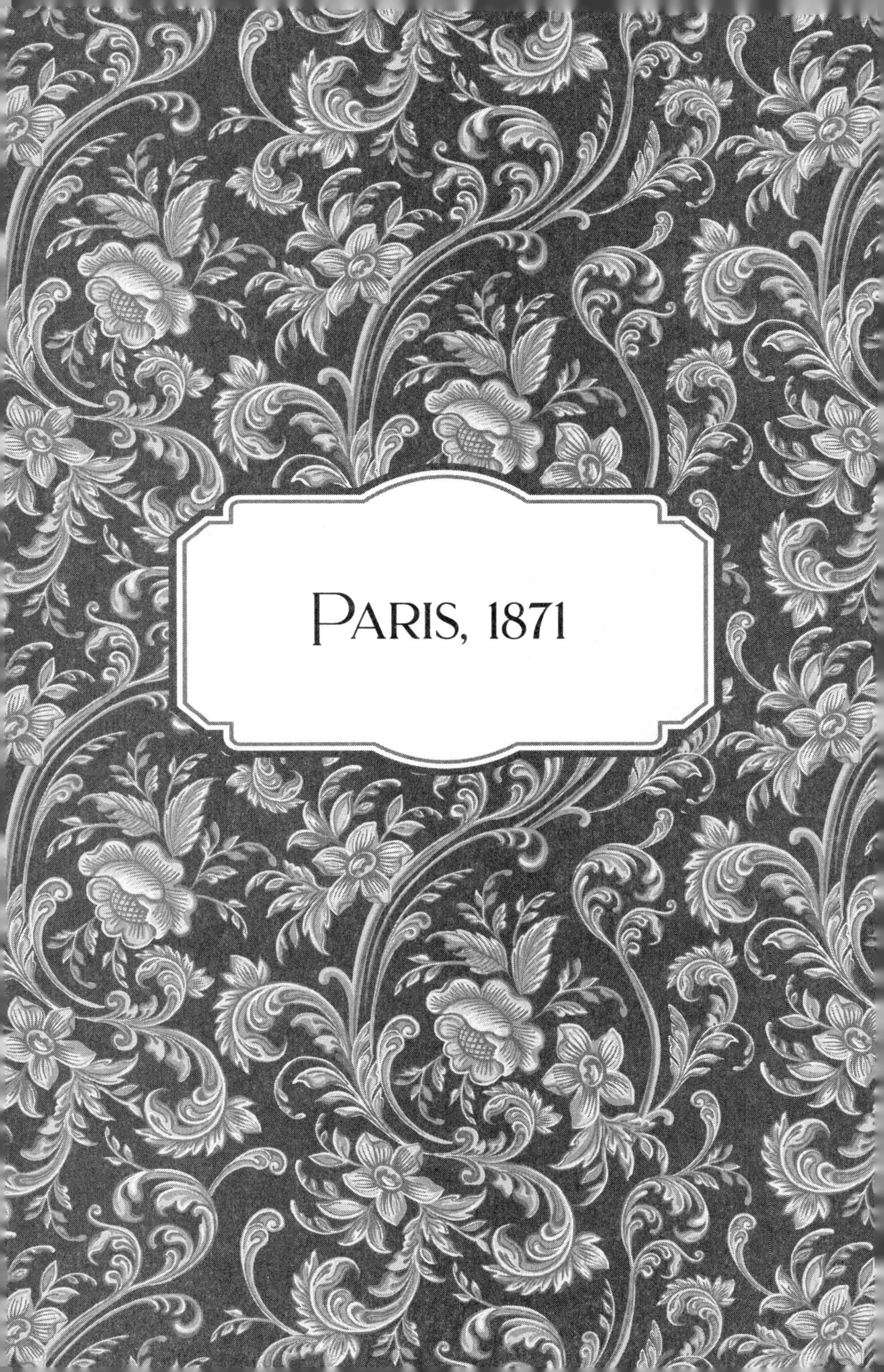

Paris, 1871

Kaleidoscope

The face in Basil's portrait is coarse as I reach out toward it, my fingers grazing the warm canvas of her skin.

Since we fled London, I've taken to spending my Sunday mornings in her company. The apartment I share with Basil has little room for anything but a dresser and our bed as furniture, but the studio attached, at least, offers a bit more space. Normally, I leave the room for him to use, but Sunday seems to be the one day he allows himself some rest. Every week, I settle on the love seat by my portrait and take my tea, scanning her features to see what new traits I might appreciate.

It amuses me to think of how this game we play has moved from an exercise I forced myself to suffer to a soothing part of my routine. It seems strange to think I used to loathe her visage, knowing how much the two of us have in common. Of course, I suppose that shared bond between us is precisely why I found her so hard to face.

I wonder, sometimes, how much she has actually changed in this past year, and how much of the shift between us is based more on my perception of her than any transformation in her features. Her traits are still so sharp as to seem unearthly, her teeth still bared behind her smile—but where she once seemed monstrous, she now reminds me of a frightened animal showing her fangs to keep others away. Even the beauty I once thought of as the lure of some carnivorous flower now feels more akin to a butterfly and the way in which the pattern of its wings imitates a predator for its own safety.

Her eyes, however, still bear a distance I've yet to cross. When I look into them, I see the measured withdrawal of someone haunted by the things they've done, hiding away beneath the weight of secrets they dare not share. Self-compassion, I've realized, comes far more easily to me than self-forgiveness. It's much simpler to feel for the scars on my portrait than to let go of the hand I played in inflicting so many of them.

The sound of keys in the door pulls me from my musings a few moments before it opens with a single gentle motion. My heart flutters as I turn toward the studio's entrance and see Basil walking toward me, then kissing me on the cheek before sitting beside me.

My looks may not have changed since the day Basil painted me, but time suits him so handsomely I often catch myself wishing I could age alongside him. Each day, he looks more at ease, more himself, rich with a depth of emotion that makes me glad I'm not a poet. I could drive myself mad trying to describe him and still find myself no closer to where I am now.

"You know," Basil teases, "I struggle to think of anyone else who would dress in their finest only to have tea with a painting."

His laughter is as hearty and warm as ever, echoing from his gut with all the force of his being. Mine is more measured, closer to the chiming of bells than the roar of the tide, but I'm glad to hear it all after the years I've spent without it. I'll admit the gossamer of my dress might be overkill for such a quaint activity, and the pearls are unarguably excessive. Perhaps one day the freedom of being whoever I want will grow stale, and I'll come to value comfort over indulging myself. For now, however, I'd rather make the most of it.

"I never know when you might decide you need to paint me again. It wouldn't do for me not to be prepared."

Basil chuckles and nests his head against my shoulder. "You look beautiful, whatever the occasion."

"Her or me?" I ask, nudging his attention over to the portrait before us. He looks back and forth, mocking contemplation, but his smile grows until he can no longer pretend to still be lost in thought.

"Both. Always both."

I smile back, resting my head atop his as his hand takes hold of mine. The quiet between us is pleasant at first, but the air grows heavier the longer I stare at the portrait's eyes. The shadows that plagued me are far less frequent than they once were, but I doubt they'll ever leave altogether. The best I can do is heed them rather than chase them away, like I'm learning to do with the portrait. Perhaps one day they might be friends of mine instead of foes.

I'm tired, the portrait whispers. The shadows weigh on me beyond the point where it might be comfortable, but they do not feel menacing, either. If anything, it seems as though they are as worn as I feel, drained by the burden of the last secret I swore to keep. *I want to let go*.

Basil's hand tightens its grip on mine, pulling me back into the plush of our love seat. Concern is written clear across his eyes, but he doesn't ask what's on my mind. He knows as well as I do that it won't prompt an answer I do not wish to share—but the vault in which I keep my secrets is cold and lonely, and the portrait is right. I've grown weary of living in the darkness.

"There's something I need to tell you."

"Then tell me."

I pull away ever so slightly, turning around to face him as I do. Our hands meet in between us, resting against the love seat. Basil's fingers paint circles in my palm as I try to ground myself, digging my knees into the seat beneath me. The words I need to say sit heavy on my chest, but I've stomached much larger weights for far longer than this. Whatever Basil's response, it will be a relief not to carry this burden by myself any longer.

"The night I left Thornhill," I begin. "You know about the fire, of course. But I'm the one who started it. I *meant* to start it. I killed Henry, Basil."

"Did you want to kill him?"

"Yes," I answer. "No. I mean . . . I set the fire knowing it would kill him. I even barricaded the doorway in case it woke him. But I didn't want to kill him when I agreed to leave with you—at least,

I don't think I did. I wanted the fresh start we discussed more than anything."

Basil doesn't flinch at my words. I've certainly wondered what he made of the fire that burned Thornhill the night I left it. The circumstances lined up too cleanly for him to think it unrelated, of that I'm sure, but he never asked whether Henry might have started it somehow, or if something had gone wrong and caused some sort of accident. Whatever theories he may have had, it's as if the two of us had some unspoken agreement to ignore the matter, lest we uncover something we could not face together.

"Do you regret it?" Basil asks.

"No."

However cold my answer might be, it strikes me as true the moment I give it. I might not be proud of it, but the longer I dwell on the thought, the more certain I grow that I have no room to regret it, either. Even the shadows around me ease as I let my words sink into the studio. I do not think we'd have the life we live if Henry hadn't died in the fire that night. I would still be looking over my shoulder, pushing Basil away lest he be caught in the cross fire between us.

"I sent him a letter telling him I was leaving," I add. "I knew it would provoke him, that he'd come to remind me of his claim on me, but I wanted to be wrong. Whatever doubts I had about my intentions, of that I'm sure. I needed to know if he would let go of me before I could start over. And then, when he played into my fears, I . . ."

"You needed to know he wouldn't follow after us."

I nod. The moment the words leave Basil's lips, my fears begin to fade away, leaving the two of us with no one but my portrait to watch us. I squeeze his hand as tightly as I can and look into his eyes, willing every fear, every vulnerability, every imperfection into my gaze. I know better than to think they'll show, but if I can trust anyone to see them regardless, I know it would be him.

"You're taking this awfully calmly," I point out.

"I've had a year to consider the possibility," Basil answers. "A fire ravages Thornhill the night you leave, allowing you to be presumed dead, and Henry just happened to be there that night? I may not have known what happened, but it would have been foolish not to wonder."

"I meant what I said in the attic that day. I wanted to be the person you saw in me. I still do. But then when I was alone, I kept thinking about how odd it would be for me to die mysteriously the very day you left London. Some part of me insisted he'd wonder, that he'd go to visit you and find his suspicions confirmed, that he'd be furious to discover his pet"—I spit the word as if it might expel the last of the venom that accompanies it even now—"would have the nerve to try and deceive him."

"You should have told me that," Basil scolds me. "We could have moved again—to America, maybe—or spent a few years traveling around so he couldn't find us. We could have worked out a solution together."

"I know. I turned into that same trapped animal you saw the moment fear showed its face, snarling and clawing at anyone in reach. The year we've shared has been wonderful, and there are times where I feel like the person you first painted, but sometimes I worry I haven't changed at all. I'm scared that anytime I feel trapped or in danger, I'll turn right back into that frightened beast you saw trembling in the old schoolhouse."

Basil studies my face, taking in every detail as he looks at me. The distance between us feels heavy, almost clinical, but the urge to panic doesn't arise. I am not a lion in a cage surrounded by uncaring observers. I'm in my home, sitting across from the person I love, someone who has seen more of me than anyone I've ever known. I cannot hope he might understand me if I don't allow him to see me.

"Maybe," he admits. "Or maybe you *were* a trapped animal. Henry watched you push away everyone around you, helped you build yourself a cage, then whisked you off to the country where he could toy with you whenever it pleased him and disregard you when it didn't. Whatever I make of your actions, it isn't hard to grasp why you felt the way you did. Do you feel that way now?"

"I feel safe," I tell him. "I *am* safe."

An eternity seems to pass between us before Basil pulls me into his embrace. I fall apart as soon as his arms wrap around me, my breath hitching in my throat as I burrow my face into his chest. "I wish you'd told me earlier," he says. "Did you think I wouldn't understand?"

"It didn't seem fair of me to ask you to."

Basil smiles, but I don't miss the hint of exasperation in his eyes when he does. "I thought we agreed not to make those decisions on behalf of each other."

We hold each other, basking in the moment far away from anything else. Light filters in through the windows, resting upon us like the gentlest of blankets. The space above us feels so open, as though we could be in a meadow or a clearing instead of a small

Paris studio. I pull Basil in as tight as I can, willing him to feel every bit of the peace I feel in this moment.

"Are there any other secrets you'd care to share with me while we're here?" he asks.

"I'm afraid to say I have no secrets left. I suppose I'll have to find some other way to intrigue you now."

I follow Basil's eyes as he looks around at the paintings that line his studio, waiting to be shown at the start of next month. Each one features a lovely young lady in various shades of historical dress, more stunning for every form she takes. Somehow, she manages to be Cleopatra staring an asp in the fangs, Joan of Arc on the pyre, Mary Magdalene at the cross, all without losing the mischievous glint in her eye that makes her so instantly recognizable.

"Somehow," Basil says, "I think intriguing me won't be much of a problem."

Looking at the series of portraits before me, what strikes me is the way time shapes their model in infinite small ways: the armor she wears squaring her figure, the regal tunics giving her a waspish, narrow shape. I see the attitudes toward her change from worship to pity to hatred so vicious as to burn her and wonder how it can be that the ages can react to the same woman in such different ways. I ask myself who she might be today, how people would treat her should she show herself. Would she be lounging on a chaise overlooking the Seine or rotting in a cell as people tried to strip her of the dignity she clings to in each frame?

Every possibility seems as likely as the one that came before, and yet none of them feel true. Why should she always find herself in grand, dramatic scenes? Perhaps, after so many lifetimes of adoration and infamy, she wants nothing more than to sit on a bench in a plain gray dress, sun-gold hair tucked into a neat, practical bun. I imagine she must have grown tired of the attention over the centuries, knowing the tragedies that worship brings. It must be refreshing to take a step back and watch the one she loves be celebrated, knowing how hard they've worked to be where they are.

"I know I normally take my Sundays to rest, but would you mind if I painted you again today?"

I shake my head. "I suppose it's a good thing I dressed in my finest for . . . how was it you put it? Tea with a painting? Although I suppose I'll have to change regardless. Who shall I portray for you this time?"

"The last portrait we did will be the final piece of that exhibit," Basil answers. "If I paint you as another figure from history, I think I might forget the world existed before we met. I thought I'd let you choose how I picture you today."

A smile cracks across my face. I'll admit it's a strange charade the two of us have started to perform. Sometimes, he paints me with a certain expression, or at a certain age, or even as a different person altogether, as he has been prone to recently. I might never change, but I trust he knows me well enough to anticipate how any feature of mine might adjust to any given circumstance. It might be guesswork, but it's as close as I can get to seeing myself in different lights.

"In that case," I tell him, "I think I'd like a simple portrait today. Why don't you picture me happy?"

Author's Note

> It is the spectator, and not life, that art really mirrors.
>
> —Oscar Wilde, preface to *The Picture of Dorian Gray*

Almost a century and a half ago, after the original serial run of *The Picture of Dorian Gray*, Oscar Wilde released a preface responding to the moral panic being stirred up over the implied relationships between Basil, Dorian, and Henry. He ends this preface with the claim that "all art is quite useless."

The first time I read *Dorian Gray*, this claim confused me. Why would any artist put their heart and soul into making something they deemed useless, and how could Wilde possibly think his work had no use when it was actively being *used against him*? These days, I read this as more of a lament than a criticism: an understanding that art depends on the people interpreting it, that there was nothing he or his book could do to stop those looking to twist it so they could make an example of him.

Four years after this preface was published, *The Picture of Dorian Gray* was used as evidence when Wilde was tried for sodomy. He spent two years in prison, then died in exile three years later at forty-six—and, while his physicians traced the death to an injury from his time in prison, many over the years have attributed his death to syphilis (despite the fact that none of the seven doctors who examined him recorded any trace of the disease).

A grim legacy, to say the least.

Working on *This Wretched Beauty*, I found it impossible not to think about Dorian Gray's history. Between the regular and targeted political campaigns to ban books by marginalized authors, the adoption of "Don't Say Gay" censorship laws, and several other actions being taken by governments across the world, Wilde's case feels less distant with every passing day.

But if art is as useless as Wilde laments, why are books treated as such a threat? How can a story be a scandal solely because of what it represents? The answer there, I think, is that the experiences we encounter, real or fictional, shape the scope through which we understand the world. Books are a window into the characters' reality, an invitation to look inward and reflect on someone else's experience. Those who approach them with hate or disdain will find within them whatever they wish to project, but to those who need it, a book can represent so much more. They're a chance to try and understand perspectives we might never encounter otherwise, or for some to see themselves better under a new light.

To those whose goal is to keep people isolated and vulnerable, there's nothing more dangerous than a bridge.

I take comfort in knowing we have a long history of telling stories that aren't allowed to be told, of hiding parts of ourselves in art for safekeeping. Whether it's Dorian hoping the version of them painted in Basil's portrait might live on where they can't, whispers from one person to another in places that are only safe so long as they stay secret, or even pulp fiction deemed too low-brow to bother regulating, queer people have found ways to reach out to one another long before we were allowed to exist in the public eye (and long before we were forbidden from it, for that matter).

I wrote this book expecting it would be restricted in some places because of who wrote it, but knowing that's a better fate than the story of the original Dorian Gray. I continue to write with the hope that those of us writing today are just the current chapter of our history, that those readers we reach—*you*—might build bridges of your own. Remembering the history of *Dorian Gray* gives me hope that a century and a half from now, the actions taken today will seem as distant and extreme as Oscar Wilde's imprisonment did when I first read *The Picture of Dorian Gray* in high school.

It's in the spirit of this ongoing history that I end this author's note by offering my own understanding of Wilde's words: The problem isn't that art has no meaning, but that it can't speak on its own behalf.

All art is quite useless—*if we don't fight for it.*

Acknowledgments

This Wretched Beauty started off as more of a pipe dream than a book, and the road that led to it sitting in front of you now is filled with more people than I could possibly list—but I appreciate all of you too much not to at least try.

To Emily Settle, my editor: Thank you for helping shape this book into the one I dreamed it would be, for your willingness to challenge me, and also for your faith in my vision. Thank you, as well, for taking a chance not only on this book but also on me, and for making me feel like I deserved to be trusted with this story. Thank you, as well, to the entire Feiwel and Macmillan teams who helped bring this book to life, as well as to cover artist Syd Mills and designer L. Whitt for putting together the cover of my dreams.

To Alexandra Levick: Thank you for being the rockstar agent that you are. Thank you for always having my back and for believing in me even when my own confidence wavered. Working with you has been (and continues to be) a great privilege. And, of course, to Soni: Thank you for being the first person to take a chance on me back in 2020, for giving me the confidence to pursue my writing, and for introducing me to Allie. My life would look much different today without the two of you.

I'd be remiss not to thank the friends who made this book possible as well. Dahlia: Thank you for all the enthusiasm you've shown about me and my work, and for being the best fairy godmother this book could've asked for. Gabe: It never occurred to me I *could* pitch to *Remixed Classics* until you suggested I look into it. Nico, Zach, C. L.: Thank you for putting up with all my rants and vents and generally unhinged antics while I worked on this book (and, let's be honest, before and after that as well). Conner, Megan, Jack, Jordan, Ellie, Gracie, and so many more of you: I never would've grown as an author if we hadn't spent all those years writing fanfic together and pushing each other. Thank you all for showing me how fun writing could be.

Camille, I know I've dedicated this book to you already, but you know I had to mention you here, too. Thank you for being the first person to read this book, and for immediately seeing exactly what I hoped it could be. Nicole and Nadia: Thank you for listening to my constant ramblings about Dorian Gray throughout our university days and for cheering me on long after that, too. Thank you to Charlie, Andrew, and Luka for keeping me sane and blessing me with days away from writing. Saffron: Thank you for the coworking sessions and for our talks about that awful movie adaptation. Et Ben: C'est un des grands plaisirs de ma vie de t'appeler à la fois mon frère et mon ami. Merci.

Last but not least, my family: I'm so grateful for each and every one of you. I don't know how I got so lucky as to be surrounded by such a wonderful group of people. Maman et Papa, thank you for believing in me, for knowing I'd be a writer since I was a kid, and for always making me feel like your love was a given. Cal and Jacinta, thank you for welcoming me into your family and being a home away from home. Thank you to my coauthors, Juniper, Bramble, and Clove, for always making sure one of you was sitting beside me or on my lap while I worked.

And to Muireann: Thank you for being there every step of the way, from listening to me ramble as I mapped out the plot to making sure I paced myself, and for giving me a home to come back to.

This one's for all of you.

About the Author

Elle Grenier is an author of young adult books and a former theater kid who lives in British Columbia on traditional Pocumtuc land with their fiancée and their three cats. They started writing at eight years old and never stopped, now striving to write the books they would've wanted to read in their teenage years. Elle studied English literature at the University of Toronto and started their master's before deciding to focus their attention on writing instead. When they aren't writing, you can probably find Elle rewatching the same three shows online, playing around with Taylor Swift covers on their lyre, or lying by the nearest body of water. When they are writing, you'll likely see them downing several cups of coffee next to a Shakespeare plush for motivation. *This Wretched Beauty: A Dorian Gray Remix* is their debut novel.

Thank you for reading this Feiwel & Friends book.

The friends who made

This Wretched Beauty

A DORIAN GRAY REMIX possible are:

Jean Feiwel, Publisher

Liz Szabla, VP, Associate Publisher

Rich Deas, Senior Creative Director

Anna Roberto, Executive Editor

Holly West, Executive Editor

Kat Brzozowski, Senior Editor

Emily Settle, Senior Editor

Dawn Ryan, Executive Managing Editor

Kim Waymer, Senior Production Manager

Rachel Diebel, Editor

Foyinsi Adegbonmire, Editor

Brittany Groves, Assistant Editor

L. Whitt, Designer

Lelia Mander, Production Editor

Gabriella Salpeter, Marketing Manager

Samantha Sacks, Publicist